The Confessions of
Joseph Blanchard

GUERNICA
PRIZE
5

**Canada Council   Conseil des Arts
for the Arts   du Canada**

**ONTARIO ARTS COUNCIL
CONSEIL DES ARTS DE L'ONTARIO**
an Ontario government agency
un organisme du gouvernement de l'Ontario

Canadä

Guernica Editions Inc. acknowledges the support of the Canada Council
for the Arts and the Ontario Arts Council. The Ontario Arts Council
is an agency of the Government of Ontario.
We acknowledge the financial support of the Government of Canada.

The Confessions of
Joseph Blanchard

Ian Colford

GUERNICA
EDITIONS
TORONTO • CHICAGO • BUFFALO • LANCASTER (U.K.)
2023

Michael Mirolla, general editor
Lindsay Brown, editor
David Moratto, interior and cover designer
Guernica Editions Inc.
287 Templemead Drive, Hamilton, (ON), Canada L8W 2W4
2250 Military Road, Tonawanda, N.Y. 14150-6000 U.S.A.
www.guernicaeditions.com

Distributors:
Independent Publishers Group (IPG)
600 North Pulaski Road, Chicago IL 60624
University of Toronto Press Distribution (UTP)
5201 Dufferin Street, Toronto (ON), Canada M3H 5T8

First edition.
Printed in Canada.

Legal Deposit—Third Quarter
Library of Congress Catalog Card Number: 2023937643
Library and Archives Canada Cataloguing in Publication
Title: The confessions of Joseph Blanchard / Ian Colford.
Names: Colford, Ian, author.
Description: Series statement: Guernica prize ; 5
Identifiers: Canadiana (print) 2023044332X | Canadiana (ebook) 20230443362 |
ISBN 9781771838375 (softcover) | ISBN 9781771838382 (EPUB)
Classification: LCC PS8555.O44 C66 2023 | DDC C813/.54—dc23

Marie Annette LeLoup
(October 23, 1956–April 24, 2021)

David Llewelyn Tate
(July 23, 1960–October 2, 2021)

Jason Simms, QC
Forest and Simms, Attorneys
931 Fort St., Victoria, BC V8V3J3
250–555–1583 • info@forestsimms.ca

June 8, 2018

To: Michael Hemming, University Archivist
    Dalhousie University

Dear Mr. Hemming,

Thank you for taking time to speak with me on the phone. Enclosed please find the material we discussed.

As I mentioned, I discovered this document among papers belonging to my aunt, Lucinda Barrow (née Pindar), after her death earlier this year at the age of 85. My aunt was a long-time resident of Victoria but was born in Halifax and spent her formative years there.

Some background: My aunt arrived in Victoria in the early 1970s, a few years before I was born. While I was growing up, I knew her as my mother's younger sister, a kind, good-natured woman who held a secretarial position in a law office. She loved us children and always had time for us. She was a devoted patron of the arts who attended plays, musical recitals, poetry readings and the like. She sometimes wrote articles on these events for a community newspaper. At some point during my adolescence I learned that she also wrote poetry and short stories, and have since discovered to my delight that some of her creative writing was published in literary journals. She was, in all respects, a remarkable woman.

When she arrived in BC, she was married to a man named
William Barrow. They were together briefly but the marriage didn't
last and she was soon living on her own, though she retained the name
Barrow, I assumed, for legal purposes. I never met William Barrow.
I'm certain he has no bearing on any of this.

I happened upon this typed manuscript as I was helping to
clear out her apartment. At first, I thought it was perhaps a novel
she had written and abandoned. But I revised my thinking when I
realized that nowhere on the manuscript does she take credit as the
author. In fact, as you will see, there is no attribution, just the title:
The Confessions of Joseph Blanchard.

This is puzzling. If she was not the author, I couldn't imagine how
or why it had come into her possession. Was she holding it for someone?
It's impossible to know.

When I read through it I was surprised to find that my aunt plays
a minor role in the story. After reading it a second time I decided to
do some research.

I have determined that the people and institutions named in these
pages are real. For instance, Frederick Gebhardt was a prominent
Halifax physician, a member of the Nova Scotia College of Physicians
and Surgeons and for some years the Director of Dalhousie's Department
of Paediatrics. He died in 1995. His wife Pauline was indeed a member
of the Board of the Halifax Public Gardens and served two terms as
president of the Nova Scotia Historical Society. She died in 2010.

However, the story this document tells is chiefly concerned with
their daughter, Sophie Alexandra. Again, the descriptions appear to
be accurate. Sophie Alexandra Gebhardt was a gifted pianist who had
achieved some local celebrity but died before she could make a name
for herself on the international music scene. I went to the trouble of
obtaining her obituary. She passed away on September 26, 1971, a
Sunday, at the age of nineteen. The notice says that she "suffered an
injury at her home" and later died in hospital. The vague phrasing
makes me think suicide. She wouldn't be the first brilliantly talented
young person, subject to extraordinary pressures, to take her own life.
But I don't believe that is what happened.

If you're looking for a more substantial connection with Dalhousie University, you will find it here: the Gebhardt family established a scholarship in her memory, the Sophie Alexandra Gebhardt Achievement Award, given annually to a first-year student in the Music Department who has "demonstrated outstanding commitment to the pursuit of musical excellence." This information is on the Department's website.

Joseph Blanchard, who has put the story to paper, claims to have worked for Murchie and Associates, the same accounting firm employing my aunt. Murchie's seems to have operated in Halifax for about 20 years starting in the 1950s. In the mid-1970s it merged with Parkland Central Financial Services, a larger firm with national reach. Eventually it was absorbed. At that point the Murchie name disappears.

Of Joseph himself, I can find nothing. The internet is a vast repository of information but has its limits. If someone chooses to disappear, there's not much anyone can do about it.

But I do recall my Aunt Lucinda mentioning a "Joseph," maybe a co-worker, possibly just an acquaintance. This happened on several occasions within my hearing while she was in conversation with my mother. I remember because of the shift in her tone when the name came up, a wistful lilt that I didn't like because it made me sad for her. Nothing was ever spelled out but I gather it was a case of unrequited love. She was fond of him, but he never gave her much notice. I never got to the bottom of why she left Halifax and moved west, why she married William Barrow, whom, according to my mother, she did not love. Truthfully, I didn't think about it. But I suppose I made a subconscious link between her departure from Halifax and this Joseph fellow and how he treated her.

Reading this story has stirred up these memories.

My interpretation is that Joseph wrote the document himself, composing the whole thing by hand in the months following Sophie Gebhardt's death. But if that is the case, why is there a typed copy buried under piles of odds and ends in my aunt's bedroom closet? Where is Joseph's handwritten original? Did Joseph really entrust my aunt with his devastating secret? The implication is that he did.

I don't know how much responsibility my aunt bears for the creation of this document. Did she somehow come into possession of Joseph's written copy—with or without his consent—produce this typed copy, and then destroy the original? But why go to all that trouble and effort? She was a busy woman who valued what little free time she had. Or is this just a sad tale of love's dark side, a fiction she concocted inspired by true events that she never got around to sending to a publisher? But if so, it seems ill-advised, from a legal standpoint anyway, to use the names of real people, whose relatives would be unlikely to appreciate seeing them reincarnated as characters in a novel.

Regardless, after reading this story my impression of Joseph Blanchard has not improved. He seems to have been a supremely self-serving individual. Cowardly and depraved. I remember hearing her remark once or twice that he was "fastidious." But I think it goes beyond that. Judging by this evidence I would say he was also paranoid with a touch of OCD. There's no question he was dishonest. It seems fortunate my aunt was able to avoid entanglement in his web of deceit.

As interesting as all of this is, I'm afraid my busy life prevents me from pursuing these matters further. I don't know if the document has any literary value or historical significance. I don't know if it is worth preserving. I will leave those questions to you and your colleagues. I trust whatever decision you reach regarding its final disposition will be appropriate.

You have my contact information if you wish to get in touch.

Yours sincerely,
Jason B. Simms, QC

Part One

One

How is it that my life, so recently a blessing, has become an intolerable burden?

For one thing, the winter just ended had been much too long as well as needlessly ferocious and cruel. Storm had followed storm with numbing regularity. For weeks, there was nowhere to put the snow when it was cleared. In the end, it was piled to incredible heights along every street, obscuring visibility and making walking treacherous. When spring arrived, the clouds moved in and for many days at a time we endured torrential rainfalls. Outside the city, lakes and rivers swelled and overflowed. Near my neighbourhood some streets flooded. People were forced out of their homes, leaving behind the belongings of a lifetime. Shops were closed and, in a move unprecedented in my memory, the universities cancelled classes and sent students packing. Like many people, I found it difficult to get around town. Finally, I decided to curtail my activities and remain indoors whenever possible.

At work a new management team had been organized with a mandate to shore up the sagging fortunes of our accounting firm, Murchie and Associates, which had seen business dwindle to perilous levels after four years of languid economic times. I had been working there for more years than I cared to count, and I regretted seeing senior employees being let go, some of whom I counted as friends. In their place a pack of recent graduates was hired, fresh-faced and unsuspecting, newly-minted MBAs in hand. We were told that the team had hit upon a strategy of injecting the firm with new blood, hoping to break free of the debilitating influence of ritual custom and antiquated tradition that prevented us from moving into the modern age and which stood in the way of real progress. According to this plan, we were told, an influx of new ideas would surely take root and flourish. Soon we would find within ourselves renewed enthusiasm for our jobs. We would willingly take on additional tasks and begin doing things in innovative ways. In no time we would acquire more clients than we could easily handle.

I admit I harboured a healthy scepticism regarding what I felt were baseless prophecies and my fears were by no means allayed when, on the day I was scheduled to address this youthful brood, I found them undisciplined, arrogant, tactless and shrill. The old ways meant nothing to them and I was subjected to bold-faced ridicule and open scorn as I attempted to explain how our bookkeeping department operated. Two young men were placed in my charge, who thereafter seized upon every opportunity to question my abilities and challenge my authority, and in general to make my life a torment. Other staff, sensing my discomfort and irritation, kept their noses to their books, their mouths firmly shut, every minute of the day. All banter ceased. The office became a mortuary, save for the corner of the room where the newcomers, seated side by side, would erupt with urgent whispers and stifled giggles throughout the day.

I was not of sufficient standing to object but even I could see that, far from reinvigorating the stiffened limbs of our firm, the new arrivals had ushered in a period of profound malaise. Nobody was comfortable with the new arrangement. Productivity took a distressing plunge. Morale sank to unparalleled depths. And though the cheery proclamations and sanguine forecasts persisted in an unbroken stream of pamphlets and memoranda from the director's office, I could not help but recognize the entire episode as a prelude to the insolvency that many of us had long feared. When we finally hit bottom—in a year, maybe two—nobody would be safe. All of us would lose our jobs.

My health was not good during this time. I had recently developed a succession of allergies to foods that all my life I had consumed with impunity and of which I had grown quite fond. With no warning—as if my body had turned against me—I found myself subject to thunderous headaches and shortness of breath if I were so foolish as to indulge in delicacies as seemingly benign as peppermints, sourdough bread, or orange marmalade. Many other foods affected me in adverse ways as well. I was advised to regulate my diet, much as I had seen my parents do in the last years of their lives, and was required to closely monitor my bodily functions and make note of secretions and discharged matter in nauseating detail. My doctor assured me there was no cause for alarm and, as consolation for my obvious distress, read aloud from a medical text which reported that allergies like mine were in some cases temporary. Some people were able to re-establish their tolerance for foods after being unable to stomach them for a number of years. Mine, he informed me, was a classic case of this sort of malady. I was not simply being neurotic.

But I was not easily comforted. I could see myself hobbling around on a cane, beset by an array of puzzling symptoms via all manner of aches and pains.

It was clear to me as well that I would be afflicted by everything from swollen joints and senility to flatulence and bad breath before the passing of too many more years. The prospect was intolerable and there were times, when my torment was at its worst, that I gave serious consideration to ending my life.

Two

~~~~~~~~~~

B UT WITHOUT A doubt the most crushing blow to my well-being came with the sudden passing of my young cousin, Sophie Alexandra Gebhardt. You may have heard of her, for even today there is talk of how brilliant—how consummately talented and beautiful she was. She received her first piano lesson at the age of five and within three or four years was receiving invitations to participate in talent shows and recitals around the province.

Soon, her name took a prominent place on the program beside, and sometimes above, performers many years her senior. By the age of ten she was a headline artist, taken seriously in the musical press and treated with deference wherever she happened to go. Her parents were of course delighted to have a prodigy on their hands. Quite reasonably, the plan was to limit her appearances to a dozen or so each year, at least until she had attained sufficient experience in the ways of the world to be capable of running her own affairs.

They enrolled her in master classes at Dalhousie University for instruction in basic composition and performance artistry. Their hope was that in an intensive intellectual setting Sophie would gain a superior education while honing her musical skills.

However, even the best-laid plans can go awry. Twelve years old when she was admitted to Dalhousie, Sophie encountered difficulties with her teachers in at least two instances that I know of. These people—failed performers themselves though I have no doubt they were quite talented—sought to develop a close mentor-pupil relationship with her and make her into something she was not. One, a renowned Beethoven scholar, wanted her to approach the keyboard aggressively and unleash in her playing a raw, untamed passion. Her regimen in these classes included a series of exercises designed to strengthen the muscles in her wrists and fingers. A reasonable goal, but the daily practice of banging on a drum with a small club for long periods was baffling.

The other teacher, a flautist of pious inclination, told Sophie that if she ever lost interest in music she could make herself useful as a CUSO volunteer ministering to the starving and afflicted in Africa. He taught her hymns and offered her a position as a church organist. The report I received was that Sophie returned home one day in tears saying that she wanted to give up her studies and devote her life to the service of those less fortunate than herself.

Though she subsequently encountered teachers more sensitive to the needs of someone her age and learned much that she was able to put into practice, the eventual result was that she left Dalhousie after only two years of study. At the age of sixteen, after a time spent in private lessons, she embarked upon a career as a soloist. Her touring schedule was initially light, her appearances limited to small local and regional venues. But she was slowly building a reputation and festival season could be busy; at peak times it was not unusual for her to present three or four solo shows in a week. She had developed steady followings among classical music enthusiasts in Charlottetown and Moncton, university towns with music programs of their own. And she had been to Montreal and Toronto, performing in schools as part of provincially-sponsored youth initiatives. A modest beginning to be sure but word was getting out and we could all see bigger things on the horizon. It did not seem unreasonable to imagine that, perhaps before her twentieth birthday, she would be playing international music hubs like London and Berlin.

Her mother was a first cousin, the daughter of my father's sister, and I was often present during the formative years of Sophie's precocious talents. Being a bachelor with no prospects of marriage any time soon, I was a regular dinner guest and thus had the good fortune to share in the thrill of some of Sophie's early triumphs. Chief among these in my recollection is the first time she played Mozart's entire K.333 B-flat major sonata without a single error. It would have been 1958 and she'd have been no more than six or seven at the time. I remember her teacher—a gruff but kind-hearted woman named Selma Kraus—leapt from her chair as the last notes faded and hugged the child with what can only be described as pure joy. Sophie remained serene as her beloved teacher bestowed kisses on her star pupil but the rest of us had never seen this side of Selma. The child was obviously a massive talent but her teacher had readied her for a night like this and their bond was plainly a deep one.

Sophie's mother, as well as her father, a physician who was struggling to establish a practice, displayed more restraint in their demonstrations of approval and, taking my signal from them, I joined in the polite ripple of stunned applause that greeted the conclusion of the piece. I knew, however, we were all faint with astonishment at what we had just beheld, for not only had Sophie played a difficult piece of music without once stumbling, she had also graced each note with what I can only call a personal signature: a fluid, tranquil quality that even on this occasion drew me in and encouraged me to explore Mozart's design—to perceive nuance and depth—as I rarely had before. As the music receded into memory and a meaningful silence enfolded us, I cast my cousin Pauline a stealthy glance and watched as her fingers disengaged themselves from a clenched position in her lap, and I realized that she too had only just begun to comprehend the magnitude of her daughter's capabilities.

Three

THE REMAINDER OF that particular evening—which lingers vividly in the memory though it was many years ago—was punctuated by lengthy silences as we each took an opportunity to reflect upon what Sophie had shown us. Sophie remained utterly mute during dinner, picking at her food and not even finishing her dessert—a concoction of cake, cream and fresh strawberries I knew she loved—before asking to be excused. Our conversation was sporadic and perfunctory, none of us directing a single remark Sophie's way, as if afraid to disturb, with prolonged attention or the sound of our voices, the surface calm of an unstable individual whose public equilibrium could not always be counted upon. This was obviously not the case at all, and I for one was uneasy at the prospect of not addressing in some conspicuous fashion the remarkable performance we had earlier witnessed. Even Miss Kraus, who as was customary had been invited to stay for dinner, and whose effusiveness was near legendary, spoke very little, having only a few tales to tell concerning the exploits of various nieces and nephews. Pauline remarked on the weather, and I contributed an anecdote from the office where at that point I had been working for some three years. I regret that my story was not more interesting because it was directly after I concluded that Sophie asked permission to leave. I remember being troubled by the thought that I had bored her and that from now on she would regard me differently, that I would not be as important to her as I'd been in the past. I didn't know what to do about this and sat quietly for some moments after she had left, struggling with an urge to apologize to everyone present for my social deficiencies.

One thought, however, persisted for the remainder of the meal, one that for some reason I believed to be extremely significant: of all those seated around the table that evening, Sophie was closest to me in age.

Normally a quiet child, Sophie was not one to draw attention to herself or her accomplishments, and I remember thinking that if the rest of us were in awe of her abilities, what must be going on within the mind of this six-year-old girl of delicate appearance as she tried to sort out what it all meant? Her rapid progress at the keyboard had been noted, but I don't think anyone had remarked upon it as anything more than what could be expected of a very bright child who showed keen interest in what she was doing. I can almost see—as I look back—how that evening marked for Sophie the crossing of a threshold that made possible everything that came afterward. She may not have seen it coming herself and been just as astounded as those of us who were lucky enough to be in attendance. Perhaps she was saddened or confused. She may have realized, as I eventually did, that from the moment the piano fell silent and Mozart's exquisite harmonies drifted into the spheres, her childhood was over and any mistakes she made tomorrow would not be tolerated as they had been yesterday. The burden must have been great and so I am not surprised she chose to leave the table early in order to take a few moments for herself.

After dinner I indulged in a brief stroll through the garden next to the house, enjoying a cigarette as was my habit then and observing a ragged stream of clouds that seemed pinned to a placid sky. I walked about in something of a daze, full of wonder and utterly enchanted by even the most trivial sights. I watched a steel-backed beetle bustle with apparent purpose over a lichen-encrusted rock, and then a sparrow as it flew from tree to tree in a design I could never comprehend. The rhythm of the heavens seemed to have somehow made a subtle shift in order to accommodate the revelation of Sophie's talent, almost as if nature itself were absorbed in rapt attention, waiting for whatever might happen next. A brief rain had fallen while we were dining and the leaves now glistened with a luminous freshness as if they'd only just unfolded themselves toward the light for the first time since the world was formed. I walked carefully, not wanting to slip on the wet grass, watching the perfect spiral of smoke from my cigarette drift upward to be dispersed by the cool evening breeze.

All this time I struggled to assess, in realistic fashion, the musical dexterity my young cousin had displayed. Especially where music is concerned, the experience itself can approach an almost mystical intensity that clouds the listener's judgment and, after the fact, encourages a fantastical interpretation of events. Later, when reason prevails, you shake your head and marvel at your own credulity. I wanted to assure myself that no such unconscious exaggeration had occurred here, and so in my mind I placed Sophie back at the piano and followed her movements and the sounds she produced as closely as I could, given my imperfect memory and the two glasses of wine I'd consumed with my meal. I replayed the sonata through in my head as she had rendered it, from the introductory theme—with its rapid cluster of trilling notes that put me in mind of a young girl running across a meadow—to the final chord that brings the whole piece to such an unequivocal yet humane conclusion. I could detect nothing strident or ill-considered; nothing that violated the spirit of Mozart's intentions (as I understood them); nothing stale or derivative. With her childish ingenuity she had revealed the vital and essential heart of the music and had conveyed this to us with the utmost skill and ingenuous charm. She was not trying to convince us of anything but only wished to send the music out to us as a gift, one that asked for no reciprocation. I realized also, of course, that she had simply been trying to please us—her audience—and had likely been nervous playing before her teacher and her expectations, and her parents, who paid Miss Kraus's wages and were entitled to see results for their money. But what left me in a state of giddy incredulity and open-mouthed wonder, with the word "genius" hovering in the margins of my mind, was that in a single stroke and with no apparent effort she had surpassed to an astounding degree the level of musicianship I would have readily granted her, and at the same time completely shattered my notion of who and what she was.

Four

M Y REFLECTIONS WERE interrupted by the soft pad of footsteps and I turned to see Pauline walking toward me through the gathering mist.

With her rounded features, full lips and arched eyebrows Pauline had always struck me as somewhat childlike in appearance. Though in age and temperament she was nothing like a child, possessing as she did an independent soul and a discerning intelligence, she presented an open, trusting mien. She was two or three years older though in many respects we had grown up almost as brother and sister, for prior to my parents' deaths we had all been very close. And since neither her parents nor mine had had any other children, we were left to weather the traumas of adolescence with, chiefly, each other for company. Absurd as it may seem, when I left home to attend college we actually wept in each other's arms. I remember, too, languishing in the depths of a crippling depression for many days after learning she was to be married. It was, to my sensitive heart, a betrayal of our friendship and an indication that our time together was coming to a close. I thought I was losing something irretrievable, something that over the years had become quite precious and to which I had grown devoted, possibly to an excessive degree. It was a struggle to keep my pain to myself because I went through a period during which I resolved to hurt her as she had hurt me, yet at the same time do and say nothing that would place our friendship in jeopardy. I understood everything that was going on, and knew I was being an imbecile, but this knowledge did nothing to soften the blow. What saved me from acting out my conflicting emotions on a public stage was that she and Frederick decided to remain in town, and I was seeing more of her these days than I had in all the years I was away at school. Of course, our lives were different now, and our immediate day-to-day concerns had shifted their emphasis away from the two of us as friends. But I would venture to say just the same that she knew me at least as well as anyone of my acquaintance. I also believe that she appreciated this distinction in my eyes.

She came up to me now and spoke these words.

"You're going to do yourself in, you know, if you keep smoking those things. They're lethal. A grown man should know better."

"Uh-huh."

She took my arm and fell into step beside me. In a gesture of playful defiance, I drew on the cigarette and exhaled the smoke in two streams through my nostrils.

"Oh, Joseph. I'm sorry. You've got enough to keep you occupied without worrying about what I think."

I shook my head. "I want you to know, my dear, that I'll listen to whatever's on your mind. Even if I ignore you, it does me good to hear you say it."

She smiled and pretended to push me away, though the result of her jostling was to draw me closer.

We remained silent for a few moments as we did another circuit of the garden. The cool air was by now creeping through our clothes. It felt like a moist cloth across my neck and I knew that Pauline's loose shawl was not enough to keep her warm. As well, the sky was rapidly giving way to encroaching clouds and the mist I had noticed only a few minutes ago was thickening to a persistent drizzle. My cigarette fizzled. Still, since Pauline seemed content with only me for company and in no hurry to return indoors, I was not about to say anything that would end our encounter. I felt the privilege of this choice she was making, and there were a few things I wanted to say while I had her to myself.

"Thank you for another wonderful meal. Someday I'm going to have to do something for you and Frederick, though I can't think of what that would be. I can't cook. And I can't entertain you. I'll have to take you out to dinner or maybe give you tickets to a show or something."

"You know very well we don't expect a thing. Frederick enjoys having you around. You're part of the family, Joseph. So don't be so silly."

"Well," I said weakly. "Just the same . . ."

I couldn't think of how to continue. Their generosity was perhaps not excessive considering that I was family but it could be overwhelming. Though, as she said, it was not something that was bestowed in expectation of return. If any expectation was involved at all, I imagine it was that I would continue to be their guest on many occasions in the future. I admit this suited me well. On my own I tended to indulge in heavy, fatty foods, or else eat nothing at all, out of forgetfulness more than neglect. So I was probably a much healthier person than I might otherwise have been. But one of the results of this arrangement with Pauline and Frederick was that I sometimes found myself spending more time in their home than I did in my own flat. I suppose it was my nature to feel guilty about such things.

Of course, I anticipated that I would someday get married and have a family of my own, although I would have to confess that I could not foresee this happy event taking place for many years to come.

It was now beginning to rain, so we took shelter under the eave. Pauline folded her arms over her chest. I gave up on my cigarette and, during a brief moment when she seemed to be looking the other way, tossed it into the shrubbery.

"Sophie's very talented," I said, glancing at Pauline to see what her reaction might be, conscious of having uttered what could only be termed a gross understatement.

"Yes," she murmured absently as she gazed out into the fading light, her eyes held by some distant, or perhaps inward, object that I could not discern. In only a few seconds the rain had intensified to a downpour, drumming loudly on the roof and forming a curtain of water that I could have parted had I reached out my hand.

I began to think, as this latest silence stretched to one minute, then two, that she was going to make no response beyond this single word. And I thought perhaps we should go in, if for no other reason than I was beginning to feel the evening chill.

But before I could nudge her toward the door, she spoke again.

"You know, it's funny—though it isn't funny at all, really. I was with Sophie in her room just before I came out here. She's in a state. She was crying. She told me she doesn't know what happened to her when she was playing earlier—she doesn't understand how she got through the whole piece without a mistake. She said it was like she wasn't there, or like she was somewhere else in the room watching herself play. I told her not to worry. But she wanted to explain it to me. And then I was thinking how I've been listening to her practice for such a long time, almost two years. I'm always here when Selma comes for lessons. So I've heard her play that piece before. Maybe not all the way through, but I've heard her playing some of the harder passages over and over, trying to get them right. I could tell she was improving. You've seen it yourself, Joseph. There's been a great improvement in her playing, especially in the last few months. I know she's still just a child. I don't want her to take all this so seriously and I certainly don't expect her to be faultless. I don't expect that of anyone. It's only in the last day or two I noticed something. It seems as if nothing is difficult for her. She's playing new pieces, but she doesn't seem to be working very hard at all. I can't explain it really, because I know things aren't supposed to happen that way. I've noticed something else too, and I can't even tell for sure what it is. I can see she's different. She said she knew when she sat down at the piano today that she wasn't going to make any mistakes. She knew that the notes were going to fall in the right order. All she had to do was hit the keys. She knew she was going to do it. And that's good, I suppose. But it seems to go beyond that somehow. And that's what I'm concerned about."

She turned to me.

"I know I'm not making much sense. Can you understand what I'm trying to say?"

I nodded. One of the things that had struck me most about Sophie's performance was a quality of effortless precision that seemed to elevate the performance into a higher—almost ethereal—realm.

"The problem now is that she seems almost afraid of what she can do. She was getting herself all worked up about it. I told her we don't expect great things from her now; things she won't be able to deliver. But I agree that it is a little frightening to see how good she is. I actually think if she tried she could play anything we asked her to. I worry though. She seems to feel it all so intensely. She's so young and I don't know what it will do to her."

Pauline's impulses were maternal and motivated solely by concern for Sophie's welfare. Her child was burdened with an artistic temperament and would, thus, need protection from the passion that was certain to take possession of her whenever she sat down to play. I realized. But I didn't see what could be done, or if anything should be done. Wasn't it all part of the creative process? The trance-like state that befalls some artists during a performance; the amplified emotional states; the frequent shifts between supreme confidence and bottomless despair? As she grew more comfortable with her abilities and arrived at a deeper understanding of the music, it was likely that Sophie's behaviour would line up with that process. What could Pauline, or Miss Kraus, or anyone, I wondered, do about it?

"I'm not fooling myself, am I Joseph?"

"Not at all."

"You saw what I saw, then. I'm not letting my imagination run wild just because it happened so suddenly."

"Be assured it was even more sudden for me. I haven't been around lately to hear her practice. At least you had some preparation. I was sitting there with my mouth hanging open."

She squeezed my arm.

"Frederick was like you," she said, relief bringing a hint of warmth to her voice. "He said he couldn't believe his ears."

"And Miss Kraus?" I asked.

"You saw her. It was like the heavens had opened up and rained gold."

"But was she as surprised as the rest of us?"

"Surprised? Hmm, no. I think she was hopeful more than anything. She said to me afterward that she knew Sophie could do it if she tried."

I nodded. Pauline had complained to me in the past about Selma Kraus's system of teaching, which apparently did not utilize modern methods such as gentle persuasion, instead relying on accuracy, discipline and the sharpness of an abruptly raised voice. As a distant relative of Frederick, Miss Kraus had his absolute confidence in her abilities. But I had no wish to explore this issue deeply. I had always listened with a sympathetic ear to Pauline's reports of how the lessons were progressing but had never presumed to offer advice. It was not my place to do so. Besides, I'd heard Pauline voice grudging approval of Miss Kraus on several occasions.

Now, there was no denying that her methods were effective.

We stood in silence for another few moments, observing the slackening rain, the dripping leaves.

Then Pauline said: "She wants to play for us again before she goes to bed."

"She must be tired."

"I told her she didn't have to. But ... anyway, we'll see how it goes."

I followed her across the porch and into the house.

Five

$\smallsmile\!\!\!\!\!\!\smallsmile$

MISS KRAUS HAVING by this time taken her leave, it was just Pauline, Frederick and myself assembled in the parlour to hear Sophie play her encore.

It was a very old house, at one time owned by a clockmaker of local renown. At this stage in his career, Frederick had neither the means nor the time to undertake major renovations and the place had retained its rustic charm. The kitchen was small, with a great deal of age-darkened wood—along with some hideous wallpaper featuring cartoonish depictions of cooking implements—giving it a cramped feel. They could fit a table in there but only just. Pauline found it drab and oppressive and wished to change a few things, the wallpaper foremost among them. But it was a well-lit space and served its purpose.

We passed through the kitchen on our way to the parlour, a small square space at the side of the house. The wallpaper in here—a pseudo-Morris print with twisting vines and flowers against a light green background flecked with gold—gave the room a patina of antique drabness. When entering this room you felt as if you were passing through a portal to the previous century. The Chelsea upright in the far corner was by far the largest object in the room. A few sombre portraits in gilt frames—Pauline's great find at an estate sale auction—put a final touch on the aura she'd evidently sought to create: a genteel age long past.

I don't know how Sophie felt about the decor. All her hours in the parlour must have left an impression on her. I had never thought the dark colours and heavy furnishings would provide much comfort to a child or create an atmosphere in which artistic endeavours could flourish. But I know nothing of such matters and she didn't seem to mind.

Frederick reclined—sprawled, really—in his armchair, with Sophie perched on his lap. He was a tall angular man with long bony limbs who was constantly moving his large feet out of the way and who struck his elbows against doorframes with numbing regularity. Despite the protrusion of knuckles and other joints, his hands—which were huge—were also remarkably gentle. At one time he'd pursued music seriously and had for several years enjoyed the tutelage of Selma Kraus. And though he came to realize that the piano would never figure significantly in his life, he still dabbled with the instrument, though more as an amusement since the demands of his new practice meant little free time.

There was nothing rough or provincial about Frederick's manner—his serenity and contemplative intellect drew people to him. His eyes always suggested traces of a lingering smile. In some ways he appeared boyish, with small round glasses, button-down sweaters over white shirts and thick hair of tarnished brass that flopped down over his forehead and which he was always brushing back with one hand. But this was at odds with his height, of which I think he was always conscious and which he sought to mitigate with an habitual stoop. Instead, he appeared to be living in constant fear of bumping his head against something.

After getting to know him I could not envision Frederick doing anything but practice medicine, though his interests ranged far and wide. It was a profession that required exactly those qualities he possessed in abundance: tact, candour, intuitive wisdom, compassion. In fact, I had already resolved to engage him as my own personal physician, though to do this officially I would first have to break off with Dr. Felix Grimes, a very gracious, elderly man, whom I'd been seeing since I was a child. Frederick, of course, was closer to my own age and had won my trust on a number of levels. However, Dr. Grimes was intimate with my medical history and had exhibited a remarkable diagnostic expertise on more than one occasion. These were the factors that weighed upon my mind as I debated with myself how to proceed.

Frederick turned to us as we entered the parlour, his glasses flashing in the light of the lamp.

"How do you like my little chicken?" he asked.

"I'm not your little chicken!" Sophie declared and grabbed her father's nose between thumb and forefinger. Frederick shook his head and made a growling noise. Sophie squawked.

"Chicken! Chicken! Chicken!" Frederick chanted as Sophie leaned forward and pushed her fingers through his hair.

"You're the chicken," she said.

"Am I then?"

"Frederick, really," Pauline said. "You're getting her all worked up. She won't be able to sleep now."

Pauline took a step or two forward, her manner indicating that the time had come.

Sophie and Frederick touched foreheads. Her blonde hair was a curtain, hiding their faces from view.

"She's right, you know."

Sophie nodded solemnly. "Can I play one more? Please? Can I play one more? Please?"

"Are you sure you want to, sweetheart?" Pauline asked in a softer tone. "You don't have to if you're too tired."

"I want to!"

Pauline sighed, defeated.

As she slid off Frederick's knee and grabbed for his hand, I noticed Pauline putting out her own hand in a protective gesture.

"Daddy will sit with me."

Frederick sprang up.

"I sure will. You'll give your old dad a lesson then, will you?"

Pauline glanced over her shoulder at me and rolled her eyes.

We resumed our regular seats and watched as Frederick clowned with his daughter.

"What do you want me to do?"

"Turn the pages."

"These pages?" he asked obtusely, retrieving a book from a nearby shelf and scratching his head.

"No, silly. Here!"

Sophie, in a flowered ankle-length nightgown with a frilly lace collar, looked like a normal child ready for bed. But as she reached upward to prevent her father from placing the wrong book on the stand, I was struck by how small she was, by the seeming frailty of her limbs and the milky translucence of her skin. Her little feet did not even approach the pedals, and her arms were much too short to allow her to arrange the sheet music by herself. Yet here she was, ready to play for us, to grant a voice to those tiny black marks dotting the page. She was about to do something that I could never hope to do, and she was going to do it well. She was so young—too young, I thought—to have achieved this degree of proficiency in anything, let alone the intricate workings of an instrument that some people spend their lives hammering away at without achieving anything of consequence.

"She's too tired," Pauline whispered as Frederick and Sophie finally settled on a piece of music. "She gets excited like this and then gets frustrated when things don't work out the way she wants."

She laced her fingers in a pattern that I knew represented anxiety. It was almost as if she was worried that Sophie would abandon her music if tonight's performance failed to meet her own expectations.

"She'll do fine," I said in a low voice, leaning over slightly to bring my lips close to her ear. But I don't know if Pauline actually heard what I said because Sophie had already begun to play.

Six

PAULINE HAD TAKEN Sophie up to bed. Frederick and I lounged with our glasses of sherry beside a blazing fire. I was going to have to leave soon, for my responsibilities at the office required me to be the first one present and I needed my sleep. But the evening had passed so pleasantly, I was reluctant to let it end. Maybe it was the sherry, but I felt myself become flushed with gratitude, as if I'd received a great honour completely out of the blue. It was a sensation of sublime well-being. I felt entirely comfortable with my station in the world; I needed, wanted, desired nothing beyond what had been given to me here tonight. Maybe I was drunk, or slightly addled by too much good food, or perhaps I had mellowed into a sentimental humour, but for a few moments I was so absurdly happy I thought I might begin to cry.

By conscious effort I managed to subdue this impulse and avoided making a fool of myself in front of Frederick for something that I could not explain. But my desire to give voice to this swell of emotion was still there, even if it had been reduced from a compulsion to a whim. We were both tired by this time and, as the evening waned, lapsed into silence, fixing a languid gaze on the fire. But I didn't want it to end this way. I didn't want to leave Frederick and Pauline with the impression that I took their hospitality for granted.

"I really can't tell you how much I appreciate everything you do for me," I said, my eyes on the fire. "Sometimes I think it's too much. I'll never be able to repay ..."

Frederick moved his hand in a succinct gesture dismissing my concerns.

"Don't even think about it. You do just as much for us," he said, though I had no idea what he could mean. "Besides, you'll get married someday. You can repay us by inviting us to your house."

I nodded and decided to hold my tongue. I didn't want to belabour the point.

A few moments elapsed and I detected a subtle darkening of mood in my companion, who seemed to slouch deeper into his chair. Or perhaps it was simply the room, which was losing its contours and growing less distinct as darkness encroached upon us. Aside from a solitary lamp on a low table beside the door, the fire cast the only illumination. Eerie shadows flickered over the walls and across Frederick's long, thoughtful face. The huge log that we had earlier lifted onto the grate was crumbling and shifting on its iron support, scattering sparks into the air, where they glimmered briefly and died. As I watched, I too felt my strength waning. My head nodded. The glass of sherry felt heavy in my hand.

But when I heard Pauline's footsteps tapping a lively measure through the ceiling, I became intensely aware of the piano bedded down for the night, silently presiding over the household like a slumbering despot, awaiting the touch of those childish fingers that would bring it back to life. And, slipping into a contemplative state, I was moved to a further awareness of the frailty of all things, not simply of life itself but of everything around us, the everyday objects and experiences that seduce us into a false understanding but which actually guard their secrets closely and in the end leave us baffled. It came to me that, if untended, connections between people can easily wither and die, in just the same way that damaged leaves of plants shrivel and drop off. I thought of my parents, who had succumbed to just such a fate, withering away to nothing from lack of use. I'd done all I could to drag them into the light of day, to nourish their spirits and sustain their hopes, to make them feel necessary. But they chose to retreat into a shadowy world of inaction and oppressive silence. I was helpless. They awaited the end as if for a train that was going to take them to a better place.

I hoped I would never again watch anyone I loved accept such a passionless, insipid fate.

"I should go home," I said, making no move to rise to my feet. "I have to get up early."

Frederick remained transfixed by the glowing remnants of the fire. I could barely make out his features in the half-light.

I drained the last of my sherry.

"Pauline doesn't want to have any more children." Frederick inclined his head slightly in my direction, drawing me into an apparent conspiracy.

"No?" I said stupidly.

"She says it wouldn't be fair to Sophie."

I weighed my words with care.

"Is that true, do you think?"

"Not sure. To my way of thinking, it's not to have any more children that might be unfair to Sophie."

Frederick came from a large rambunctious family and grew up in a house swarming with all kinds of relatives of all ages. However, Pauline's experience had been identical to mine: that of an only child. I had no way of knowing which of these two childhoods would be better, for anyone. Certainly there were times growing up when I had been lonely but it became for me a condition essential to living, normal, neither beneficial nor harmful. Though I had had friends whose families were large, I could never imagine being a child in a house full of other children. I still could not imagine entering into a lifelong competition for the attentions of my parents.

These concepts were alien and somewhat frightening to me and I could only guess that Pauline harboured similar reservations. But we had never discussed this topic in the context of her marriage with Frederick and I found myself reluctant to explore the matter with him. If a conflict was brewing between them regarding the potential size of their family, I would not take sides. This was something they would sort out privately or not at all.

Frederick sighed and settled back into his chair. He seemed content to remain where he was, though we were now sitting in almost total darkness.

"It's late," I said, finally making the effort to rise to my feet. My legs were stiff and heavy and I wondered for a moment how I was going to manage the walk home.

"Didn't mean to drive you out," he said in a morose tone, from the shadowy depths of his chair. I had never seen him quite like this—the melancholy side of his character so plainly exposed—and the idea of him burdened like the rest of us with troubling questions to which there existed no easy answers gave me a bit of an unpleasant start. I certainly don't expect anyone to be happy all the time—least of all myself—but when someone you know well who has always found a way to derive some measure of satisfaction even from life's afflictions suddenly shows you a darker aspect, you can't help but look for reasons.

I did this now, recalling a brief episode at dinner, which even as I brought it to mind appeared to be nothing. It was a fleeting image of the five of us sharing a laugh over something, a remark I believe Selma Kraus had made, and then of Frederick glancing up and of Pauline lowering her eyes, as if she had been witness to some indecency. Frederick eyed her sternly, for no reason that I could see. I'd thought little of it at the time, but I now wondered what I had missed and what it could have meant.

"No," I said. "It's not that at all. I'd happily stay up all night if I didn't have to go to work in the morning."

"Well, you know, there is a spare bed."

I smiled, though it was much too dark for him to see this.

"Thanks, Frederick. Not tonight."

"Ah, well …"

I had slept at their house many times before, most recently mere weeks ago. And I would likely be doing so again at Christmas unless I happened to make other plans. I didn't want to impose needlessly.

I pulled on my jacket. Frederick stood, yawned, stretched his limbs, and went to switch on the ceiling light. The room leapt into painful focus. I shielded my eyes.

"I'll give you a lift home, if you like."

I could see now how exhausted he was, his skin pale and creased, his eyes sunken, appearing shrivelled in their sockets.

"Actually a walk is just what I need."

The living room opened on to the front vestibule. It was from here that stairs led to the upper floor.

"I want to go up and say goodnight to Pauline, and Sophie, if she's still awake. I'll just be a minute."

Frederick folded his arms and leaned his shoulder against the wall. I could sense him drifting off to sleep even as I ascended the stairs.

Seven

~~~

I WAS NOT surprised that Pauline decided to remain upstairs with Sophie rather than join us in front of the fire. She often left Frederick alone with me, imagining, I suppose, that we would communicate spontaneously with each other in that brawny vernacular that women seem to think men assume in their absence. I realized that she wanted us to know and like each other, to form a bond exclusive of her influence. And I had no trouble with this whatsoever because it was a simple thing for me to do and because I knew it pleased her. I wanted to please her, to let her know in the small ways available to me that I valued her friendship just as I always had.

On some level, I suspected, she suffered a measure of guilt for having—in her eyes—abandoned me, her childhood friend and soul mate; for having thrown me over and fallen in love and embarked upon a life of her own. With Frederick and me as friends, she could welcome me into her home without having to regard us as rivals for her attention. When I visited I was there, also, as Frederick's friend.

But the fact was that, even though almost seven years had passed and I felt at ease in his company and enjoyed discussing almost any subject with him, there persisted between us a relic of our old formality that I doubted would ever be completely dispelled. And I don't mean to imply that I felt in the least slighted by this. It was simply his manner of dealing with people; all people, not just me. He was shy—possibly because of his height—and he tended toward introspection rather than displays of gregarious fraternity. He could appear hesitant and timid, even among those he knew well. I had attended many gatherings at their house—usually an assortment of friends, relatives, colleagues, neighbours—and noticed that, while Pauline played the congenial hostess and seemed to be all places at once, Frederick made it a habit to linger in the background, to frequent the kitchen, or else select a chair and remain seated in it for most of the evening.

People would then cluster and circulate around him, as if he were the sun and they the planets. Women would sit on the stool beside his feet, men would pull chairs away from the table and situate themselves close by so they could hear all he had to say. It was not just his medical associates who held him in high regard. People of various backgrounds and professions sought him out but in his manner was the tension and unease of someone who cannot bear intimacy. I suppose I was the person closest to him after Pauline and Sophie. But this does not mean we were like brothers.

A light was coming from Sophie's room. Pauline was seated on the edge of the bed close beside the lamp and holding a book. I couldn't tell immediately if she was reading aloud—I didn't hear her voice, but in intimate situations she often spoke in tones so low her voice fell to nearly inaudible levels. Upon drawing closer however I could see it was a thick book with pages greyed by dense blocks of text. The title caught me by surprise because *Anna Karenina* is such a grave and oppressive story and I thought she had read it years ago. But I remember her telling me how much she'd loathed it and how Tolstoy was surely no better than an ogre and a tyrant to dream up such a hideous fate for a free woman.

Sophie seemed to have fallen asleep.

"Hi," I said softly. As Pauline turned, the light caught her hair and made it a blaze of gold.

"You're leaving?"

"I can't believe it's this late. I'm not going to be any good at work tomorrow."

She rested the book on her lap.

"Is she asleep?" I asked in a whisper.

"Yes, but I didn't want to leave her alone. I don't know why, really. She was over her ... upset, I think." Indeed, Sophie had seemed very calm after playing her second piece. "I guess I just wanted to be with her."

"Well, you certainly didn't miss anything. We took turns falling asleep in front of the fire."

Sophie moaned and shifted her head on the pillow, turning it away from the light. As she slipped one arm from beneath the blanket, the sight of her tiny limbs and the pale, soft skin touched me once more.

The glorious music I'd heard earlier sounded like a mature, highly-trained artist at her peak. It was impossible to reconcile it with the seraphic image before me. I had nearly forgotten the short piece she played after dinner, the Chopin *berceuse* in D-flat. But after Pauline's comment I could once more hear the fragile dignity of its theme and variations and feel my blood pulse in concert with its delicate rhythms. It is a piece of great subtlety, weighty with pauses and solitary notes left dangling in the air.

But Sophie handled it with aplomb, not forcing anything, allowing the music to achieve its own balance and flow and to express its full range of emotion through a kind of surface tension between push and pull, light and dark, restraint and exuberance. She appeared to toy with the music, allowing it one moment to lead her where it would, the next reining it in, grasping it tightly as if it belonged only to her. Indeed, as she played, her face radiated the confidence of ownership, not simply of the music but of her ability to convey it. No longer was she the spectator at her own recital, breathlessly in awe of her own prowess, fearful of any sudden disturbance that might upset the fragile equilibrium she had achieved. She now seemed in total control, even closing her eyes as she played, daring the music to confound her by indulging this whim and yet leaving her performance unblemished. Her hands darting over the keys were like water, their unbroken movement full of fluidity and grace.

"You really should go home, Joseph. You're in bad shape."

To my embarrassment, I had allowed my head to nod and my eyes to droop shut.

She smiled.

"Poor boy," she murmured, laughing softly with maternal forgiveness. "Too much wine."

I leaned over and kissed her lightly on the forehead. Her hand brushed my cheek.

"Thank you for tonight."

I went around to the other side of the bed to give Sophie a kiss, my usual practice whether she was asleep or not. I was sorry to have missed my opportunity to tell her at length how much I had enjoyed her playing but on her way to bed she had offered her cheek for a kiss and I decided it could wait.

As I bent down to place this second kiss on her cheek, imagine my surprise to see her eyes wide open and feel her arms encircling my neck in a sturdy embrace. The sudden weight of her threw me off balance and I had to support myself with my arms to avoid being hauled down on top of her.

The strangest part of this encounter—which left me dizzy and out of breath—was the look in her eyes. While I do not mean to use the word "desire" in its erotic sense, her eyes searched mine in an audacious and unchildlike manner, probing deeper and deeper still until I stood exposed before her. Then, after a second or two, her eyes lost their focus and I understood that she was not awake.

Beside me, Pauline gently unwound Sophie's arms from around my neck.

"There you go," she said casually.

Freed, I retreated and straightened my collar. I hoped that I had not emitted a gasp and appeared steadier than I felt. I understood, of course, that it was a meaningless incident but was troubled by a sense of having stepped over a line. I did not want to meet Pauline's eye while guilty confusion was no doubt obvious on my face.

As we left the room—just as Pauline was shutting the door—I caught one final glimpse of Sophie in bed where she lay framed by the silver oblong of light from the window She may have been smiling, but since she remained in sight for only a moment, I could not tell for certain.

"Well," I said in a hoarse whisper as I struggled to regain my voice, "what do you think that was all about?"

Pauline seemed to dismiss the incident altogether.

"She's been sleeping poorly for a few weeks now. She's been having bad dreams too. Sometimes I hear her whimpering in her sleep. Frederick says there's no need for concern, it's just a phase she's going through. But I haven't seen any improvement and sometimes, when I hear her and go in to look, she's sitting up in her rocking chair rocking away, eyes open. Anyone would think she was awake but she's sound asleep. I don't know what to make of it. I don't think she knows what she's doing. At least, I've never woken her up in the middle of one of these … episodes. Sometimes I stay up with her, but usually I lead her back to bed. When I hear her crying again I know she's having another dream."

"Does this happen often?"

"Often enough to make me worry."

Downstairs Frederick was nowhere in sight.

"It could be Frederick's right." I tried to sound reassuring. "It's probably something she'll grow out of."

"Well, if it doesn't stop soon I'm taking her to a specialist. I can't let this continue, Joseph. She wakes up exhausted and cranky. And I'm not getting any sleep either because I'm listening for her all night."

Just as we reached the bottom Frederick emerged from the library—a small room to the left of the hallway—with a slender book in his hand.

"Look, Joseph, I almost forgot again," he said, appearing distracted, pushing strands of hair from his eyes. "We talked about this last week—or it might have been the week before. I meant to give it to you long before this."

He handed the book to me. It was frayed and blackened somewhat along the edges, obviously well-thumbed. The cover depicted the very image of desolation, a slender willow tree bent amidst a blasted landscape. The title, *Rites of Passage: The Collected Verse of*

Peter Surrey, did not seem familiar. Frederick's features sagged with disappointment at my lukewarm response.

"I'm sure we talked about him." he said. "You remember. It was just last week." He paused and drew his eyebrows together. "Wasn't it?"

He looked to Pauline for an answer. She shrugged.

"Oh, God. Maybe it was someone else."

"I don't think I've ever heard of him," I said. "But I'll borrow it if you don't mind. It looks interesting."

"Don't feel you have to, Joseph," Pauline said. "You know how Frederick gets things all mixed up in his head sometimes."

"I was sure it was you," he said, gazing at me with dismayed perplexity and then at the book. "Surrey was a physician as well as a poet. He was only young when he died. Thirtyish. He killed himself."

"Oh, well then. I have to read it now."

Pauline retrieved my coat from the closet and I slipped the book into the inner pocket.

"Thanks," I said again. "For everything."

"Here," Pauline said as she pulled an umbrella from the stand. "You'll need this."

The rain had indeed persisted, though more softly now. I was surprised that I had so thoroughly lost track of both the time and the weather. I did not like to be caught off guard. However, it had been an unusually eventful evening: revelatory, rewarding, unsettling. It signalled a departure of some sort, the commencement of a new chapter in all our lives. At the time, I may not have thought about it in precisely those terms, but the notion was there, taking shape at the back of my mind.

I kissed Pauline on the cheek, shook Frederick's hand and took my leave.

Eight

THE WET SIDEWALK felt slippery and my breath created tufts of steam in the damp air. All around me tidy, darkened houses exuded an air of snug and prosperous security, for this was an exclusive neighbourhood, one with many dwellings constructed on a grand scale, girded by high wrought-iron enclosures or stone walls.

It was just past midnight, but I felt no danger walking alone along these tranquil avenues with their pristine uniformity, sculpted shrubbery, and antique streetlamps. I visited Pauline and Frederick as often as three times a week and frequently covered the entire distance in an automatic fashion—almost as if sleepwalking—while allowing my mind to wander. Often I reached home completely unaware of the time that had passed, my head filled with images that bore no relation to these deserted streets.

Tonight, my thoughts returned to the many things I had witnessed during the evening, from Sophie's extraordinary musicianship to Frederick's peculiar confusion over the book of poems. I wondered now if it had been wise of me to borrow the book after all, considering that he had obviously discussed it with someone, likely a colleague, who would recall the conversation and then ask Frederick if it was still available. Frederick would then be compelled to explain that he'd loaned it to someone else, forced to relive his mystification and embarrassment over the matter. This would be painful for a man who took great pride in his intellect, even if, as

Pauline had so blithely pointed out, he sometimes "mixed things up in his head."

I resolved to read the book over the next day or two—to study it and be prepared to make a few intelligent observations—and then return it at the first opportunity.

My solitary steps raised a hollow clatter in the still night air. The rain had slackened to mist and so I closed the umbrella and continued on, tapping the steel tip against the pavement.

In my mind there remained the ghostly echoes of the music Sophie had played, the two pieces blending together in my memory to create a hybrid that possessed features of both compositions: the rhythmic order of the Mozart, the ardent lyricism of the Chopin. Because I lacked all but the most rudimentary musical education, it always astounded me to watch another person wrest untainted emotion from any instrument, especially one as expressive as the piano. I had been attending concerts for most of my life, and possessed an elementary critical aptitude, a basis on which to pronounce one musician's talent superior to another's. I was not a novice in these matters, for as with Pauline and then Sophie, parental duties included the offer to take up music if we so desired. It was soon clear that my enthusiasm far outstripped my talent. Although I studied the piano briefly when I was quite young and later played French horn in my school band, I learned very early that my delight in making music was not shared by those who were unfortunate enough to find themselves within hearing range of my performances. My musical ineptitude was a source of great disappointment to my parents, who always measured their own successes against those of others, and when they saw children my age making such an eager display of their skill at the piano or violin—witnessed the rapture and pride on the glowing faces of other parents—they interpreted my lack of proficiency as a personal failure and were ashamed. They became even more humble and contrite than before, and, seeking to make amends, threw themselves with renewed vigour into their community work. I can see all this now as part of a larger pattern of behaviour. But at the time all I knew was that I had let everyone down, myself included, through laziness, lack of discipline, poor posture, what have you. Never mind that I won a prize for mathematics, or that my physics project was singled out for special honours and was among those selected for an inter-school science fair held in the Studley Gymnasium at Dalhousie University, or that my elocution instructor claimed I was among the best students she had ever taught. These were minor accomplishments—after all, there was a mathematics prize awarded every semester, two hundred projects were displayed at the science fair, and the elocution instructor was known to be generous with praise. These childhood triumphs therefore lacked distinction. My father loved that word, "distinction," and would utter it with a covetous gleam in his eye as if it were some consummate state of being that he could never hope to attain, like sainthood. I don't seem to remember him ever accomplishing anything of "distinction" himself, which may have accounted for the permanent aura of mourning that infiltrated our home and, like a shameful secret, tainted the years we lived together.

We had a nice house, actually. It was large, with much more space than we ever used or needed, and an attic that in my solitary fantasies I pretended was a magic cavern containing wonders of every description. But by the time I was old enough to form impressions of the world around me, the curtains were tightly drawn over closed windows, even in summer. This was done as a concession to my mother's weak eyes and delicate constitution, or so I was told. However, my earliest memories of my mother are of an efficient and bustling little bun-haired woman who appeared untroubled by physical infirmity. In fact, she appeared to my childish eyes boundlessly energetic, always cooking or cleaning, always up to something that required a great deal of effort and sprightly movement. Not until much later does she appear in my mind as a wretched recluse like my father, sitting at the table drinking coffee hour after hour, interested in nothing, content to allow her days to slip quietly into the dustbin.

There may well have been an illness involved—mental if not physical—but my parents were not the sort of people to discuss such matters in the presence of a child. I was left to draw my own conclusions. The impression that remains with me is that they preferred the house that way: faded, dreary, silent, cheerless.

Tonight, my route home took me down a narrow street lined on one side with tenements and vacant lots overgrown with weeds, and hemmed in on the other by a huge warehouse with most of its windows broken. I had only taken a few steps when the sound of laughter and the sight of two men emerging from an apartment building brought me up short. One of them lit a cigarette but instead of moving off in one direction or another, they slouched beneath a nearby streetlamp. They were a fair distance away and likely hadn't even seen me. I could easily have turned back and found a better path that would have delivered me to my flat with only a brief delay. But tired, not thinking straight and because I saw no rational alternative, I decided to keep going.

It was as if circumstances had hunted me down and cornered me, cutting off every other possibility until I was left with this single, unappealing option. I like to believe that I am not unduly nervous or timid. I tend not to shrink from a confrontation if I believe the outcome will be constructive. But neither do I seek such encounters unnecessarily. As I drew closer and saw nothing threatening in the pair's behaviour, I realized nevertheless that my action was pure folly. How could I know what they were up to? Or how my presence might impinge upon their designs? That they were lounging in the street after midnight exchanging secretive murmurs should have been enough to alert me to potential danger. But with a stupidity born of exhaustion, I refused to let myself be intimidated. I saw only my flat and its homely comforts. I told myself that very shortly I would be in bed, asleep.

They glanced my way as I neared and shared a look of casual complicity. One scuffed his toe against the curb and raised his eyes to mine. As if in response to a signal, the other tossed his cigarette into the street. I broke into a cold sweat, my heart pounding out a demented warning in my chest. But it was too late now. They'd seen my face; the only way was forward.

I continued on.

I can't say what they were thinking as I drew near, looking proper and affluent in my long coat, gripping the umbrella, which may have looked like a thick walking stick. The lamplight cast a milky circle on the wet street and my rhythmic steps echoed shrilly in the night. I kept my head up, fully awake now, my eyes focused and unblinking. A frightful physical pain shot through my body, so keen and intense was my state of awareness, as if my limbs were set to explode. I prepared myself for the flash of a knife blade or a fist suddenly raised against me and tensed the hand that gripped the umbrella, my only weapon. Surely I could overpower them. In this neighbourhood, at this time of night, they were likely to be either drunk or hungry or in some other way disadvantaged.

Almost up to them, I felt like I was about to step blindly off the edge of the world into a void.

Then, with a swiftness that quickens my breath whenever I recall that night, I was close upon and then past them. With an ambiguous grin the smoker stilled my blood by grunting, "Evening . . ."

I gave a cautious nod.

They were behind me. I waited for the sound of footsteps chasing me down, for the heavy grip of a hand on my shoulder. Silence. Then a muffled exchange followed by a hoarse laugh. At the far end of the street I turned and hurried beyond the margin of their concern.

In the weeks and months that followed, I was haunted by dreams of derelicts and hoodlums accosting me in deserted alleyways, shoving me up against brick walls, demanding payment in exchange for my life. Without exception I emerged unscathed from these imaginary encounters, leaving my would-be assailants face down in the dirt after a brief scuffle. For a time I stayed away from that part of town more scrupulously than before and avoided walking alone late at night. However, as the weeks and months passed, these visions became less frequent and eventually stopped altogether. I resumed my old habits.

But the raw, brain-numbing fear of that moment remains with me to this day, leaving a bitter taste in my mouth and transcending memory. It has become a marker in my life separating all that had come before from all that followed. That incident has become part of who and what I am. It brings the entire evening leading up to it into vivid relief against the inconsequential routine of my life. I see Pauline and myself standing sheltered from the rain beneath the eave; Selma Kraus peppering Sophie with kisses; Frederick's mildly amused expression as he turns the pages as Sophie plays.

Then there are the textures, sounds, and smells of a more tactile memory. These sensations remind me of how things once were and cause me to reflect upon how radically things have changed. I am no longer the person I was. I feel like an old man and, in the manner of old men, take comfort in the past. But strange as it seems I still have much future to look forward to, much of my life left to live. At some point I will have to decide if it is worth the trouble to continue on, given my fluctuating health, the problems I've lately encountered in the office, the incessant foulness of the weather. I try to tell myself that, though I have lost a great deal, much remains for me to cherish, but somehow the words have lost their lustre. I exist from day to day but with Sophie gone my life is an arid place. The sun and moon are two faces of the same unfriendly creature. Night and day fuse into a chain of hours, minutes and seconds from which there is no respite. I see time stretching ahead as a monolith without features, blank and grey. I want no part of it.

But for now, I cling to this contemptible life, coward that I am.

Part Two

One

⌒

I FEAR I have misled you, my reader, by portraying myself as other than what I truly am. That is, I have suggested that I am honourable and worthy of your respect. I now admit that this is not the case. I am in fact a wretched creature whose life is an elaborate sham, an exercise in deceit. At one time I even fooled myself into believing I'd attained a degree of respectability and fell into the habit of accepting the courtesies of others as if they were my due. However, as you'll soon see, I strayed from the path of decency and lapsed into a state of internal exile, as if split into a private life and another life for public display.

To all appearances my conduct was above reproach. I performed civic and work-related duties and met my social obligations as always. But privately I developed appetites and surrendered to passions that can only be described as detestable. Outwardly unchanged, I allowed a craving for what I thought was love rule my actions. At every step, though I knew it to be wrong, I justified my hunger for pleasure with spurious rationalizations and deplorable excuses. I told myself that I could not help myself, that it was not my choice. When it was over I regarded with renewed clarity the people who loved me and looked up to me, who were generous toward me and invited me into their home. To my shame I not only deceived but betrayed them and continue to do so to this day. With one effortless act of treachery I was able to conceal the truth and escape a world of pain, a world I deserved.

Of course I cannot be sure my reputation is safe, or that the facts of the matter will remain hidden. I have no idea if direct evidence exists that would cast light on the contemptible part I played in this tragic affair. All I can hope for is the courage to reveal everything before a day of reckoning arrives. This will require great determination and some sacrifice and, in my weakened condition, I feel unequal to the task. Thus, if I fail in my resolve to make a verbal confession, this journal will stand as a record.

Only one other person in the world knows about this. She is sitting here with me, pen in hand, taking down everything I say. My dear Lucinda. In the end I was able to persuade her to delay her departure for just a little while.

And so, before proceeding further, I pledge not to burn these pages. I intend that upon my death they will find their way into the hands of those whose lives I so thoughtlessly destroyed.

Two

⌒

THE EVENTS I am about to describe occurred in the spring and summer of 1971, last year. Thirteen years had gone by since the evening I recounted earlier. Over that time, I had been fortunate enough to gain the favour of some senior managers at work who appreciated my efforts on behalf of the firm and saw to it that I received regular pay increases and was considered seriously for promotion whenever opportunities arose. After a rapid series of advancements, I was appointed Director of Bookkeeping, a position of considerable responsibility, one that placed me in charge of a staff of thirty clerks and typists. This meant that in only five years my salary had more than doubled, while my needs remained virtually unchanged. I still lived in a shabbily genteel two-bedroom flat on Walnut Street, near the university. I still took the bus or walked. Material things had never interested me, and other than books and record albums I owned no possessions bought for the sake of vanity or the thrill of ownership. I continued to buy the same ragtag assortment of groceries I'd always done and indulged only in the odd bottle of wine.

More often than not I dined with friends and relatives. My improved circumstances, however, allowed me to reciprocate all of the many invitations. I was disinclined to encourage people to visit me at my flat, which suffered from a bachelor's casual neglect. Not a conscientious housekeeper, I often saved my domestic chores for rainy afternoons, or let things accumulate to crisis proportions. And so, I delighted in the simple pleasure of being able to take the people I cared for most out to dinner and sometimes to stage plays. My most frequent companions were Frederick and Pauline and Sophie when she was available, though a number of others favoured me with their company on a regular basis. In short, I was living a life that, had I been granted a vision of it as a child, I would have gazed at with disbelieving eyes, wondering who that man could be with the long coat and the beard greying in such a distinguished fashion. When I presumed to speculate on the future, continued advancement and further success did not seem an unreasonable expectation.

This was only last year.

I was thirty-seven years old.

Sophie had lately turned nineteen, a fact that caused Pauline to grow dreamy and sentimental and to muse upon the early years of her marriage, as she had been nineteen when she met Frederick. She would talk about the little house they had lived in, about Sophie's first piano and the sensations of trepidation and wonder at discovering Sophie's talent. All of this had become part of family lore, a private mythology in which we all played various roles. I was usually the guest or onlooker; my function was to bear witness. I could verify much of what Pauline said, though with regard to some events my recollections were hazy. We must all share the blame for turning an ordinary family history into an extravagant and fanciful odyssey. Memory gives rise to hyperbole.

Ours was a common enough story of modest means transformed into affluence through ambition, talent, luck and simple hard work. There were no lengthy periods of deprivation or hardship, no serious obstacles to overcome. The past flowed seamlessly into the future to become our present. If Pauline occasionally exaggerated the stringent economies of the early years of her marriage, who was I to contradict her? Their first house became in her retelling little more than a hovel with draughty windows and an unreliable supply of running water. Sophie was often characterized as a capricious child of artfully mischievous tendencies. I held my tongue though my own memories were of a house that exuded a cosy warmth from every corner even with the fiercest winter winds howling outside, and of a polite child who seemed passively compliant even when tired or ill. I concluded that these embellishments caused harm to nobody, and if it gave Pauline pleasure to rewrite her story in this fashion, why should anyone spoil her fun?

The years had been kind to all of us. Frederick had become—as I predicted he would—a leading figure in the local medical establishment and was frequently invited to speak at official receptions and formal dinners. Recently he had been appointed to the Board of Directors of the Victoria General Hospital. His practice had flourished early and continued to do so after relocating to larger quarters and adding several associates. In only a few years he had been able to move his family into an imposing residence a few blocks away from their first house, a sprawling brick edifice at 1220 Young Avenue with twin pillars and a portico out front, six bedrooms and nearly as many baths.

It sat squarely in the middle of a half-acre of impeccable grounds upon which a squadron of landscapers and gardeners occasionally descended to prune and groom every square foot. Within the house, Pauline was kept busy planning meals and arranging social events. The subdued character of the decor, which tended toward off-whites and intricately patterned tile and wallpaper, was largely her doing, Frederick's input being limited to silent indications of approval. Pauline engaged a cook—Mrs. Radcliffe—to prepare the food for the frequent parties and gatherings, but otherwise prepared most meals. The only other regular staff was a maid, an amicable young woman named Deanna who, given one of the upstairs bedrooms, lived on the premises. Even I was assigned a room—a sizeable corner space with its own bath—for my visits had continued unabated throughout these many years, and I sometimes remained overnight.

Sophie's musical career had leapt forward in the meantime. Her affairs were handled these days by a booking agency which arranged tours and monitored the globe for demands for her talents. The concert year ran from September to April during which time she would give upward of fifty performances. She travelled a great deal and had become accustomed to doing so on her own. Sometimes, if the distance was vast and her absence prolonged, she was accompanied by a young woman from the agency named Grace Cabot, who had become a good friend. During the summer, Sophie tried to remain at home with her parents as much as possible, restricting her appearances to a few recitals in the immediate area.

Mostly she practised and sought to expand her repertoire, which already included a great many solo pieces by Mozart and Beethoven, Schubert and Schumann. There had been talk of adding some of Bach's Toccatas and Fugues to her summer recital list, as well as a few pieces by Ravel. But at the point at which I pick up the thread of my story, this was all speculation. Possible effects of a repertoire change on her audience—which had come to expect a standard set of works—still being debated.

Sophie's most pressing concern regarded an invitation from the Music Department at Dalhousie University to lead a master class in piano theory and practice. Her inclination was to turn it down, for the pressures of performing weighed heavily on her slender frame, and by the time the concert season came to a close she was grateful for an opportunity to relax and enjoy non-musical activities. When I saw her toward the middle of the month, she appeared eerily pale, her skin having taken on a jaundiced tint as it sometimes did when she allowed herself to become exhausted.

I dare say I had grown very fond of my young cousin. I count myself extremely fortunate to have attained a place among Sophie's inner circle of friends, for as she left her childhood behind she developed a fiercely independent nature and, as adolescence took hold, defended her privacy with a passion that some regarded as unreasonable. All during her school years she developed no close attachments to other children her age but even within her own family—and I am thinking here of her many cousins on Frederick's side—there were few whose company she would tolerate for more than an hour at a time. Her talent seemed to distance her from the world of childish amusements, for she always had one foot set firmly in the adult world, where every word and gesture can carry unintended meaning.

Other children regarded her with suspicion, perhaps even fear. Their gaiety and chatter withered in her presence and her efforts to join in seemed like appeasement rather than for her own entertainment. I believe they thought she looked down on them, and this may be so, for she could be harsh in her criticism and rarely endured the attentions of foolish people. In her mind, other children fell almost without exception into this category. She seemed to genuinely prefer the company of adults.

To put it simply, she was not like other children. She was sober and reflective to such a degree that for a long time Pauline was convinced there was something wrong with her. I hope we were fair to the child Sophie. I never heard her express resentment over the way she was treated, even with the mountain of expectations that were heaped on her shoulders at such a young age. I am certain we did not mistake a serious and solitary nature for commitment to art. She possessed an authentic and undeniable talent that as far as I could see she wished to share with everyone. But, strange to say, none of us ever expressed our thoughts on this topic. The assumption was there, from the day her gifts first appeared before us in all their radiant splendour, that she would devote her life to music. Nobody questioned this.

In April of last year Selma Kraus contracted pneumonia and died soon afterward of congestive heart failure. She was in her eightieth year. Not in regular contact with her, I was shocked by the news. Frederick had evidently been visiting her in the hospital every day and when I spoke with him later he indicated that he had got over his initial anxieties and was satisfied her recovery was well under way. But then one evening, for reasons that left the doctors scratching their heads, she fell into swift decline. Her strength waned, her heart grew weary with the struggle and in twenty-four hours she was dead. It happened so quickly that nobody thought to call her relatives until it was too late and so she died alone, with only a young nurse to comfort her. Her younger brother flew over from Bonn to put her affairs in order but while awaiting his arrival Pauline and Frederick took it upon themselves to make arrangements for the funeral and burial in a picturesque Lutheran churchyard outside of town.

When Pauline phoned me on Thursday with news of the death and to inform me of the visitation schedule and of the Monday service, she did not explicitly request my attendance at any of these events. And since I had not enjoyed as close a relationship with Miss Kraus as had the rest of the family, I assumed I would be paying my respects over the weekend at the funeral home and heading to the office as usual on Monday morning. The matter thus settled, I gave it no further thought.

Toward the close of business on Friday I received a second call, this time from Sophie, who informed me that her mother had changed her mind and wanted badly for me to come to the funeral.

"Well, it's certainly no problem," I said, puzzled somewhat by the urgency of her tone, though I was familiar by now with her tendency to be overly dramatic at times. "But you realize of course that I didn't know her all that well. Certainly not as well as you did."

"That doesn't matter," she said. "As long as you can come, it'll make Mom happy. She would have phoned herself, but she's got all these arrangements."

"It's the least I can do, isn't it," I said as I reflected on the situation, at the centre of which I envisioned Pauline wringing her hands, hoping enough people would attend to make a good show. "Your mother asks so little of me."

"Do it for me too, Joseph. Please. I don't like it when you do everything for her."

As she made this comment I noticed her voice modulate ever so subtly, as if the muscles of her throat had tightened. Her remark was followed by a brief laugh.

"I don't do everything for her, Sophie. Do I?"

"It looks like it sometimes. At least to me."

"That doesn't bother you, does it?"

I couldn't imagine why it would. I had never made a secret of the common history that Pauline and I shared. Frederick didn't seem to care. And Sophie was familiar with the story. Nothing had ever been held back.

My question—purely rhetorical in intent—was supposed to be playful; it was supposed to provide her with a chance to laugh the whole thing off.

"Well, you know. It sort of looks sometimes like you're in love with her."

This comment, as well as her serious tone, caught me by surprise.

"Sophie, she's my best friend. We grew up together. We share everything." I sighed, somewhat at a loss. "But you know all this. I don't have to explain it. Of course, I love her. I'd have to be the worst kind of monster not to."

After a moment she murmured, "I guess ..."

"Sophie, you don't sound pleased. Is something the matter? Can you tell me what's wrong?"

"It's nothing."

"How's your practising coming along? How are you doing with the Ravel?"

There was a brief pause.

"I don't want to talk about that."

"All right," I said. I tried to think of a graceful way to say goodbye.

"You don't have very many friends, do you?" she asked, catching me by surprise again. I felt colour rise in my face.

"I do all right." For some reason beyond my comprehension I added: "Probably better than you know."

I heard her emit a short, unpleasant, laugh.

"Likely," she said.

"How about you?" I asked, pressing forward against my better judgment. "I'll bet you have lots of friends."

"I don't have any friends."

"Sophie, that's not true and you know it. Listen to yourself. You sound like a brat."

"Does that bother you?" she asked, mimicking what I had earlier said.

"It bothers me a great deal because I know you. I know you're not really like that."

"You don't know, Joseph. You don't know me at all. You don't know what I'm really like."

"I think I do, Sophie. And I also think we should bring this conversation to a close. I have to get back to work and I can't see that we're getting anywhere."

Again, a pause.

"Fine," she said.

"I'll probably see you at the funeral home on Sunday. But if not, I will be at the funeral. Tell your mother I promise to be there. Okay?"

I waited, expecting her to hurl a peevish retort or some piece of sarcasm my way. But this did not happen. At last, her bad temper seemed to have spent itself.

"Whatever," she said. "G'bye."

Three

A s you can imagine, this exchange spoiled the rest of my Friday afternoon and evening. I was supposed to dine with an old friend from school whom I had not seen for years and who was going to be in town for only one night. But toward five o'clock when my mood failed to brighten I called Arthur at his hotel and cancelled, pleading a migraine and stomach cramps. I would not have been good company anyway, Sophie's inexplicable behaviour having consumed my thoughts so thoroughly that any effort to feign interest in casual conversation and reminiscence would have been painfully obvious to my friend.

After the office closed I walked home, forgetting in my preoccupied state that I'd intended to dine out and therefore had no fresh food in the house. As I walked I replayed in my mind the conversation with Sophie, trying to locate the exact point at which our perfectly cordial exchange began to sour into a verbal jousting match. It seemed to me that my attachment to her mother should not be of any concern to Sophie, and that it was grossly unfair of her to suggest that whatever small courtesies I was lucky enough to be able to perform for all of them were actually done for Pauline alone.

Financially speaking I had always been in a position of inferiority to Frederick, and so had never seen the point in giving them expensive gifts. Instead, I sought unique items and kept my eyes open for antique sales and estate auctions where I might happen upon treasures of a singular nature, one-of-a-kind oddities. I had come across several unusual specimens of late Victorian design—in particular a splendid floor lamp fashioned of wrought-iron and crowned with frosted glass in the shape of rose petals—which I purchased and gave to Pauline and Frederick as occasions arose.

I gave Sophie books and ornaments that I felt would appeal to an adolescent girl of high intelligence, though I suppose there is always the chance I misjudged the appropriateness of some things. However, there could be no question in anyone's mind that my intentions were anything but forthright and honest—I did what I did out of familial attachment—and Sophie was the one person who should have been able to see this without having it explained to her.

It was plain, though, that I had displeased her and in some mysterious way turned her against me. I brooded over this all of Friday evening (as I prepared a can of beans for supper and consumed several glasses of wine) and through the day Saturday as I performed my weekend chores. I resolved, of course, to clear up the matter at the first opportunity. But I resisted phoning for the simple reason that I hoped she was suffering mental anguish of a severity similar to my own. Also, I did not want to place myself so soon in a position of entreaty. My opinion—and I was confident she would share this opinion with me once we had talked the matter over—was that if any blame were to be assigned it would be mostly her burden to carry. I could not see, frankly, that I had done anything wrong. My only crime—if it could even be described in terms so harsh—was failing to put an end to the conversation sooner than I did, and this was largely a failure of nerve; I did not want to appear rude.

I was disappointed, therefore, to see that Sophie was absent when I arrived at the funeral home on Sunday. When I asked Pauline why, she lifted her chin in annoyance and informed me that her daughter had been "indisposed" for a day or two and was at home languishing about and feeling sorry for herself and being generally moody and uncooperative. I found this report somewhat encouraging, for, though I disliked the idea of Sophie preying upon her mother's nerves in such a selfish manner—particularly in a time of bereavement—it indicated, unless I was seriously misreading her conduct, that she was troubled by what had passed between us and was unwilling to encounter me in public before she could apologize to my face.

Still, I was unable to completely free my thoughts from this unpleasant episode and kept returning to it in search of an explanation even as I conversed with various persons gathered around the open casket to pay their respects to the late Selma Kraus. Many young people milled about—former students, I guessed—as well as older individuals and I heard more than one young man inquire after Sophie and then droop with disappointment when Pauline delivered a shortened version of the explanation she had given to me. It occurred to me then that I had never heard tell of Sophie forming any sort of romantic attachment, something that, though certainly none of my business, would surely have come up in conversation had there been any likely prospects lurking on the horizon. The two or three young men I noticed—grave, temperate, clean-shaven youths, each in a dark jacket befitting the occasion, each possessing the slender build and slight stoop of the serious student or musician—looked to me to be more than eligible. And it was also plain that, whatever affection they may have borne for Selma Kraus in her capacity as teacher or colleague, their real purpose today was to see Sophie.

As the crowd swelled, I decided not to prolong my stay. Preparatory to taking my leave I sought out Frederick and we exchanged a few words of admiration for the deceased. He informed me that she had not suffered, that her illness—though it took such a disastrous turn toward the end—was quite brief overall and had caused her little discomfort.

We shook hands and I began the arduous task of wading back through the crowd toward Pauline. However, on the way I encountered a rather short, stout, elderly gentleman with a beak-like nose whose air of weary distraction and of being totally removed from his element led me to the conclusion that he was the brother of Selma Kraus. The instant our eyes met he grasped my hand as if he'd discovered a familiar face amidst a throng of strangers.

"And how are you?" he asked, with such enthusiasm and delight that I began to fear that I really had met him before.

"Joseph Blanchard," I responded to his glance of inquiry. "I'm sorry about your sister."

"*Danke*," he said as he released my hand and clutched my elbow in a tight grip. "But is good, eh? Many people."

"She was well liked," I said, and found myself loudly enunciating each syllable with exaggerated precision, as if someone had told me he was deaf as well as German. Hoping to make myself heard more easily, I bent toward him. "She had lots of friends, lots of students."

"Ya," he nodded. "I saw you over there with ... uh ..."

"Pauline." I completed the sentence for him. "I'm her cousin."

"Ah," he said, nodding again as if this cleared up some conundrum that had been weighing upon his mind. "But the other one. The young *fraulein* ..."

"Sophie," I said, hazarding a guess.

"Yes, Sophie."

He raised himself on his toes an inch and glanced around the room.

"She's not here," I said in an even louder voice. "Not feeling well today."

"Ah," he said, nodding. "She's a bit ..." Here he left a blank for me to fill in. "... in the head. You know?"

"What?"

He looked confused.

"In the head," he repeated, now touching his right temple with his free hand, his other still gripping my elbow. "She's ..."

"Confused?" I ventured, though I suspected this was not his intended meaning.

"Not like ..." He closed his eyes and seemed to concentrate. "I do not know the word. My English is not so good."

"Oh well," I said and shrugged. "It doesn't matter."

I tried to ease my elbow from his grasp.

"No, no," he protested. "I will find the word."

I could see my afternoon slipping away as he sifted through the limited supply of English words at his disposal. Ten feet away, Pauline was engaged in conversation by a tiny, quivering, birdlike lady with bleached skin and tear-filled eyes, wearing a fur jacket and long white gloves. I was reminded that Selma Kraus had been a larger than life presence at the hub of a broad circle of intimate friends who had now been cast adrift by her death. She had also served the community well and brought culture and elegance into the lives of many people in the form of music. I resisted, unsuccessfully, the notion that Sophie's absence today was a disgrace.

My companion cleared his throat with a guttural resonance that seemed to shake the room.

"Excuse me," he said with a bright smile. "I try to improve my English on this trip."

"Not at all," I said, the urge to flee eased somewhat by the thought that I had nothing else to do anyway.

"*Fraulein* Sophie, I mean to say, what she is, is strong . . ."

I must have appeared confused, for he rushed into an explanation.

"In the head," he said, tapping his temple.

"Headstrong!" I said as the curtain lifted and the light came on.

"Yes, headstrong," he said, repeating the word with a note of triumph in his voice. "It means . . . ah—*Wie sagt mann das auf eng-lisch?*—she does what she likes. No?"

"Yes, she does what she likes. That's Sophie."

"Yes," he said, grinning and nodding like a puppet. He then added with inexplicable emphasis, "Splendid, eh?"

"Very much so," I said, not keen to prolong things by exploring what he meant by this. "But I'm afraid I must go now."

"Good, eh?" he said, nodding, but refusing to loosen his grip on my elbow.

"Yes, very good. But I have to talk to Pauline."

"Eh?"

"Pauline? Before I leave?"

I began to drift more forcefully away from him.

"You are leaving?"

"Yes, I'm afraid. I must go."

"It was good to see you again . . . uh . . ."

"Joseph," I reminded him as we shook hands.

"Ah …" He nodded.

I backed into the crowd, smiling foolishly, treading on toes and murmuring apologies as I went.

For a moment I loitered to one side as Pauline completed the task of comforting the pale-faced lady, who was shaking her head and discreetly applying a handkerchief to her nose. Pauline rubbed the woman's crooked back and whispered something into her ear, and I saw the old head tremble as she nodded in distraught agreement. Indeed, the degree of genuine sadness that accompanied this death—the death of a woman who had lived a rich and active life right up until the very end—struck me as a convincing demonstration of how firmly other people can become rooted in our lives. And I could not unsee the hurtful memory of the ill-attended visitations held for each of my parents upon their deaths, and how some people had turned up out of idle curiosity because of the widespread impression that my parents had died long before they actually drew their last breaths.

Finally Pauline was free.

"I see you were talking to Werner."

"So that's his name, is it? He never got around to telling me who he was. When I saw him I assumed he was Selma's brother. He just looked like what I thought Selma's brother should look like."

"Werner Hölderine. He's an architect. Quite an important one apparently, if what he says is to be believed. Did he tell you any war stories?"

"We didn't get into that, I'm afraid."

"He will. He'll tell you everything you ever wanted to know. And then some more. If you come for dinner tonight you'll hear it all. He's told us once already but I don't think that will stop him from telling us again."

"I think I might give dinner a miss tonight, if you don't mind," I said as we watched Werner snag the arm of an elderly gentleman in tweed who then stood close by, his head inclined, nodding occasionally, listening with rapt concentration, as Werner spoke and gesticulated in illustration of some point. "He's a nice enough fellow, but …"

I allowed this comment to trail off into the realm of unarticulated common understanding. But what had come to mind the instant Pauline issued the invitation was that I felt unprepared to encounter Sophie in a social situation considering what had so recently passed between us. I needed an opportunity to speak to her alone first.

"How are you holding up?" I asked.

"Oh, I'm all right," she said, granting me a brief smile. "Death is never easy. But it doesn't help that Sophie's being such a little witch about it."

"I suppose it hit her pretty hard."

"Maybe. But she hasn't really seen much of Selma these last few years. I don't think that's really it. All I know is that she's not herself. She just sits in her room. To tell you the truth, I'm sure there's something else on her mind. But I can't do anything for her if she won't say what it is."

"She'll snap out of it. Young people are stronger than we give them credit for sometimes."

"Oh, I'm sure she'll come out of it, like you say. But in the meantime she's driving me wild with her pouting."

"Maybe I'll try talking to her after the funeral."

"Oh, you've decided to come then. That's so good of you Joseph. I know Frederick will appreciate you being there. He's very good at hiding his pain, as you well know, but I know he'll miss her terribly." She paused and surveyed the crowd. "Yes, you talk to her. See if you can get any answers. Lord knows, these days I can't."

I opened my mouth, intending to ask if Sophie had passed along my message but it was clear that she'd neglected to do so.

We'd drifted over to one side of the casket and together observed the progression of young and old faces making their way forward. A few of those present were in some obscure way related to Frederick and therefore also bore a relation to Selma Kraus. Second or third cousins somewhat removed, relatives by marriage, uncles more or less. Many of these people I could not recall having seen before.

"I guess I'll take off," I said. "You don't really need me hanging around, do you?"

Pauline shook her head.

"No, I'm fine. We'll stay till the end." She consulted her watch. "Another hour or so." She took my hand and gave it a light squeeze. "Thank you for coming."

"It was no problem," I said.

"These things are always a problem."

"I don't know about that."

She smiled.

"Oh, and by the way, we're having a reception tomorrow afterward, back at the house. It's for whoever wants to come. So feel free."

"I always do, you know."

With this I left her standing on her own at the outer edge of the crowd, looking tired and somewhat wistful. Her face, turned in profile, seemed paler than usual, her large eyes stood out in bright unhealthy fashion from the waxen skin around them. I had the impression of many wearying concerns draining her strength. The situation was, of course, anything but normal. Though grief did not appear to be a pressing issue, the occasion did call for a certain grim reserve, a conscious toughening of exposed surfaces. Pauline was good at this and, like Frederick, could appear placid and untouched by the emotional turbulence around her even when her heart was breaking.

As I made my exit I sought out Frederick's eye, and we exchanged a brief signal of mutual acknowledgement. His height always made him the pivot of any gathering, the nexus of attention. People—relatives, friends, acquaintances, colleagues—mingled about him in a series of waves, each pausing for a chat or a few words. The irony of this was apparent, at least to me, as I caught sight one final time of Selma Kraus resting in her casket, enveloped by the sweetness of roses and the ponderous scent of lilies, but largely ignored now except by those of her generation who would soon be following along the path she had already taken.

Four

T HE NEXT DAY—Monday, that momentous day—there were no clouds. And as the sun progressed upward, its heat seemed to radiate not from the sky, but from somewhere deep within the earth's hidden core. Everywhere birds were singing. Trees quivered in the warm breeze.

I awoke early and made my way to the office where I got in a few hours' work before catching a taxi uptown to Grace Lutheran. Sophie's behaviour still weighed upon my mind, but not to the oppressive, exhausting degree of the last few days. I was eager now to meet because I wanted to find out what was troubling her. And I felt that, as a near relative, but neither parent nor guardian, I was possibly in a position to elicit a closely protected secret or two that she may have felt awkward disclosing to Pauline or Frederick. Not that I was so confident of myself that I was sure she would tell me everything. I had simply reached the conclusion that my value to her as a friend had always been obvious and that her rudeness the other day was an indication of her faith in our friendship. That is to say, she knew she could wound me with words and still come to me later to talk, that we would remain friends. We both understood that I could never be irreparably offended by anything she did or said.

None of this had ever been stated openly and there was probably no reason why it should have been. But I suppose I owed it to her to make some sort of general declaration of my respect and admiration for her, if only so she would realize that I didn't take her for granted.

Her extraordinary accomplishments were rarely discussed in her presence. Frederick had mentioned to me privately on a few occasions that he believed it to be unwise to heap too much praise on the shoulders of the young and impressionable. He'd heard of terrible things happening, he said, when juvenile virtuosos were constantly lauded. The immature ego is a ravenous creature, he told me. Parents should be mindful of what they say and not treat the gifted young person like a prince or princess.

The most they can and should do is provide an environment in which their offspring's talent is likely to flourish. Words spoken without heed to their ultimate effect can be destructive, and ill-considered praise can be every bit as harmful as undeserved criticism. Nobody, he concluded, wants to create a monster, because once you create it you have to live with it. I agreed this was a prudent strategy. After all, the applause of an appreciative audience, good reviews in the press, the occasional fan letter and a steady stream of bookings in prestigious venues should provide nourishment sufficient to sustain the hungriest of egos.

But I also felt that I could say a few words to Sophie about my reaction to her talent without bringing cataclysm raining down upon us all.

The church was crowded, and since I was one of the last to arrive, I seated myself near the back among the other stragglers. I strained to catch a glimpse of someone I knew, but to little avail. Near the front I noticed one head peeking above the rest which could have been Frederick's, but I knew I'd be seeing everyone later anyway and so relaxed into my place in the pew. Pauline had informed me that Frederick would be getting up to say a few words of eulogy, so I had this to look forward to.

As I arranged myself, I was still occupied with the question of whether Sophie had recovered from her funk to a degree that would enable her to attend the service this morning. Or, perhaps more to the point, was she here willingly or had she been coerced? Because she had to be here. She would have been given no choice in the matter. Pauline could be forceful when she had to be and I was confident

Sophie would have concluded that she could not back out of this morning's ceremony even if she were inclined to do so.

As the congregation settled and the churning organ music soared from background to foreground and the mass began, it grew much warmer in the church, in keeping with the unusual conditions outside. After a few moments I became conscious of feet shuffling, of cloth chafing against cloth, of throats being cleared, of bodies at odds with themselves. Like myself, many people, in the expectation of cooler weather, had come overdressed, some in long wool coats over suits. I felt the rising temperature within my own clothes and the stale exhalations of many people wafting over me. In a short time my discomfort grew severe, reminding me of days spent sitting in a stuffy school-room in early June, flies lazily circling the light fixtures and the sun's magnified rays assailing thirty children through a wall of windows, trying my utmost to concentrate on the teacher's words.

The priest's nasal intonation and tentative speaking style—full of awkward pauses of bewildering length—did nothing to dispel the general atmosphere of discomfort. The loudspeaker system buzzed throughout the service, and at one point during Frederick's brief eulogy the elderly gentleman next to me began snoring softly, his head bowed as if in reverent contemplation.

Regretfully, my mind wandered, and I found myself gazing around the unfamiliar interior of the Grace Lutheran Church as if in search of an anchor for my thoughts. Having been raised Catholic, I was struck by the ascetic nature of my surroundings. The Lutheran faith was alien to me; Lutherans appeared to have limited regard for the iconography I was used to—images of the Virgin, of Christ on the cross. The service was familiar and, at the same time, not familiar; though, to be frank, it had been so many years since I had attended a service of any kind that the entire experience felt surreal, as if I had been removed from the present day and transported back thirty years to a time when attending church on Sunday morning was done in the normal course of things.

My father's funeral nearly twenty years ago was the last time I had entered a Catholic church. Before this, my attendance had been sporadic, a matter more of convenience than anything else. I was curious, but, ultimately, indifferent. My parents had failed to kindle within me the fiery ardour I would need in order to carry the light of religion all the days of my life. I suppose I thought of this with regret and regarded it a loss; but I had also never in any way sensed that my progress through the world had been impeded by my failure to embrace my Catholic heritage. It seemed for me to be very much a thing of a past long dead, though paradoxically whenever I happened to stroll by a church of any denomination, my mind would conjure an image of myself inside, sitting in the pew between my mother and father; bored maybe, or sleepy or otherwise disgruntled, but always to some degree contented because we were all there together. Prior to my illness, our family had been active members of the parish of St. Lawrence's Catholic Church.

The truth of the matter is that I was equally fascinated and repelled by the notion of organized religion. I'm not sure why this was so. I can still recall my father holding the wooden doors open so my mother and I could pass through. I remember the vaulted ceiling, the stained-wood interior, the heavy scent of the oils used to treat the wood finish, the service that, to the child that was me, seemed to go on forever, the sense of awe at all this solemn ritual. The building was new at the time, and its modern design left beams exposed and favoured natural surfaces over stone or plaster. Elevated recesses held statues of Jesus and Mary and various saints, all of them vaguely smiling down at us, bathed in a soothing golden glow. The confessional, which reduced me to weak-kneed terror, was on the right as you approached the altar, which was itself covered with carpet as red as blood. I could recall these details vividly, even though I had not set foot in St. Lawrence's church for nearly thirty years.

This prolonged absence was brought about by my parent's estrangement from each other after my illness. Like almost every other activity in which we had partaken as a family unit, churchgoing was sacrificed to the twin gods of gloom and self-indulgence. I suppose I could have attended a Lutheran service with Pauline's family—I spent so much time with them—but for some reason this never happened; the possibility was never even raised. Maybe they thought I was still going to church with my parents. Or perhaps they suspected I wouldn't be interested. It could even be that they felt that allowing me to tag along with them to their own church would be perceived as an attempt at conversion. And though I can't see now how my choosing a new spiritual path would have made any difference to my parents, I can understand that Adele and Willard, Pauline's parents, would have preferred not to become involved in this issue.

I had received my first communion not long before my illness, and by all accounts it was a momentous event. It made me feel grown-up, proud, important. But this is as far as my initiation into the Catholic religion went. My father stopped going to church altogether. My mother, who had served on committees and joined various church groups—and who had always approached the religious side of things with a gleam in her eye—continued to attend without suggesting that I accompany her. I regarded this as strange but did not question it. I watched and waited, believing that someday she would whisper that she wanted me beside her in church that morning, or just tell me I was going with her and that was that. But though her devotion to her faith became stronger as the years went by—even when her drinking was at its heaviest—it never again became something she was inclined to share.

When I was old enough to begin asking questions, she simply responded that religion was a personal matter, something between you and whatever version of god you chose to worship. Her neglect of my spiritual welfare left me with many more questions, none of which I asked—mostly because of other children at school complaining bitterly about confession, Sunday School lessons, summer church camps and the like. I kept quiet and tried to feel grateful that I was being spared these torments.

Still, there was within me a craving to be a part of something larger than myself. Around the time I turned nine or ten, I began going to church on my own, mentioning it to nobody, not even Pauline. It was not shame or anything like it that kept me quiet. I just didn't want to discuss my religious feelings with anyone until I had made up my mind. I was by no means a regular churchgoer. I went when I felt like it, when the weather was favourable, when I had nothing better to do. I enjoyed the music, the communal spirit. I even drew some measure of satisfaction from the mass itself; the familiarity of the text was reassuring. It was like seeing a play re-enacted week after week with subtle variations in cast and timing. I knew my own role and never missed a cue to stand or sit or kneel.

But I was an oddity, a child attending Sunday mass on his own. I never once accompanied my mother, and in fact made a point of attending a different service if I knew or could guess which she was going to, often not going at all if I wasn't sure. I knew people were observing me and taking note. Some bestowed a smile or greeting upon me. I did not mind this. The priest himself, Father Andrews, a very tall man in his sixties with a stooped frame who had a Dickensian air of long-suffering deprivation about him, spoke to me on many occasions after mass. What bothered me, and in the end compelled me to discontinue my attendance, was that my absence was remarked upon. People asked where I was or what had happened if I missed a week or two. I tried my best to bear with this, for the concern of these people, whom I didn't know and who didn't know me, was well-intentioned. However, I could see these innocent questions leading to others of a more personal nature, and my worst fears were confirmed when Father Andrews ushered me aside after one service and broached the subject of "troubles at home," referring obliquely to the concerns of "fellow parishioners." I knew then that my private affairs had become the stuff of other peoples' conversations.

I did not return to St. Lawrence's after this, switching to the Catholic Church of St. Agnes after a few weeks had passed. It was a long, strenuous uphill walk from home and I soon discovered that the parishioners of St. Lawrence's had been truly blessed by having Father Andrews to preside over their flock. The priest at St. Agnes, a Father Myers, was a different species altogether. He was much younger, but he was portly, balding and humourlessly earnest. His lengthy sermons were filled with too much hellfire and damnation for my taste. Even worse was his supercilious air, as if the only reason he descended from the summit each week was because he felt sorry for us corrupt mortals, who despite his courageous efforts were going to spend eternity dodging spears of flame while he sat comfortably at God's right hand.

I didn't stay at St. Agnes for very long.

In the years that followed, my attendance at church became even more irregular. I would go once or twice every few months, then only at Christmas, then every second Christmas. After my parents died I devoted myself to my studies and gave up going altogether. I thought about what I was missing, but only rarely, as one recalls with fondness the special times shared with a friend who moved away and with whom you wish you'd been able to keep in touch.

I started, as if a loud noise had wakened me from a nap. The priest's sonorous drone echoed through the cavernous interior. I arranged myself furtively and glanced to the left and the right. I was sweating; my collar chafed my neck. Nobody appeared to have noticed my lapse. I was wishing now that I'd taken a seat at the end of the pew instead of in the middle in order to facilitate a quick escape. As it was, I had no choice but to wait.

The walls were running with moisture when at last the casket was wheeled in solemn procession up the broad centre aisle and carried out the front entrance by the six young pallbearers. As we turned to leave, the building itself seemed to exhale a grateful sigh.

Five

⌒

I STEPPED OUTSIDE into the light, my coat over one arm, happy just to be able to stand upright and stretch my legs. People milled drowsily about, squinting as if they'd just spent a long time underground. The pallbearers rolled the casket into the gleaming hearse and then entered into discussion about something. Soon they were all laughing.

I took a few steps away and lit a cigarette. Drawing in the smoke and expelling it upward, I felt instantly revived and energetic, as if awakening from a lengthy and undisturbed sleep. Evidently, I was not the only person with an inclination to do precisely this, for, as people flooded from the church, I found myself surrounded by a gaggle of tobacco enthusiasts, young and old. As I backed away to avoid bumping elbows I kept an eye on the door, waiting for Pauline or Frederick to emerge.

An older man stationed himself next to me and remarked: "A bit stuffy in there, don't you think?"

"I suppose they could have opened a window or two, or maybe the doors."

"Wouldn't have hurt. People around me were dropping like flies. I don't think I've shed that much moisture in one hour since my wedding." He wiped his face with a handkerchief and returned it to his pocket.

As I laughed, a breeze swooped down upon us and the cool air wrapped itself around me. I shivered and was conscious of my skin tightening beneath my shirt, though the sun continued to beat down upon us with a searing intensity.

"Yes, I think I got a bit overheated. But just the same I'm glad I could pay my respects. She was a remarkable woman."

"You were a student?"

"A friend of the family actually. My cousin—"

"My son, Alfred, took lessons for years. Can't say it ever amounted to much but she did her best. Best discipline in the world, music. Better than the army. Did him a world of good. He went into medicine. Cardiology. Lives in Boston. That's why he's not here today."

"Ah."

"I'm not musical myself." He tapped the side of his head. "Tin ear, I'm afraid. It's the wife. She plays harp. Lovely instrument. I can't make head or tails of it. It's all a complete mystery as far as I'm concerned. You know, those notes, sharps and flats. Another language. Like Chinese. Not for the likes of us, I'm afraid."

He nudged me and raised his furry eyebrows chummily as if our shared inability to understand music actually constituted an advantage of some sort, though I'd made no such admission. I dropped my cigarette and crushed it out. I put on my coat.

"Seems a bit chilly just now."

He didn't seem to be listening.

"These musicians, they're uncommon specimens. If you know what I mean."

"Yes, I suppose I do."

As my companion prattled on, Pauline and Sophie appeared in the doorway, Pauline fanning herself with a folded pamphlet. I realized with a startled shock of recognition that until that instant, I'd for years regarded Sophie as a younger, slimmer version of her mother. There was something within me—residual from our linked childhoods I suppose—that always absorbed Pauline's presence first, and her daughter's secondarily, as if it were something of lesser importance. Sophie often seemed shadowy next to her mother, as if she were still searching for a voice and a place to stand that would be hers alone. By contrast, Pauline had no doubt about where she stood, and filled her space with full assurance that she belonged and that nobody was going to forget she was there.

This surprised me because I hadn't been aware that my manner of regarding these two women had favoured one at the expense of the other. I suppose our perception of the people around us is always shaded by the past, by our own experience, or by factors we don't understand. For all of us there comes a time when a veil falls and for the first time we realize that our parents are old and helpless, or that our children are human beings in their own right. Today, watching Sophie and Pauline on the steps outside the church, I saw that my perception had shifted. Now, that Pauline was a slightly plumper, shorter version of her daughter.

Pauline stood back from the step in a smartly-tailored navy dress, her face pink from the heat, her mouth drawn tight. She appeared agitated and cross. Sophie, in a cream dress with jacket and matching purse and shoes, appeared serene, gazing around the parking lot with the cool detachment of someone with no stake in the proceedings. With a subtle curve of her lips she indicated amusement and, dare I say it, contempt for those around her. I chalked this observation up as a trick of the sun and my light-headedness in the extreme temperatures. Undeniably she was resplendent, her own person. And though I'd often seen her on stage, bowing and accepting the adulation of an audience, I'd never seen her as poised as she was today. Only her hair, sheared off close to her head, had changed. It gave her face more definition, and though it still hid her ears the new coiffure threw her features into relief, accenting the fine bones of her forehead, cheek and nose.

When a couple of people attempted to engage her in conversation, she replied with a curt shake of the head, as if they'd asked a question she either couldn't, or didn't care to, answer. In the meantime the birdlike lady, who appeared every bit as distraught now as she had the other day, had seized Pauline by the elbow.

Werner Hölderine and Frederick had joined Pauline and Sophie on the steps and they all began moving off together. I quickly extinguished the second cigarette I had lit and followed them, for I assumed I would be riding with them to the cemetery.

Six

IX OF US rode in Frederick's Mercedes to the old Lutheran cemetery, located about forty minutes outside the seaside town of Chester. Frederick drove, with Pauline and Sophie beside him. I occupied a window seat behind Sophie with Werner Hölderine at the other side. Between us was the little bird-lady whose name, to this day, escapes me.

The leather upholstery seemed burnished for the occasion, as if Frederick had spent hours pampering it with exotic oils. The odour of cleanser lingered, for the car was still relatively new. This aroma mingled pleasantly with various personal scents, Werner's cologne and the women's, particularly that of the bird-lady lady, with a potency that soon overwhelmed the others. During the drive the conversation meandered. Pauline expressed disappointment with the service, with the church itself, with the priest, even with the flowers, which had begun to wilt before the service got underway. Frederick made some placating comments and asked my opinion on the matter. Werner offered a few observations and indicated he was quite pleased with the way things had gone, an opinion shared by most of us in the car.

The bird-lady emitted a raspy sigh and, leaning forward, placed a purple-veined hand on Pauline's shoulder.

"It's of no consequence, my dear," she said, her voice gentle, though quite robust for her slight frame. "Selma was watching and she approved of it all, I can assure you. She loved ceremony and this was exactly what she'd have wanted."

She glanced at both Werner and me in turn and nodded, as if the matter were now settled. I smiled.

"Well, it's very good of you to say that," Pauline responded fractiously, unconvinced, "but I think it's disgraceful—"

"Pauline," Frederick said, one hand in the air, "It's over. Everyone did the best they could. Did anyone know it was going to get this hot today? No. And people usually have more tolerance for discomfort than you think they do. So save yourself some heartache and don't dwell on it."

Pauline was fanning herself with a stiff piece of official-looking paper that she'd taken from the glove compartment.

"Yes, I suppose I'm more susceptible to the heat than most. Maybe it wasn't as bad as all that."

"It wasn't bad at all," I said, as Sophie leaned her head against the window, gazing out, exhausted or bored. "Frederick, I enjoyed your eulogy very much."

"Also, I did too," Werner said. "Thank you, for myself and for my sister."

Frederick gave a terse nod in acknowledgement.

The conversation continued, sporadic and casual. The bird-lady, evidently noticing me for the first time and unhappy with the silence that had descended in the back seat, decided to question me about my connection to Pauline and Frederick, my job and myriad other things. Words in the front seat were masked by the hum of the air-conditioning system and from this point on none were directed toward us in the back. I recall a number of random sensations: the unrelenting sun approaching its zenith; the rising temperature of my body and the return of the feverish light-headedness that had afflicted me earlier in the parking lot. But most of all, I was distracted by the skin of Sophie's exposed neck, the tilt of her head resting against the window, the shape of her lips as she turned to look out the window. I knew my purpose here today was twofold, that besides augmenting the congregation, I was expected by Pauline to draw her daughter aside and, if not get to the bottom of what was troubling her, to at least scout out the territory. However, the more I considered this task the more daunting it appeared, and I was having great difficulty convincing myself that I was up to it. I was dismayed at how nervous I was at the prospect of speaking to her alone. In all likelihood, she was not going to want to answer my questions and this caused my breath to catch in my throat. Above all else, I disliked pushing people in directions they didn't want to go. It was the only part of my job that I detested. As supervisor of a large unit, I inevitably had people in my charge who either refused or were incapable of adequately performing their duties. I was not a rigorous administrator (quite the opposite, in fact) and so was always disheartened when someone could not meet even my relaxed standards and needed talking to. Sometimes there were tears and in those cases I would inevitably learn the sordid, messy minutiae of some employee's life. Spotting such a situation on the horizon, I would procrastinate and agonize, sometimes for weeks, before eventually dealing with it.

It will seem odd that I have not mentioned a relationship with a woman aside from Pauline. I have been "involved" in affairs of the heart, having formed close attachments in school with various people, male and female, a few of whom I kept in touch with. From an early age, however, I suspected that my inability, or rather, disinclination, to form intimate relationships was evidence of a serious deficiency in my character. When I was younger, others within my social circle entered easily into such matters of the heart—these could be loose and informal or passionate—flitting by the month or the week from romance to romance like bees among flowers. I used to observe my friends at school dances, huddled in corners away from the sweaty throng, engrossed in conversation, revelling in the nearness of each other's bodies. My envy was great, for I had no concept of what was right for me and wanted only to follow the crowd.

Certainly there were girls to whom I was attracted, but I had no idea how to approach them without seeming a complete imbecile. We talked, as classmates who shared academic interests in common, but I recoiled from conversation on a more personal level. Even when they appeared to reciprocate my unstated feelings (and this did happen more than once, in secondary school and again in university), I resisted. How, I thought, can I be sure I'm not misreading the signals? Interpreting body language was never my strong suit, so how was I to know what that smile, or that warm whisper in my ear, really meant? People smile at each other all the time and it means nothing. Terrified of rejection, I convinced myself I was wrong. My instincts told me I had a choice: I could remain aloof, shielded from unruly passions, an unfulfilled observer, emotionally inhibited. Or I could become intimate with someone, speak openly and at length about my feelings—in other words, sacrifice my privacy so that the relationship might survive and flourish.

Of course, my instincts were never this articulate. It was never a matter of making a conscious decision. Like most people in their late teens I was at the mercy of hormonal upheavals and psychological squalls that I didn't realize were taking place, let alone understand. All I knew was that whenever I found myself in a situation that required disclosure of any kind, I began to back away, taking refuge in distance and silence. And whenever I overcame my initial anxieties and actually formed a romantic attachment, it always turned out to be a horrendous mistake—a disaster and a source of humiliation for all involved. Eventually I convinced myself that I preferred being on my own.

I'm saying this only to clarify my position on this day. I loved Sophie dearly and had spent many pleasing hours in her company but was not (I was now convinced) the first person to whom she would turn were she suffering emotional distress. I could certainly talk to her and endeavour to uncover whatever issues were weighing upon her mind. After all, there was our telephone conversation of last Friday still unresolved. That would provide a starting point and I'd see how things evolved from there. But I was uneasy when I envisioned myself sitting beside her and trying to imagine the words we might exchange. She was not easily compelled to do something outside of her natural inclinations and I'd already been wounded by the sharpness of her tongue. In short, I felt the burden of my mission every bit as heavily as if I were sitting in my office waiting to inform some unsuspecting soul that his services were no longer required.

Frederick steered the car off the main highway and turned onto a secondary road. Now sitting up straight, Sophie was glancing around at the scrubby and altogether forgettable scenery. The odd farmhouse contributed a veneer of charm, but more as feeble panacea to the pervasive rural melancholy. Granted, there were cleared fields and graceful trees; tractors tilling vast stretches of property; men in overalls labouring here and there. But there were also fences falling over, abandoned vehicles shedding rust, barns with caved-in roofs.

Eventually, Frederick pulled the car off the road onto a bumpy unpaved lot. The hearse had arrived and within seconds two more cars pulled off the road and parked.

The sky was clear, the air still and the heat brutal. Struggling with mild vertigo and a suspicion that I was going to be unwell, I left my coat in the car and joined the others. Pauline uttered more complaints and fanned herself vigorously. The bird-lady took Werner's arm, somewhat to my relief, and led him toward a little white-washed church, the old Lutheran church of St. John's. Sophie followed a short distance behind her parents, in her high heels treading with care over the uneven ground. Knowing my role, as always, was to play the gallant, I assumed a position by her side and took her arm. There was no hesitation at all in her response, which was to cling to me tightly.

We strolled thus, side by side, the short distance to the grave, heralded by the cajoling songs of birds and the high-pitched trills of insects teeming in the tall grass.

"I'm so happy you came today," she said, smiling up at me, squinting against the sun. "I was sure I'd frightened you off the last time we spoke. I'm sorry. I don't know how to explain it."

"I don't want you worrying about that," I said. "I assumed you weren't feeling well. When you didn't come to the funeral home yesterday, I was sure I was right."

"Well," she said, squeezing my arm, "I'm feeling much better now."

"Even in this heat? I'm afraid I'm fading fast. If I fall down, I hope you'll pick me up."

She gave me a teasing smile. All this while I was coming to realize that my sudden hyper-awareness of everything sparkling around me—of each blade of grass; of the jewel-like splendour of the sky; of the sponginess of the earth beneath shoe; of the gentle pressure of Sophie's arm in mine—was in fact signalling the onset of illness. I was growing feverish and would likely collapse into extended bed-rest on my return home. I know the cycles and levels of tolerance of my body, and having in a short time experienced the sweltering and airless conditions within the church, the chill air from the car's air-conditioner, followed by murderous heat, I could easily predict the outcome.

"Joseph, stay with me," she said. "Just hold on and don't let go."

She was watching workers preparing to lower the casket, using thick canvas straps, into the open grave.

"I won't," I said, perhaps too softly, for she did not respond.

The service was executed with dispatch. Werner was given a clump of earth to toss into the grave. The priest read stock phrases from his mass book. We stood about in a circle, wearing grim faces. The bird-lady wept quietly. It is restorative, I suppose, to see things through to their final stages. I, for one, felt a sense of completeness, of having fulfilled my obligation to Selma Kraus. I've always main-tained that the death of another presents an opportunity for a cool assessment of one's own life, a chance to give some thought to ar-ranging one's affairs. It's a selfish belief, I know, but at this stage the departed is well beyond our influence and will neither appreciate, nor benefit from, tears and wringing hands.

But at some point my thoughts lost their focus and from then on I heard only portions of the priest's words. My back to the road, I heard a rumble commence far in the distance and creep toward us through the trees, gradually increasing in volume to a thunderous clatter that drowned out the priest, birds, and everything else. For a moment I felt as if I were standing within an assembly of the deaf, for no one showed any sign of being troubled or distracted by the noise. The priest continued to speak, though it was impossible to hear what he said. When the car with the defective muffler was finally past and had rounded a bend, its roar receding to a distant echo and then to silence, I began to wonder if the noisy diversion was a product of a feverish brain unable to concentrate on the business at hand.

After the ceremony people seemed momentarily unsure whether to rush to their vehicles or to linger in the wholesome country air. As hot as it was, nobody appeared in a hurry to leave. Near the church Pauline was chatting with an elderly man unknown to me. The young pallbearers sauntered off, lighting up cigarettes, chuckling over some private joke. Then next to me Sophie stirred and my brain jolted into gear, causing me to remember my promise to her mother.

"Are you all right?" I asked. "I don't think there's any rush to leave, if you'd like to take a walk around."

"It's really hot, isn't it?"

"Yes, but it looks shady back there," I said, pointing to some trees.

We followed a path to a grove of maples and spindly poplar at the back of the churchyard. Behind the church an enormous old lilac had yet to bloom. Sophie's arm slipped out of mine and she took my hand. Hers was cool and light and I felt revived at her touch.

"You know, Sophie, your mother's worried about you. She thinks there's something bothering you and it upsets her that you won't talk to her about it."

She seemed to shake her head.

"There's nothing wrong with me. It's her. She's always after me. She never leaves me alone."

"Well," I said, "she's your mother. Nothing's going to change that. And mothers are always going to be concerned for their children."

We stood beneath a large maple. From here the church seemed tiny and immeasurably distant. Figures shimmered as they moved slowly in a gauzy haze of heat and dust.

"I'll be moving out soon," she said, releasing my hand and leaning her back against the tree. "I don't think she can stand to let me go. She's got nothing else in her life." Her eyes were suddenly level with mine. "Absolutely nothing. For her, I'm the sun and the moon and the stars."

Something vaguely insolent and self-satisfied drifted into her expression.

"Maybe you're giving yourself too much credit," I said. "I don't see that her concern is unreasonable, especially if you're behaving oddly and refusing to do things that you should be doing out of simple courtesy."

She glanced around and seemed to consider this.

"Grace says I should stand up to her and not let her make all my decisions for me."

"The girl from the agency. What does she know about your mother?"

"She's my friend."

"Maybe so, but does that mean she knows what's best for you?"

"Does my mother know what's best for me?"

"At least she has your welfare at heart. The agency makes more money if you perform more. Your friend might have other motives for the things she says."

"Well, maybe I want to perform more. Maybe I want to move into a place on my own."

"Sophie, there's nothing wrong with any of that. But can't you discuss it with your parents before you decide that they're going to say no? You owe them that much, surely."

She tilted her head, considering me with a kind of languid exasperation, as if she doubted I could be serious.

"Oh, Joseph," she said, her expression difficult to read. "You're always so reasonable."

During a pause we looked closely at one another. She was clearly disappointed in me; not, I realized, for defending her mother so much as for saying exactly what she expected me to say.

The silence stretched to a minute, then two. She gave me an enigmatic smile and lifted her gaze to the distance, across hilly terrain and into pine forest. I swayed slightly, feeling as if the heat had penetrated my bones and was now emanating from within.

"Maybe we should get back," I said.

"My God, it's so hot!" She shrugged off the jacket. Beneath it the dress was suspended by narrow straps. Her shoulders and arms were otherwise bare. "Could you hold this for me?"

She handed the jacket to me and closed her eyes as she pushed one hand repeatedly through her hair.

"Sophie, are you feeling all right? It is hot, I know. Maybe it's too hot. I should have saved this conversation for another time."

"No. Now is best."

"Well, we should head back anyway—"

"Joseph, you never see me, do you? You look at me, but you never see the person who's here."

Her tone was all at once impassioned and her eyes, brimming with tears, pinned me to the spot.

"I know you don't even try because if you did you'd understand. You'd know who I am and what I want. But all you can see is my mother's little girl. Like her, you can't or won't see that I'm all grown up. My mother has pictures everywhere of a little girl in pigtails playing the piano. You've seen them. It's not me. It's a shrine to someone who's gone. When she looks at me, that's what she sees. She still thinks I'm six years old. I'm tired of it. I'm tired of being treated like a child because I'm not a child."

There were tears streaking her cheeks. I took a step forward and wrapped my arms around her.

"Sophie—"

"I've got to get away from her. I've got to. I can't be her little girl anymore."

I laid my hand on the back of her head. Her hair was fragrant and infinitely soft. I was suddenly aware that other than brushing against her inadvertently, or a quick kiss on the cheek at Christmas, I hadn't touched her in years. I hadn't held her since she was small.

"Joseph, you can see that I'm not a little girl, can't you?"

At this point I admit to not knowing what to do, or say. For all my experience living in the world and all the mental preparations I had made for this encounter, the moment utterly baffled me. I eased my embrace but she remained pressed firmly against me, her face an inch from mine. In spite of the blindness she'd attributed to me, I was painfully conscious that she was no longer a little girl. That she was a beautiful woman.

Her forehead sloped upward smooth and unblemished, her nose was small and rounded at the tip. Her questioning eyes were a pale blue and her lips curled playfully. I felt the return of my vertigo. I stood there and said nothing as she leaned upward to press her lips against mine, did nothing as the thrust of her kiss made itself felt in my groin. The moment is vivid in my mind as I write this: the glare of the sun glancing off the church, the ruined headstones rising out of the earth like craggy teeth.

Then she heaved her body against mine, crazily, lifting one leg. I breathed the moment in, inhaling along with it the outrage I was committing. At the same time I was disengaged from it, as if unacquainted with the person standing in my place filling his lungs with her scent. For one astounding instant I clutched her to me, my hands riding the supple length of her. A murmur half escaped from her throat and then seemed to catch there, making me think I'd somehow hurt her. I recall every detail with surreal clarity, shocked—each time I relive it—to notice myself in the midst of this scene when anyone else could see instantly that I didn't belong.

I can't claim to have behaved faultlessly every day of my life, to that point. But with this single repugnant act all my virtuous deeds were expunged and whatever good works I might have accrued may just as well not have happened.

Seven

OUR BODIES SEPARATED but our eyes met. Stricken and fighting for breath, I left her standing beneath the tree and made my way back toward the church. Unable to locate the route we had taken earlier, I wandered through the long grass, my progress halted again and again by headstones and tangled undergrowth. I heard a voice that could have been Sophie's calling my name but I didn't look back. I tried not to think about her standing there alone, flushed and weakened by our embrace. I felt like a long-distance runner approaching the finish line, the goal within sight but the strength needed to reach it rapidly fading. The church was only a few metres away, but the distance seemed insuperable. My entire body rebelled at the thought of crossing even that brief stretch. I felt like each step sliced a year off my life, yet even that seemed a trifling price to pay for being able to put greater and greater distance between myself and what I'd done. Sweating, I wavered between rage and humiliation, prepared to lash out at the first accuser. The dread of discovery that swept over me as I groped my way toward the church remains my close companion, my trusted ally, as does the foreboding that we had been spotted in the arbour by someone who understood immediately what was happening and who was preparing to make my life hell on earth.

Somehow, stumbling through the bushes and using the building itself for a support, I managed to propel myself around the church to the parking area in front, where Pauline was tending to the bird-lady's distress. From the expression that passed over her face, I can only imagine the shock my appearance must have given her. Within seconds there were many hands laid upon me amidst a general outcry of alarm. Soon Frederick was by my side propping me up, and I was conveyed with much more gentleness than I deserved into the back seat of the Mercedes. The only words I was conscious of uttering were, "The heat, the heat," which came out involuntarily because at this point my craving was for quick relief and nothing else.

"Sunstroke, in all likelihood," I heard Frederick say as they hustled me into the car. I was in no position to argue.

Through all of this my eyes were wide open. Fear of succumbing to my illness fed my brain with adrenaline and kept me awake. I saw as if through a telescope people hurrying to my aid and demonstrating a level of concern that, had I been in any condition to do so, would have made me shudder with embarrassment. I understood with aching clarity that, having betrayed their trust, I could no longer trust any of them, that I had defiled the moral fabric of their lives and made myself their enemy. I was hiding a secret that, if it were to see the light of day, would mark me as an abomination. Most frightening of all, however, was the realization that I could not trust myself. I lay quietly, but when I sensed my attention flagging and my eyelids growing ponderous, I began to panic and started to flex muscles somewhere in my body, moving my head, or stretching an arm or leg. This struggle to remain conscious would not end until we reached town. Was there a possibility that I would utter something revealing while in the throes of delirium? I didn't want to find out.

Pauline sat with me in the back seat and cradled my head in her lap. Sophie and the bird-lady got in front with Frederick. Werner, I assumed, rode back to town with someone else. When the air-conditioning came on I began to feel better. But my entire body had been enfeebled by the spell I'd suffered, and every second I was aware that I was in the grip of a fever that was clearly overpowering my efforts to fight it off.

Pauline stroked my forehead.

"I'm sorry about this," I said. Uttering these few words left me weary beyond description.

"Shhhh."

"Not going to vomit, are we?" Frederick asked, glancing over his shoulder. I could understand his concern.

"No," I said.

"Just let me know," Pauline said. "We'll stop the car."

"I'm all right," I said, recognizing the absurdity of saying this given my obvious affliction. I even tried to demonstrate my imminent recovery by attempting to sit up, only to sink instantly backward with a groan, my head rioting in protest.

As we drove, I tried not to dwell upon what had just taken place between Sophie and me but every few minutes found myself back in the churchyard with her in my arms. I must have been truly out of my mind, I thought, though even temporary madness could not excuse what I'd done. My exhibition of lust had been just that, made a hundred times more odious because of the object of that lust. There was no question that Sophie was a willing participant—in fact, if I may be permitted to say so, the incident seemed to have occurred at her instigation—but in my capacity as an elder cousin and mentor and friend, I should have been able to take control of the situation. I should have pushed her away. I should have spoken to her sternly, without regard for her feelings, for any wounds I inflicted would heal soon enough. My duty was to protect her and guide her and do everything in my power to ensure her safety. Reasonably or not, I sometimes feared that her beauty and talent might attract the attention of someone who didn't have her best interests at heart. But I was the one who had betrayed her. I had taken advantage of a shared moment of weakness and given her a rude push along the pathway to disgrace. My only hope now was to apologize and pray that she would forgive me.

These reflections left me depressed. I could see that she would be well within her rights not to forgive me. If she refused to speak to me or have anything to do with me from this day forward, I could hardly raise an objection. And what if she were to come to me and threaten to tell her parents? What argument could I seriously advance that would convince her that this was the wrong thing to do, especially since I knew in my heart that it was the right thing to do?

I watched and listened. Silence prevailed for the most part. Pauline absently stroked my forehead, the bird-lady made some observation or other to which nobody responded. I could detect nothing in Sophie's manner to indicate that she was upset or in any way distressed. Her calm seemed almost unnatural, as if she'd swallowed a sedative. She was likely just tired, as I was, sluggish from the heat and the exertions of the afternoon.

During the entire trip back I struggled with what to do. Should I confront Sophie immediately and settle the matter once and for all? Should I spend some days recovering my strength before taking on this monumental task? I realized that every minute of delay merely confused the issue and that my silence might be interpreted as complicity. However, I was swayed toward the latter course of action simply because of my physical state. I was not in any condition for an encounter that would involve tears and recriminations. The thought of it made my head spin with renewed vigour and flooded my mouth with bile. For a few days I wanted to be left alone so I could relax and fight off this damned fever.

So it was with no little alarm that I came to understand, after passing through stages of denial, that I was being conveyed not to my apartment on Walnut Street but to Frederick and Pauline's house. I tried again to sit up, but Pauline with one hand exerted a gentle pressure on my head to keep me down, an indication itself of how weak I really was. When she made a remark about taking me in through the back way so I would not have to confront all the other guests, I knew I was not being given a choice and that this assumption of my illness as their own responsibility was, to Pauline and Frederick with their instinctual generosity, nothing more than the appropriate response.

Eight

A NY ILLNESS IS disorienting, even for the strongest individual. The body performs inward gyrations as it attempts to expel the invading forces, and about all we can do is place our trust in those who know best and try not to interfere as the battle is waged. I remember being ill as a child with whichever virus was going around at the time and lying in my room with the curtains drawn. Thinking about my friends perhaps passing my house and wondering, briefly, if my condition was improving. I imagined brows wrinkled with concern and serious discussions in subdued tones, though why this should be the case I have no idea because whenever I was out and about and another of our number was laid low, I rarely gave it a moment's thought. I suppose it's difficult to conceive of oneself being so ill and nobody really caring.

Illness turns the mind inward, reduces the margins of our concern to our body, and then to our immediate surroundings. How, we might allow ourselves to ask, can this be happening to me without others feeling it as well? My childhood home, being very much like a convalescent home at the best of times, was in fact ideal for recovering from maladies such as croup and influenza. There was no clamour to interrupt my rest, no voices calling, no telephone ringing. The windows were closed, so I was in no danger of exposure to drafts. I was attended with droop-eyed solemnity by both parents and indulged to such a lavish extent, with creamy desserts and sugar-coated cookies and other delicacies that I didn't normally get to eat, that in order to prolong my confinement I sometimes let on that my ailment was worse than it really was. My only visitor during periods of illness was Pauline, for whom I would routinely stash extra treats to be shared over tea.

This is not to say that being ill is a holiday and I guarantee it certainly was not for me in the days following Selma Kraus's funeral. I have little recollection of that period, which lasted for almost a week. My room with its private bath was my world for this time. I did not leave it until I was strong enough to descend the stairs unaided. My infection ("a bug of some sort" was Frederick's diagnosis) left me prostrate and woozy for days, unable to eat anything but consommé and dry toast. I suppose I was fortunate to have such compassionate and conscientious relatives nearby, for I cannot imagine how I would have survived had I been left to my own devices. There were times when I could not manoeuvre my limbs sufficiently to negotiate my own way to the bathroom. I slept a great deal; or, I should say, I spent many hours in a state very much like sleep.

From a long sleep, one expects to awaken refreshed and invigorated. However, the state of unconsciousness into which I slipped left me depleted and anxious when I emerged from it, as if I'd spent hours wrestling demons. I'd emerge into consciousness at odd times, unsure where I was and how I'd got there. At night I trembled with cold, perspiration dripping from my body, my hair flattened to my head, my stomach grinding and empty. Sharp, random pains made me envision someone jabbing a straw doll with pins. Patches of skin on my limbs became irritated at the slightest contact until the only relief came from throwing off the covers to avoid the maddening and fiery itchiness. For a few days at least, my discomfort was severe. I was quite sure that none of this was life-threatening—Frederick's cool and casual presence by the bedside as he administered some medication or other assured me that I was not in mortal danger. However it is difficult to retain a lucid perspective when your body is under attack from within, and there were many occasions during the early days of my sickness when I would have welcomed with open arms the release to be found in death.

I have slight recollection of the comings and goings of others to and from my room. Pauline and Frederick stand out, of course. I can see Pauline sitting in a chair reading or helping me to a sip of water, and I'm sure that she took charge of feeding me when I was at last able to eat. Toward the end of my convalescence, Miss Pindar from my office arrived with a card signed by numerous of my co-workers along with a box of chocolates, which I squeamishly handed over to Pauline immediately upon Miss Pindar leaving the house.

As I regained my strength my mind naturally returned to Sophie and the incident in the churchyard. And I wondered if she had been in to see me, though for a variety of reasons, all of them selfish, I hoped that she had not. It also came into my head that it was possible I had been contagious during our moment of closest contact and I directed many silent appeals heavenward that she be spared the torment I had endured.

I can recall one thing about that week with utter clarity. During the day, as I lay in bed, either alone or with someone in attendance, slipping into and out of my feverish oblivion, I was aware of music playing elsewhere in the house. Sophie's music room was on the ground floor at the back, in an extension built solely to accommodate her instruments (the old Chelsea, a new Steinway), and as she played, the strains floated upstairs and penetrated the fog encircling my brain. I was thankful for this, though not consciously so at the time, for it provided a focus for my attention whenever I drifted close to the surface, enticed my thoughts away from any physical distress. She seemed to be reviewing her entire repertoire, for I remember the Mozart sonatas—a dozen of them at least—some Beethoven and Schubert. Occasionally there would come the skipping cadence of a Chopin waltz, or something whimsical and irreverent by Erik Satie.

She was exploring new material I didn't recognize, repeating some passages up to thirty and forty times until she'd perfected them, sauntering through them now as if she'd been playing them all her life. I knew the Ravel and I could easily distinguish the Bach but there were other much more turbulent, almost violently impressionistic pieces among those she played that left me dazzled yet at a loss. I suspected that the composers were Russian—possibly Scriabin or Prokofiev or Rachmaninoff—for the music suggested freedom of expression gained through enormous struggle—but this was only a guess.

Early in her career Sophie had gravitated toward music with a spirited countenance, pieces that cavorted and relied on lilting melodies and straightforward themes and variations. By contrast, her new repertoire was very often harshly dissonant, the central motif formless and wrenching, bringing to mind images of devastation, a sense of passion gone awry. She struck thunderous chords and battered the keyboard without mercy. Sometimes there was nothing for me to grasp as I tried to follow the piece, a pattern emerging only upon the recapitulation that followed quickly upon the initial performance. I don't suppose I was bothered by any of this, for the music seemed only to form a soundtrack to my illness, carrying me through intervals of temporary relief and intense misery. Sometimes I felt as if I could easily get out of bed and walk downstairs and out the door. Seconds later I would be semi-conscious, every muscle aching, barely able to move my arms.

The music served another purpose as well. Though to my knowledge she never entered my room the whole time I was there, it nonetheless made Sophie, the mere fact of her being in the house, a major element in my recovery, every bit as healing as the drugs prescribed by her father and the soups prepared by her mother.

Once the worst part of my illness had passed, I had ample time to reflect upon what had transpired on the day of the funeral. The passage of several days had eased my anxieties somewhat. I was confident now that we had not been spotted in the midst of our embrace. And the continuing attentions of Pauline and Frederick were enough to assure me that Sophie had revealed nothing to her parents.

The unseasonable heat had passed and we were now burdened with the cooler temperatures and incessant rainfall more in keeping with April in Nova Scotia. From my bed I could look outside at the branches of a huge old ash tree against the grey sky. As the wind wildly circled the house, often raising its voice to a howl, the tree's limbs rose and fell, rose and fell, nodding as if in agreement with a point being made again and again. Heavy rain always makes me anxious, for when I was living at home with my parents, the rain sometimes found its way indoors, either through a defective window casing or by working its way beneath a shingle and gaining entrance through the roof. It often seemed to depend more upon the direction of the wind than its force, strong winds being no guarantee that leaks would result. My father was forever taking precautions, nailing extra sticks of wood above window casings in the hope that they would reroute the water, caulking everything within reach, securing the shingles to the roof with tar. Some of his efforts solved our problem for a while, but the leaks always recurred with the inevitability of the weather itself. My anxiety was inspired by the sight of him emerging from the basement carrying his mismatched tools with the understanding written in the lines of his face that he was about to spend the better part of his Saturday afternoon doing something that would not make the slightest difference.

So as the rain poured down in great heaving swells, my stomach muscles spontaneously tensed, though I knew very well not one drop was getting in this house. I found it impossible to sleep while it was raining, but by Friday I was beginning to feel like I'd slept enough to last me several months. I was sitting up in bed, reading a book from Frederick's library, feeling like I should be making an effort to return home and resume my life. The rain pummelled the roof. Between volleys, I could hear Sophie playing. I knew that I still had before me a dialogue with her that could very well prove distasteful. But the timing of my illness had pushed everything back by a few days and I was hoping that, like me, she had taken advantage of the intervening time to ponder the events of that Monday.

I set the book aside when Pauline knocked on the door and came in. She looked like she'd been exerting herself with some strenuous activity. A few loose strands of hair hung over her forehead. She wore casual slacks, a checked apron.

"Looks like you're improving," she said cheerfully, seating herself in a chair beside the bed. "I'm beginning to think you might live." She fiddled with her hair, prodding the unruly strands into place.

"Oh, I think I'll pull through," I said. "I'm feeling pretty strong now. I'll get out of bed today. I might even go home this afternoon."

"Don't hurry things, Joseph, please. Wait to hear what Frederick says. You've eaten almost nothing all week, remember. I don't want you doing too much too quickly and ending up sick again."

"Well, I think it'll do me good to be up and around and doing a few things. I don't intend to go jogging around the park yet."

She was silent. But still I sensed her disapproval.

"I don't know what I would have done without you and Frederick. I know I wouldn't have been able to take care of myself. I probably would have died."

"You aren't an inconvenience, you know. It's no different than having a healthy house guest. Probably less trouble overall."

"Still, I mean ..."

The rain fell, a percussive downpour. Then with startling abruptness it stopped, and Sophie's playing leapt to the foreground, the largo of a Beethoven sonata.

"She's been practising like crazy all week. You've probably heard her. I suppose the weather's been so poor, and there's not much else for her to do around here. I don't know what you said to her the other day, Joseph, but it worked wonders. She's back to her old self. I hadn't heard her laugh for ages. It's been a relief, these last few days. It's like living with a different person."

My whole body clenched at the mention of "the other day."

"I don't think I had anything to do with it," I said, forcing myself to look upward into her eyes. "We didn't talk much. It was too hot for a serious discussion."

"But did she say anything about what's been bothering her?"

There are truths that hurt even as they heal and truths that cause great pain to little purpose. I decided, rightly or wrongly but mostly to spare myself the agony of causing needless grief, that I couldn't tell her everything at once.

"She says she wants to do more concerts. She also said she wants a place of her own. I told her she should discuss it with you and Frederick."

For a moment she remained silent, as if waiting for me to conclude a half-finished thought.

"That's all? We've been through that with her. She can do more concerts when she's ready and I think she's almost ready. What she has to learn is not to exhaust herself and to eat properly when she's touring, because you know she gets hyper and can't eat. And then has no strength left when she needs it. As for the other thing, Frederick's told her he'll consider paying rent on a studio for her but I think it's ludicrous. She's only nineteen."

I shrugged.

"She seems capable," I said weakly, unsure why I was even promoting Sophie's position in this matter since I shared Pauline's doubt that Sophie was equipped to live on her own.

Pauline tilted her head.

"There's capable and there's capable. She's certainly capable of opening a can of soup, but she's never shopped for groceries in her life. I can't remember if she's ever prepared a meal for herself. She could keep an apartment clean, I suppose, but she doesn't do these things without prompting. You should see her room. It's a fright."

"Well, you know I was never one for housekeeping," I said. "But I've managed to survive. So far, anyway. I haven't opened a closet and had everything fall out on top of me yet."

There was reproach in her narrowed eyes as she replied.

"This isn't a laughing matter, Joseph. She's my only daughter and I'm concerned for her. I don't want her starving or living in filth. And it's not only that ..." She paused and knotted her fingers together in her lap. "She is a young woman, and ... well, things can happen. I don't have to go into detail. But we both know the city isn't as safe as it used to be."

"Things can happen anywhere. Anytime. She doesn't have to be living on her own for things to happen."

Her lips tightened.

"Thank you, Joseph. I didn't need to hear that."

I shook my head.

"I'm sorry. God, I'm sorry. I didn't mean … I guess all I mean is that you can worry too much. Sophie travels all over the place. You can't be with her every minute of every day. It might do you both some good to loosen the ties a bit."

She rested her hands on her knees.

"That's the kind of thing that Frederick says. He seems to be prepared to let her walk out the door any time she wants. Well, I'm sorry, but I think she needs more supervision than that."

"Supervision," I said. "What kind of supervision?"

"Well … supervision. Advice … about how to live her life, I suppose. And who to get involved with. Surely I don't have to explain."

I must have appeared puzzled.

"For God's sake, Joseph! I don't want her running into the arms of the first young man who comes along with a dozen roses. I want her to marry well, into … you know … society. Maybe a doctor. Someone with credentials. I want her to be secure." She sniffed haughtily. "These musicians. They're so flighty. They're all *artistes*." She raised her chin and affected an exaggerated flip of the hair. "None of them know the first thing about paying bills or fixing kitchen faucets or anything useful. They're always worried about their hands. The boys who come to see her are barely out of diapers. And they're just gaga about her. She needs someone who's not going to indulge her every whim."

"Look," I said. "All I'm telling you is what she said to me. She wants to move into a place of her own. I don't know if she understands what that involves or not. She might do very well. But if it doesn't work out she can always move back home, can't she?"

"Of course!"

"Well, then," I said. "I've done my bit for the family. I've relayed the message. I think she'll be okay whatever you decide. She'll be moving out on her own eventually anyway. It probably doesn't matter if it's not today or even next week."

For a few moments neither of us said a word. The rain continued to drum an unbroken rhythm against the window but more gently now, as if it were losing heart. And the music, which had entered a lyrical section, mixed soothingly with the muted patter of the rain. I felt myself beginning to drift off.

"Can I get you anything?"

"I'm fine."

But there was a suggestion of melancholy in her tone and a hint of it in her expression as well, in the subtle pursing of her lips, in the creases around her eyes that resisted her attempts to smile as she took her leave. And once again I suffered a fleeting sense of having disappointed someone I cared deeply about, as if I had simply confirmed her fears, taken her to the brink of some ugly chasm, revealed what was in store for her and left her to sort it out for herself. Perhaps she really did want assurance that Sophie would never grow up and leave home. Or maybe she needed to be told that her daughter loved her and would continue to do so even after she moved halfway across the world. Maybe she didn't know what she wanted. I could be sure of very little, only that I knew something about her daughter that I could not reveal and that the burden of this knowledge bore down on me with the pressure of a thousand petty obligations. I couldn't just walk away from what happened but at the thought of exploring the implications, of uncovering the intent behind the kiss, my extremities grew numb. I couldn't convince myself it meant nothing. A benign rationale—that weakened by the heat we'd fallen into each other's arms by chance—just didn't stand up to scrutiny. Pauline's report of Sophie's transformed behaviour made that clear.

Nine

I NEITHER EXCUSE NOR defend, nor even really understand, the events of the next few days. But by any standard my conduct was shameful.

I'm getting ahead of myself.

I remained a guest at Frederick and Pauline's overnight Friday and then hurried home Saturday morning, declining Frederick's gracious offer of a drive in favour of a taxi, for which I gratefully paid, glad simply to be taking care of things myself for a change. Dinner the previous evening had been informal, the four of us seated around one end of the long mahogany dining table. Not sure what to expect, I was somewhat nervous to find myself in Sophie's company for the first time since the funeral, and was unable to eat much of Pauline's rice and shrimp pilaf, which I normally devoured with enthusiasm. For dessert there was lemon tart, followed by strong black coffee. Frederick, as was his custom, offered me one of his imported cigars. But this I couldn't face, whether because the pungent tobacco turned my stomach or because I was conscious of falling further and further into his debt, I can't say. Conversation at the table was never lacking, and Sophie contributed her share. She seemed completely at ease, untroubled by thoughts of her mother's interference, moving out, or her identity as a grown woman. It was as if these issues had been settled to her satisfaction. She laughed frequently and extravagantly from deep in her throat. Seated across from her, I was unable to take my eyes off her for very long and our glances met again and again. She was dressed simply in faded jeans and a forest-green sweater that exposed her neck.

Throughout the meal I was fiercely conscious that the pantomime she and I were performing was not only for her parents but for ourselves as well. Without a word having passed between us, we'd apparently concluded that it would be to our advantage to make everything appear as normal as possible. Beyond this, I have no idea what occupied her mind. The words she uttered carried no suggestion of hidden desires, no hint that she and the person seated across from her were conspirators in deception. Her parents supplied most of the conversation, as was usually the case. And as the evening progressed and the wine took effect (I drank very little), we all became more animated and willing to laugh and be somewhat silly.

Outwardly I would have great difficulty distinguishing this particular evening from the countless others we had spent in each other's company over the years. The ebb and flow of dialogue, which drifted easily from one subject to another—all followed familiar patterns. But beneath the façade of an unexceptional occasion resided a layer of meaning that showed itself whenever Sophie's eyes met mine. This happened so often I still can't believe that Pauline and Frederick remained oblivious to our silent exchanges. Numerous times I glanced up from my plate to discover Sophie watching me, her gaze unguarded and candid and displaying no concern that I had caught her in the act. In the same way, my eyes were drawn to her even when I was engaged in discussion with one of her parents. And when she noticed me looking at her there was nothing in her face or manner to indicate she was in the least perturbed by my attentions. Occasionally I'd see that her lips bore the slightest shadow of a smile, as if someone had singled her out for praise or said something she found secretly amusing. At other times I'd be surprised by the graveness of her expression, for there had been nothing in the conversation at that point to warrant it. I'd look up and catch my breath, losing myself in the regal blue of her eyes, which, now that her hair was short, shone with dazzling intensity against the white of her skin. I found none of this disturbing, for I had grown accustomed to the physical Sophie, to the adult beauty she had attained. I believed her appeal was purely and innocently aesthetic; that much like a painting or a sculpture she was there for all, including me, to behold and appreciate.

Eventually she retired to the music room, where she performed the Turkish Rondo, *Für Elise* and some other light pieces. Shortly after this we all went to bed. I slept fitfully, bothered by the food in my stomach—which sat, inert as a boulder—and hopelessly agitated by visions of Sophie. In these half-dreams, she appeared in a formal white dress with white gloves, a wide-brimmed hat with veil, and stood among crooked headstones and knee-high grass. Face turned away, head down, she wandered from stone to stone in the bright sun, apparently searching for one in particular. I saw her as if from a great distance and knew with wrenching clarity that I had to speak with her. When I called out, there was an obstruction in my throat and I couldn't raise my voice above a whisper. As I approached, she floated farther away until she was out of sight and I was utterly lost. As I drew near where she'd been standing, I awoke.

Ten

M Y APARTMENT WAS not tidy but neither had it been left in the crisis state I had begun to imagine as I lay in bed at Frederick and Pauline's, unable to do anything about it. A few items in the refrigerator cried out for immediate disposal but, other than plants wilting on their stalks, nothing caused alarm. I performed a few mundane chores—changing the bedsheets, doing some laundry, washing up a few encrusted dishes—and then left to buy groceries.

The day was cool but the sky was jewel-like and brilliantly clear. A breeze disturbed the trees but harsh weather seemed unlikely. I headed along Spring Garden Road toward the downtown core, the location of small specialty markets stocking fresh produce and imported foods. Once I'd passed the Public Gardens the street was busy with people out strolling, simply enjoying the day, or shopping. The air was cool on my neck and I was suddenly aware of a profound appreciation of life's bounty, as if it were on display for my personal gratification: the street, the fragrant trees, the shelves bursting with their profusion of brightly-packaged goods. It was a feeling I'd had before, but perhaps because of my recent illness it seemed extravagantly intense. Maybe I'd re-entered daily routine too quickly, for to my dismay my eyes were brimming with tears and I was in danger of making a fool of myself on a city street in broad daylight. It was as if my emotions, rampant and unconstrained by reason, were determined, like a mischievous child, to exploit my weakened condition.

I paused to wipe my eyes, feigning the removal of a piece of grit. Shaky and feeling fragile, I continued on.

I found everything I needed, including a bottle of Chianti, and decided to return home before I was completely drained of energy. The exercise was bound to do me good, but Frederick had warned against ignoring my episode and with the "hubris of the healthy," as he put it, presuming I could carry on as usual. I made my way back along the main road and took a detour through the Public Gardens, which had only lately been cleared of winter debris and re-opened. The Gardens is a large square in the heart of the city. Expanding from a circular pond in the centre, the meticulously groomed land-scape and sculpted pathways are home to hundreds of preening waterfowl and endless varieties of trees, shrubs and flowering plants. Even at its busiest at the height of summer the Public Gardens is a pleasant retreat from the commotion of the city, separated from the lush terrain by only a few metres. Since my office is nearby, I often take my lunch here and spend my hour reading or, like the ducks, basking in the sun and watching the passers-by.

I speak casually about the day but in truth my mind clung ob-sessively to thoughts of Sophie. I felt beyond help and I could not imagine what I was going to do. Our kiss was almost a week old and since that time our only direct exchanges had taken place mutely over dinner. We had spent ten seconds alone in each other's company, hardly time enough to address the weather never mind the weighty topic of misplaced affections. Nothing had prevented me going to Sophie as she played piano after dinner and speaking my mind, ex-cept my reluctance to do so. The mere thought of a discussion about emotions made me weary. But I knew it was up to me to repair the damage. I had to set her straight on matters of the heart even though I didn't understand or want to think about them myself.

And so, I was unprepared for the encounter when it came. Seated on a bench, Sophie wore a trim taupe dress, black cardigan and dark glasses and appeared to be reading a book. When she saw me emerge from behind a massive rhododendron, she dropped the pretence of reading. My breathing slowed and for a moment it was like someone was standing on my chest. Blinded by uncertainty, my whole being reeled and I had a momentary vision of myself split in two, half running toward her and half running away. She was someone I'd known her entire life, someone I'd held on my lap and fed from a spoon. Now I was a stuttering wreck because the wide smile on her face said clearly that she was pleased to see me. No doubt a stronger, wiser man would have seen a clear path forward, a way to set things right and avoid all that followed. But I was weak. All I could see was her.

Stuffing the book in her bag, she rose to greet me. My confusion must have been manifest.

"You're not happy to see me, are you, Joseph?"

"I'm always happy to see you," I said, smiling at last.

She stepped forward and in seconds our hands had found each other and, just as I had in the cemetery, I relished the cool contact of her skin.

"I wanted to see you. I wanted to make sure everything was all right between us." She looked up at me. "Is everything all right between us?"

It was too easy to smile at her and say nothing. I wanted to tell her we shouldn't be together like this, that it was wrong of her to seek me out for this purpose. But even as I began framing a statement to this effect, all notions of propriety were banished to the back of my mind, hustled out of sight like a gift that's grossly inappropriate to the event at hand.

Struggling for words, "we're fine" was all I could manage.

"I came over this morning to see if you were all right. But you were on your way out. I didn't want to hold you up, so I followed you—I hope you don't mind. I wandered along behind you, looking at things in the stores. I felt like a complete idiot, spying on you like that. I didn't know if I should show myself or just go home, so after a while I came back here to wait. I thought, if he comes along and finds me, then it means I did the right thing."

"You did the right thing," I said, squeezing her hand, appalled that I had so easily abandoned my role as her guardian.

We reached the edge of the Gardens and exited in silence through the iron gate. Warmth expanded my chest and all at once a strange glow brightened the sky, houses and people walking by, making everything and everyone appear supremely affable, flooded with benevolence.

"I think something happened the day of the funeral," she said, turning thoughtful. "I feel like I grew up all at once, or finally saw myself the way other people see me. When we kissed it was like a door swinging open. You took me through and now I'm a different person living in a different place. All week I've been thinking about it, trying to figure out what happened. I wanted so much to talk to you about it, since it happened because of you."

"Sophie," I said, seizing the opportunity, "I'm very sorry. I took advantage of you and I shouldn't have done it. I must have already been coming down with flu or whatever it was and then the horrible heat ... I didn't know what I was doing ..."

My voice trailed off and I wondered if she was as willing to excuse my behaviour as I was.

"No, it's okay. Really. I don't want to ..."

"Sophie, what is it?"

She wasn't crying, but she kept her face away from me.

"I have this feeling, like I'm a little girl and you're this grown-up person who's only putting up with me because you're too good-natured to tell me to go home."

As she finished speaking her voice cracked.

"But you just said that the other day it was like you grew up. Why don't you feel like that now?"

She shook her head. "I don't know."

"You have to remember we all doubt ourselves from time to time. It's natural. I sometimes feel exactly like that. It's like, you look around and you think: I don't belong here. And you start to wonder if people are only putting up with you for the sake of appearances."

"So you're not tolerating me just to be nice?"

"Hardly," I said.

"I'm one of your favourite people in the whole world?"

I used to tell her this when she was small and I was surprised and delighted beyond all reason that she remembered our conversations of years ago.

"In the whole world," I said.

She smiled, and, wrong or right, I was content. I could assume credit for having set her mind at ease for the moment. It would be simple now, if only I could find the right words, to send her on her way and then meet later at her parent's house and talk in the familiar yet subtly detached manner we always had, probing no deeper into each other's thoughts than empathetic friends normally do. I told myself that the episode was concluded. But then I looked at her and I could see—as she kept her eyes to the ground and took each deliberate step—that she was at odds with herself, fighting an impulse that carried her along even as she struggled against it. And yet I still believe—even now, even after all that's happened—that she was very much in control of her actions that day.

She held the reins firmly in both hands and, had she the least desire to, could have changed the direction of events. Though I was much older and seemed to have steered the conversation toward instruction of an inexperienced person on one of life's dilemmas, I sensed she was letting me believe I was leading when in fact I was the one being led.

I could have told her to go home. I could have pleaded exhaustion or an upset stomach or chills or sore feet. Instead I pretended it would be cruel to hurt her, that she was infinitely fragile, that she needed me as an ally and mentor and that, if I deprived her of my friendship, she would be utterly broken. But the truth is I hated the thought of being alone and couldn't imagine how to continue without her. I lacked the resolve necessary to deprive myself of her company and the touch of her skin. She was young and lovely and intelligent and I was alone. That is all there was to it. I flexed my fingers against her hand and felt the response of her smaller ones. To be fair, I confronted my self-deception, looked it squarely in the face and then strolled serenely past it. We approached my place in silence, still clutching hands as if they were the anchor keeping all of creation from spinning out of control.

Without a word, we entered the flat.

I put away my groceries as she looked around the place. I could not recall the last time she had been here. She paused before a dark brooding landscape I'd picked up at an estate sale and walked on without comment. Still wearing her sweater, she held her hands clasped behind her back. My hands were cold. My heart wobbled.

When I turned around her sweater was draped over the back of a chair and she was out of sight. I noticed her white canvas sneakers with laces askew, abandoned on the floor. I followed the sound of her movements and found her in the living room where she was scanning book titles, her index finger grazing each spine in turn. The whole room seemed unkempt and vaguely repugnant, a depressing and harsh depiction of bachelor life. Dust coated the magazines littering the coffee table, as well as the table. The picture above the mantel was just perceptibly crooked and grimy blinds all but obscured the sunlight. I saw her bare feet on my hardwood floor, imagined dirt between her toes. She did not belong here, appeared out of place. And yet I was grateful she had come.

"Hi," she said, turning with a smile.

Then we were facing each other, standing close and looking into each other's eyes. Lifting a hand to my neck and with subtle pressure, she guided my mouth toward hers. We kissed shyly, both of us smiling but hesitant. It could have been a minute or an hour that we stood there, playing with the kiss, touching each other lightly. Occasionally I surfaced and heard traffic whizzing by outside, felt air growing cool and warming up again. At one point I heard a rattle as the paperboy shoved the newspaper through the mail slot. Our bodies pressed into one another, we explored each other with our mouths. I kissed every part of her face, felt the moist urgency of her lips and the heat of her tongue on my eyelids. Every now and then we would open our eyes and take each other in. I see her yet, her face aglow, her hair gorgeously tousled by my fingers. I fed on the softness of her skin, wishing I had more hands to stroke her with. When I began undressing her, she made no movement or sound. I drew down the zipper at the back of her dress, let the straps fall from her shoulders. She stepped out of the dress as it sank to the floor. I helped her with her undergarments. When she was naked, we kissed again and she pressed herself to me as she had that day in the cemetery, lifting her leg, rubbing her inner thigh against me. I let my hands roam up and down the length of her. I leaned into her and kissed her sweet little breasts, then all down her stomach. She gasped and said something as she grabbed my hair. We were into it now. I was past saving myself and could not hope to save Sophie, even if I'd wanted to.

We moved into the bedroom where, with Sophie's help, I quickly undressed. I stood over her as she lay on the bed and simply stared, absorbing the beauty of her flawless skin, the supple lines of her slender young body. Had I ever envisioned this moment? Dreamed about it? Craved it? It seemed impossible, and yet ... smiling, she reached out to me. I took her hand. She giggled and drew me down, without hesitation taking hold of me. My thoughts scattered and I lost myself in her. In a very short while the deed was done and we were curled into each other, alone with our thoughts. My only comment was, "you weren't a virgin, then," to which she replied "no" matter-of-factly, as if nothing could be less important. I didn't pursue the point and for a long time there was no talk. I reached for a cigarette and to my surprise she calmly lifted the lit cigarette out of my hand and—her eyes on mine—drew from it, as relaxed with the act of smoking as I was. I believed, in that moment, that life as I had known it had changed utterly, that from this minute on my only reason for drawing breath was to protect this child from the consequences of what I had done to her.

Part Three

One

T HIS IS HOW my young cousin and I became lovers. I'm not offering excuses, nor am I seeking exoneration for my actions. I am merely recording facts. And the fact was that we both discovered much within the other worth pursuing.

It will seem odd that a girl of nineteen would find anything of interest in a liaison with a man nearly two decades her senior. I admit this was a concern. I became obsessed with keeping her satisfied, which to my mind meant providing material for her amusement and entertainment. I wondered if my flat was good enough for her and even thought briefly about moving to brighter, more agreeable quarters closer to the shops and cinemas where she enjoyed spending her free time. I looked over my collections of books and recordings and saw that my tastes could easily be those of a man twice my age. I wondered about myself as well and, above and beyond my physical attributes (such as they were) and my performance in bed, concluded that my habits of dress were eccentric and hopelessly inconsistent with the fashions of the day. I could foresee a moment fast approaching when she would declare I was a bore and a pathetic embarrassment, shrug off the burden of my affections like an old coat and take up with someone closer to her own age. I suffered doubts both vague and specific. A dozen times, maybe more, I resolved to end our affair before Pauline or Frederick or an acquaintance happened upon us in a compromising situation. I saw calamity around every corner, disapproval in every eye. At times our situation seemed little more than a scene from a comic opera. I suffered visions, when asleep and when awake, in which I appeared as an old buffoon bent double with age and leaning on a cane, while she, still nineteen, guided me along with a hand on my elbow.

It was not that I doubted her love for me, for she never seemed to weary of my company, never wavered in her affections. But I had been conditioned by social norms to believe that our sort of love was not only unlikely, but impossible; that a difference in years inevitably outweighs other factors that might compel two people to develop a physical bond as well as deep and lasting fondness for one another. There is no disputing that we came from separate generations and that our assumptions and prejudices were dissimilar. I relied upon formality and convention in my dealings—even with those I knew well—respecting the emotional barriers people erect around themselves. Sophie was less inhibited in expressions of affection or discontent and in her assessments of other people. It was nothing for her to dismiss one of her mother's elderly acquaintances as "a miserable old fart," and to do so within earshot of everyone, including the maligned party. On one occasion, at a gathering of some sort, she told a priest that his opinion on abortion was "crap." If she was angry, she would think nothing of making a public display. If she felt like laughing, she laughed. Pauline could ignore this but I was easily shocked. And once Sophie had seen me drop a napkin or two to conceal my mortification, I believe it amused her to say and do outrageous things just to watch me drop napkins.

But it could be that the differences that appeared to set us apart actually brought us together. Sophie found most people her own age frivolous and tiresome. Her generation was preoccupied with all things shallow or simple-minded and anything that could be easily consumed and digested. They demonstrated little desire for self-improvement, little interest in the historical record of where we come from or the science of where we are going. Sophie, different from her peers in attractive and endearing ways, was grateful for whatever facts she happened upon and blessed with an ability to turn them into knowledge. And whenever she slipped into the ways of her contemporaries, she did so with an ironic gleam in her eye, laughing at herself the entire time. I sometimes even found myself defending her generation against her criticism, suggesting that if she troubled herself to explore more deeply she would actually find many attributes worthy of admiration in the young people of today.

Thus, our relationship was built upon more than physical attraction. Though our passion was short-lived, it did not for one minute diminish in intensity. We took each other into our hearts from the beginning, aware from the outset of the obstacles that stood in our way. Not once did we swerve from our original purpose, which was to complete each other in the way that a puzzle is complete when all the pieces are locked into place. On occasion our differences surfaced and we separated. But we always came together again, our love all the stronger for the time spent apart. I consider my relationship with my cousin Sophie Alexandra Gebhardt to be the single worthwhile accomplishment of an otherwise squandered life. And though there is nothing admirable in what I did, and though I admit my actions damaged the lives of people I love—and even knowing what I now know to be true—I can say with confidence that I would not have done a single thing differently.

Two

I N THE WEEK following our first time in bed together Sophie and I met privately about half a dozen times. Each reunion was a great relief to me because the moment we parted I began to fret over what had occurred, shouldering the blame, formulating exit strategies from what I knew to be a scandalous, alarming predicament. Once we were together, my guilt vanished and I lost myself in the innocent yearning of her eyes, in the allure of her young body and the tranquil beauty of her soul. We spent most of that Saturday afternoon in each other's arms, intermittently dozing, and consciously (in my own case) not speaking of what had just happened. Lying beside me, she appeared happy, composed and as regally confident as I had ever seen her. We shared a cigarette, then another. At one point my telephone rang and with blissful nonchalance I ignored it. Sophie burst out laughing. And then we were both laughing, perhaps at each other, perhaps at the thought of the outside world trying in this puny fashion to distract us from our euphoria. When we talked, our conversation gravitated toward the irreverent and the inconsequential, as if we couldn't possibly have anything to worry about. For almost five hours that afternoon, lying in bed together seemed the most natural thing in the world and nothing less than what we deserved. And when toward seven in the evening she finally left to go home and dine with her parents, we stood at the door and indulged in a long kiss. Then she declined my offer to accompany her at least part of the way and I watched her walk down the street and around the corner, waving to me until she disappeared. It wasn't until after she was gone that I realized we'd made no arrangement to meet again.

As it happened she was at my door very early the next morning. I took a moment to answer the knock, for I imagined in that instant Frederick waiting to wallop me senseless for what I had done to his daughter. I knew this was unlikely—for one thing Sophie would have told him nothing, and for another, he was perhaps the gentlest person on earth—but my mind was quick to envision catastrophe. I was still in a state of anxious trepidation I can only compare to how a professional spy must feel when, having committed an act of treachery in which he'd betrayed his country for selfish reasons, he suddenly finds himself burdened with a conscience.

When I saw it was Sophie, my first thought was that she had come to rebuke me for having taken shameful advantage of her youthful naiveté and to give me fair warning so I could pack my bags and leave town before she told her parents about us and took her story to the papers. But even before I saw the smile on her face I knew that I was tormenting myself needlessly. I opened the door and instantly we joined in a fierce embrace. Once again, we went to bed; once again, neither of us found any reason to leave the flat or venture any further than the bathroom for many hours. I considered going to church to try to cleanse my soul or at least feign contrition for my sins but I couldn't leave Sophie alone in order to partake in a ritual that to a large extent symbolized the barren existence I had endured before this weekend. I had never before been tempted to view my life as menial or drab. But it was dawning on me that I had also never allowed myself to experience passion or to hunger after something with an unquenchable appetite, never allowed myself to lose control even for an instant. In only a day I had attained an understanding of myself that would have eluded me for years had not Sophie slipped past my emotional bulwarks. I had been a sad case: a timid man who out of fear of the unruly had denied himself sustenance from another's love.

There were practical considerations, to be sure, and I saw these massing on the horizon as one glimpses approaching storm clouds.

The need for secrecy was uppermost in my mind. Looking at it from the perspective of Frederick, Pauline, or their social circle, I could find no mitigating factor that might excuse what I was doing, no possible interpretation of events that would situate my behaviour in a favourable light. I was not so blinded by lust that I failed to anticipate how perverted my actions would appear to the wrong people. And I wanted to avoid causing anyone pain. To this end, when I was alone I plotted vague measures that would safeguard our secret, pictured us behaving with discretion at every step, never holding hands in public, meeting only in my flat or perhaps at a country inn miles out of town. The thought of engaging in deception under these circumstances did not trouble me, for I convinced myself that it was undertaken solely for the benefit of others, that I was being big-hearted and considerate.

On the other hand, it wearied me to think of maintaining this deception for an indefinite period. When I looked at myself, which I did as seldom as possible these days, I found I neither trusted nor fully comprehended my new persona, one so estranged from the upright and principled individual I used to be. I realized that understanding would come with time, but until then I had to continue playing my former self when in polite company.

I returned to work early Monday morning, hopelessly in arrears and soon in a panic over how I was to make up the ground I'd lost in the previous week. I sorted through the papers heaped on my desk and attempted to set a few priorities. There were reports to write and meetings to attend. I discovered several outstanding accounts still to be settled and an unpleasant personnel problem I'd been avoiding for weeks leapt to the forefront. And yet, despite the urgency of work, I kept drifting off, head in the clouds, always trying to drag myself back to the matter at hand. I was happy in a way that had eluded me for years and I wanted to declare this in a loud voice—to the people in the office, strangers on the street, to all my friends, Pauline and Frederick included. And yet I could not speak of it.

How long could I live this way, and how long could I expect Sophie to live this way? How long before the first cracks appeared?

Three

A T THE END of April, I presented Sophie with a key to my
flat. It seemed logical, for I trusted her without reserva-
tion and could find no argument against taking this step
once she suggested it as a matter of convenience. And of
course I wanted her to feel she could come and go as she pleased,
even if I could not always be with her. My faith in our relationship
and her feelings for me seemed to grow by the day. Still, I was weak-
kneed with anxiety as I stood in the hardware section of the department store and watched the man behind the counter fit my key into
a template, power up his grinder, and in a matter of seconds produce
a duplicate. I could only imagine what the woman in line behind me
was thinking, for why else does one have extra keys made? My apprehension was not alleviated when later that week I pressed the key
into Sophie's eager palm. I knew I was not plotting to steal her away
from her parents. So why did I feel that I had committed yet another
unforgivable trespass against decency?

We had been involved for about three weeks and it was now
early May. The weather was improving, but for the most part the sky
remained overcast and intermittently doused the city with drizzly
rain. Sophie's summer schedule was beginning to develop more precise contours. She had accepted the university's offer to lead some
classes in the Music Department, mostly because she wanted to see
if she was up to the challenge but also because my flat was no more
than a three-minute walk from the Arts Centre. While she was in

the office of the department chair, a Dr. Ritchie—a slow-moving behemoth of a man but a brilliant organist whose concerts I had attended on many occasions—the subject of chamber music came up and in short order she found herself contracted to join a group of exceptional students who were looking for a pianist to make up a quintet. She didn't ask for my opinion, only announced her intention to take part in this project as if I couldn't possibly object. And I didn't object, not to the proposed enterprise itself. But I was left wondering where we were going to find any time to spend together, what with my office job and her multiplying commitments.

When I questioned the feasibility of adding this latest project to her list of activities, purely for reasons of time, she grew impatient with me.

"Oh, Joseph, it won't take long to practice these pieces. He said they meet on Saturday mornings and there's never anything else going on then."

She was sitting at the window seat, gazing out at the rain, chin resting on her arms folded on the sill. This was Thursday afternoon, around five. I'd left work early when she phoned to tell me she was here, frantically hailing a taxi as if I'd been informed of some family crisis that demanded my intervention. She was wearing one of my most expensive white dress shirts (imported from England) tucked loosely into jeans. Her feet were bare. After making love she had rifled my closet, found the shirt, and claimed it for her own with the pointed accusation that I hadn't given her any presents since we'd begun our liaison. This was true enough since I didn't think it would be wise for me to buy her things and have her attracting attention with jewellery she would have to explain. I was lying in bed smoking a cigarette watching her and when she said this she turned to me a smile both lovely and provocative, daring me to utter a protest. I was not about to tell her to put the shirt back.

I must have appeared downcast, for she beckoned me to sit beside her. I put my arms around her and drew her close. She wrapped her arms around my neck.

"It won't be forever, Joseph. Just for the summer. And it'll be new repertoire."

"But then you'll be off on tour again and I'll never see you."

Her response was to touch her forehead to mine.

"I'm sorry. I shouldn't be so selfish. The concert hall is your life. I'm going to have to accept that."

"You could come with me."

I shook my head. "I don't think that would work. You're going to be busy. I'd be a distraction. And anyway, how would I get the time off?"

The rain descended heavily in vertical sheets. The street was awash; the few people who were out clutched broad umbrellas or held raincoats over their heads. Occasionally a car sped by, splashing water in every direction. The dark sky grumbled. For a moment I cast my thoughts forward in time and could see only that it was going to be nearly impossible to spend more than a few days together here and there once the concert season began.

"What are we going to do?" she asked a moment later, in a small voice almost drowned out by the thrashing rain.

I held her tightly and pressed my face into her shoulder. When I looked up she was crying.

"I'm so happy here with you," she said, wiping the tears away. "I don't want to be anywhere else."

"You don't have to be anywhere else, Sophie. Not right now."

I kissed her forehead and smoothed her hair.

She still seemed distraught.

"How could this have happened? I mean, why do we have to keep it a secret? If it's what we both want? I'm old enough to make decisions for myself. I'm old enough to be in love with whoever I want to be in love with."

"I know. You're right. We just have to be careful. There are other people involved. It would break your mother's heart if she found out. I don't want that to happen. She doesn't deserve it."

I expected a saucy retort, for from her perspective this was probably one more instance of her mother controlling her life. She turned her head and gazed out the window. The rain had slackened.

"I wonder sometimes if I really want a career in music. I think it would be so easy to just walk away from it and be a secretary or something. There wouldn't be any pressure, none of this worrying about what people want to hear."

"You don't want that, Sophie. You'd go crazy working in an office all day like I do."

"I know." She spoke without hesitation, as if she'd considered it before and dismissed the idea as ludicrous. "But I've been performing on stage since I was six years old. I don't know anything else. That's not normal, is it? I mean, I haven't lived a normal life. I don't even know what a normal life is. You'll think I'm awful for saying these things. I know it's a gift and a privilege. It's a rare thing, to be able to perform and make people happy. Everyone's done so much for me. I'll never be able to repay what I owe. And I love what I do. It's not that. But sometimes I can't help it. All these questions build up and my thoughts just go there and I'm thinking about people who wake up in the morning and do what they do all day and then go home. They have supper and they turn on the television or they read a book. I know they have lots to worry about. Nobody has it easy. But they don't have to worry about what they're going to play when they get up on stage in front of two thousand people six months from now. Bach or Ravel or Rachmaninoff. They don't have to worry about learning new pieces, the phrasing and the tempo or whether or not Debussy really meant mezzo-forte when, you know, some of the scholars have doubts. Normal people don't think about things like that."

I had thought about this before—Sophie declaring she'd had enough and wanting to quit—and wondered how her parents would react. But somehow it didn't seem a real possibility. She'd never do such a thing.

"What do you want to do then?"

She shook her head.

"I don't know. But I wish I had a choice. It's like all my choices were made for me a long time ago and now I'm stuck with them. Other people have choices."

I laughed.

"Do you think I chose to be head of bookkeeping in an accounting firm? It's not like I woke up one morning when I was five and decided I was going to be an accountant. That nothing was going to stand in my way. It's more like I went to school and then to university and somewhere along the way it occurred to me that if I was going to live a decent life I had to find a profession. But none of it was planned or thought out in advance. I got a business degree and started applying for jobs and accepted the first thing that came along. I didn't have much say in the matter. I couldn't afford to be choosy. Not many people in my situation can afford choices like that."

"So what you're saying is that we're all trapped."

"Well, no. Not trapped exactly—"

"I feel trapped sometimes. Like I'm stuck inside a bottle and can't get out."

"Well, I feel like that too. It's not just you. Lots of people feel like what they're doing is a dead end."

"What's the point then? Why do we bother?"

I laughed and took both her hands into mine.

"What's so funny?"

"You are. You're so serious."

"Joseph, I am serious." She scowled. "Please don't laugh at me."

"I'm sorry," I said. "It's just that I can't imagine you doing anything else but playing piano. Most of us get no satisfaction from what we do. It's just a job. We go in there every day and do what we have to do. Maybe we can take some pride in being good at it. But in the end, we put up with it because it pays the bills. We have to look somewhere else for ... fulfilment, I guess. If I could play an instrument well enough to make other people so happy that they lined up to hear me and actually paid me to do it, there's no question I'd be gone from Murchie's in a minute. You say these things, but I think you really do know how lucky you are."

"Oh, believe me, I know how lucky I am. I know I live a privileged life. That's what makes it so hard. I feel like I should be happy all the time because I'm not out on the street begging for food. But I'm not happy all the time."

"Sophie, nobody's happy all the time. Don't expect so much from yourself. And don't put yourself through this. For most of us it's enough that we're happy some of the time. You're happy when you're playing. I know that for sure."

"And how do you know that?"

"Just by the look on your face. If you could see yourself . . ."

"Luckily I can't."

"I like watching you," I said, and it was true. Even if I were deaf I'd still enjoy watching her at the keyboard. She radiated delight, sheer exultation in the act.

The rain continued to pour down. It was approaching six o'clock. The sky was a pallid grey. Soon it would start to get dark.

She looked around my small, cramped living room.

"I wish you had a piano in here," she said.

"Where would that go, I wonder?"

"How long have you lived here?"

I calculated.

"Almost twenty years, if you can believe it."

"My whole life," she said absently, gazing around the room.

I followed her gaze and tried to see what she saw. I suspected she was viewing the flat with a head full of romantic notions, either of moving in here or of finding a place of her own. It was tempting for me to think this way as well, though the first of these scenarios was out of the question. All I could see when I looked around was twenty years of muddle, a bachelor's humble sanctuary, a place to hang my coat and put my feet up. I was never able to keep it as clean as I wished. I'd often resolve to do this or do that—scrub down the kitchen cupboards, change a light fixture because the old one bored me—but these decisions usually came to nothing as other commitments took over. Mrs. Ryan, my landlady, had told me on the day I moved in that if I wanted to change the colours I should feel free to buy a bucket of paint and a brush. But I'd never taken up the offer and all the walls had gone from a sheer white to a dirty beige. I knew my smoking was to blame but I so seldom had visitors that I'd let the flat fall into comfortable decline. The next tenant would want to change everything and it was likely that Sophie was viewing it as a potential occupant. But for the moment it was still mine and I was quite happy with it as it was.

"Do you ever think of moving?" she asked.

I shook my head.

"I don't want to move."

She seemed perplexed.

"You could afford a bigger place," she said. "Something grander."

"I don't need bigger and grander," I said. "I have this and it suits me very well."

She smiled and ran her finger along my chin.

"You're in a rut, Joseph. You need shaking up."

"I like my rut," I said. "And you've given me all the shaking up I need."

We kissed.

"How long have you loved me?"

She was staring into my eyes.

"All your life," I said. "The first time I met you, you were a day or two old. I fell in love immediately."

"You know what I mean. How long have you ..."—she looked down away from me and then back up again—"wanted me?"

I knew precisely what she meant.

"How long have you wanted me?" I asked.

She didn't answer right away but she didn't take her eyes from mine.

"I saw you one day," she said. "Summer, a couple of years ago, at the house. Everyone else was in the backyard because it was so hot. You were there too. The doors were open and I was playing, just bits and pieces. It was one of my mother's parties and I was so glad you were there because it meant I'd have someone to talk to. Then you got up and came back toward the house. I watched you. I saw you look over your shoulder at the rest of them. It was like you were sneaking away. You came up on the veranda and stood by the door and listened to me play. I could hardly see your face because the sky was so bright behind you but I could see that most of the time you had your eyes closed. But then sometimes I saw you watching me too. The feeling came over me that we could speak to each other silently. We didn't need words. And I knew you had more to say to me than you had to say to any of them."

"I remember that day," I said. "It was the first time I ever heard you play Bach. You were wearing a white dress."

"Then my mother came and found you. She took you away and I felt the loss. It went straight to my heart."

"I had no idea. I thought you had a boyfriend."

"He thought he was my boyfriend. But I cured him of that."

I vaguely recalled a gangly youth with thick glasses looking awkward in a tuxedo.

"What was his name?"

"Taylor," she said. "Taylor Lucien Bradford. He plays violin. He's very good. He was my prom date and we went to a few movies together but I wasn't interested in anything long-term and I told him so."

"That was mean," I said. "How did he take it?"

"He was upset for a while. He didn't speak to me much after that. But I see him around now and he seems okay." She kept looking at me. "So?"

"What?"

"How long?"

I placed my hands on either side of her face.

"I can't say, Sophie. I just don't know. Nothing was clear in my mind until you came here and I could see that you wanted to be with me."

She tilted her head.

"What about the funeral? When we kissed? You do remember that?"

"Yes, of course. But ... Sophie, you're putting me on the spot."

"What spot is that, Joseph?"

She was still smiling, but a hint of irritation had crept into her tone.

"Sophie, I've loved you since the day you were born. I watched you grow up. I've always felt we shared a rapport, some sort of understanding. I can't describe it. But that day you mentioned, when I came and stood in the door and listened to you play, I remember you were so beautiful in your white dress. Angelic. There was something magical about that whole afternoon. But I never thought about you ... you know, that way. Never for a single moment did I imagine I could be so fortunate." Her eyes didn't waver from mine. "This is so difficult."

"What's difficult about it? It's just a simple fact."

"But I couldn't love you when you were seventeen. I couldn't want you in that way. It would have been wrong. I couldn't plan for this to happen. I couldn't even hope for this to happen. As beautiful as you were and as much as our friendship meant to me, I could never dream of approaching you as if I wanted you sexually. Don't you see? I would have had to be some sort of monster to do that."

"And besides, you thought I had a boyfriend."

"Yes. That too."

"So you never thought about me the way I thought about you. Because I dreamed about you, Joseph. Every day I dreamed about us being together."

She said this accusingly, as if I'd deceived her or failed to live up to my part of a bargain.

"But I couldn't dream about you. Not when you were seventeen."

"You dreamed about me later, then."

"I didn't ... I ..."

"You never dreamed about me?" Her tone was incredulous. "Not even once?"

Her eyes were bright with hurt, with the injury I'd done her.

"Maybe," I said finally, not looking at her. "Maybe I did. But if I did, it wasn't because I wanted to."

"So you did dream about me." There was something else in her eyes now, a glint of triumph. "Were they nice dreams?"

"Yes, they were all nice dreams," I said, opting for exaggeration. "Very nice dreams."

Her mouth relaxed into a smile as she leaned forward.

"You should just see the look on your face."

She laughed and clapped her hands. And with her laugh the tension broke and I realized how close to absolute panic she'd pushed me. My face was hot, my body drenched in sweat. Blood rushed once more into my frozen limbs.

"My God, Sophie. Why did you do that to me?"

She leaned back against the wall and plopped her feet into my lap.

"I only wanted to know."

"Well now you know," I said, stroking her feet. "I lusted after a seventeen-year-old girl."

"As long as it was me," she said, beaming, her eyes quickening with her victory. "It was me, wasn't it?"

I looked at her and then away. The sky had assumed a dusky tint and in the houses across the street some lights had been switched on. The rain had stopped but the sound of water dripping through the eaves was loud. A sensation of faintness swept over me along with a wave of relief. I couldn't believe she'd tricked me so easily, with just a pout and a subtle shift in the timbre of her voice. I had believed her displeasure to be real, so real that it meant the immediate withdrawal of her affections and I had become wild with terror, for I was no longer able to regulate my emotions. I saw this now and understood what it meant.

I had been in love before in my life, repeatedly, many years ago, but it was always a shallow, adolescent infatuation, one that glowed like the last coals of a fire and then quickly cooled to ash. The thing that horrified me most about those fleeting but intense escapades of the heart was that the person whose affections I craved seemed to hold absolute sway over my disposition, determining with a glance or a giggle the direction my mood would take. I could find myself strutting like a peacock at full fan simply because some girl I liked turned toward me in the cafeteria with a smile that would melt ice on the moon. I was sure this was the real thing and would spend my day concocting a fantasy in which we fled the banality of life in Halifax, Nova Scotia and spent the rest of our years together on some island paradise. If the next day the same girl ignored me, or, worse, spoke affably to someone I considered a rival, I would imagine tossing myself off a cliff and having her find my smashed body, too late for her to see her mistake and realize our hearts were aligned in a unique and beautiful way.

"Don't be angry with me Joseph, please."

Her voice alarmed me with its pitiable urgency. Tears hovered at the edges of her eyes. She'd drawn her legs up and folded her arms around her knees and she looked all at once so small and frail in my shirt that was far too big for her, and dreadfully young and innocent.

"I'm not angry with you," I said, adjusting my face into a smile. "I could never be angry with you."

"You looked angry."

I shook my head.

"Not with you."

"I didn't mean it."

"Didn't mean what?"

She wiped her eyes with the sleeve of the shirt.

"I think I frightened you. I was only kidding around. I'm sorry."

"I over-reacted. I'm sorry."

We watched each other for a moment, and then we were both laughing as if nothing could be funnier than two people stumbling blindly over each other's intentions as if they were rocks strewn in our path. I took her again into my arms, grateful for the heat of her body, for the fruity perfume of her hair. We kissed each other long and hard and it was a moment before I remembered we were sitting next to the window where anyone strolling by could glance in and catch us in the act.

Shortly, I phoned for a taxi and sent her home, having first elicited from her a promise to change her clothes as soon as she got there and to hide the shirt at the back of her closet. In her absence my flat seemed to collapse into a state of dreariness. I could not help but notice all its blemishes and be appalled by them: the grimy walls, the worn and scratched hardwood floor, the plain-as-potatoes kitchen cabinets painted pale blue by someone who by now had probably been dead for thirty years, even the bathroom tile with its blackened grout—together it indicated long-term neglect.

Deciding I couldn't stay there, I phoned for another taxi to take me to an inexpensive downtown restaurant where I slouched into a booth and consumed an overcooked steak with mealy vegetables and an entire carafe of watery house red. For distraction I'd brought a newspaper with me but in the flickering light of a single candle flame I couldn't read more than a few lines. Against my will my mind kept returning to the confession I'd made to Sophie and I wondered if it was in fact an accurate account of past desires. My memory steadfastly refused to yield an answer. I could not recall ever having observed the adolescent Sophie with lustful eyes. She grew into a dazzling young woman very early, but I certainly never behaved toward her in a manner that I or anyone could have deemed inappropriate. I valued her youthful good looks—I'd have to be a stone, not to—but only as a parent or guardian might, with pride tempered by anxiety over the fact that she seemed to be maturing much too rapidly. All the while she was growing up I maintained a physical distance between us, or perhaps I should say there seemed to be a distance between us which I hesitated to encroach upon. But whether this was a deliberate artifice on my part or simply something that happened, I couldn't say. At a certain age I suppose she became shy of me, or perhaps of men my age in general. There was a period of maybe a year or two when she had difficulty looking me in the eye. I could recall her in demure fashion presenting her cheek to me for a kiss on birthdays or at bedtime, seeing it glow scarlet at my touch. She might have been eleven or twelve.

Later she gained confidence and became more outspoken and seemed to fear very few of the challenges that social occasions can present to younger people. From the age of fifteen or so she normally joined in the conversation, often sat next to me at dinner and never displayed the least trepidation if our glances happened to meet.

None of this was unusual, I dare say, though I am hardly an expert.

But since my feelings for her had taken on a physical dimension, I concluded there had to have been a time when I first imagined the possibility of this happening. So when would this have been? After our first kiss in the churchyard I was stunned that I could allow such a thing to occur. I viewed it as a violation and castigated myself for what I regarded as almost criminal weakness. But before that first kiss, had I ever thought of kissing her? Had it ever occurred to me that she was an attractive young woman and that I wanted her to know how I felt about her? If kissing her was wrong, then perhaps I had not tried to kiss her all those years because I knew it to be wrong. And if I understood that it was wrong, then at some point I must have given some thought to the wrongness of it. In other words, I had been tempted and managed to control myself. Until that day in the churchyard.

Could this be true? Had I desired her all along? Had I simply been lurking in the shadows, waiting for an opportunity to unburden myself, to force my affections upon her? I had no idea. I could not tell if I was recalling fact or if I was assembling a fiction out of fragments of memory. It was likely she had entered my dreams long before recent events had made a muddle of my life, but if she had ever played more than a casual role I was unable to remember this now.

The waiter looked at me oddly when he presented the bill. I suppose I had been mumbling aloud and I can imagine that my sullen demeanour was off-putting. My gloom had deepened as the wine disappeared from the carafe and by the time I was done I could not imagine being more disgusted with myself. The restaurant was decked out with tacky black-and-white celebrity photographs, people who were long dead or whose careers had fizzled ages ago. It made my heart sink to see them. Humphrey Bogart, Richard Burton, Clarke Gable, Vivien Leigh—they all stared into that nether distance with their false smiles and dead eyes, a reminder of things to come. It was almost midnight when I stood to leave on legs turned to rubber. I scattered some money on the table and staggered out the door, saying nothing to the cashier who asked me if I'd enjoyed my meal.

The street was still damp with the recent rain but the sky had cleared. I fumbled through my coat pockets until I found my cigarettes. Once I'd lit one and pulled the smoke into my lungs, I felt better. The sidewalk glittered beneath the streetlamps. I strolled along Barrington Street, feeling more or less right with myself and with the world again. I was having an affair with my younger cousin but she was a grown woman who could make decisions for herself. She had said so and had also told me that she'd known of her feelings for at least two years. So even if I had been sexually attracted to her then, or longer, where was the harm? I was not aware of having plotted the affair, of having lured her to my bed after manipulating her affections. I was not even the first to have sex with her, a fact that caused me more perplexity than concern or jealousy, but which I knew was none of my business. What was my crime? Why was I so worried?

I turned up Sackville Street, heading home. My mood brightened somewhat as I decided I didn't have to justify myself. As long as Sophie's happiness was my principal concern, I could not possibly cause her any harm.

And then a few steps ahead of me a couple emerged from a side street. I could hear them talking but could not make out individual words, which were spoken in harsh whispers. Though they shared the same slender build, he was taller. The man kept taking the woman's hand and each time he did this she jerked her hand from his grasp. Suddenly they stopped walking and the woman spun around and shook her finger in his face. The man turned his head and spat on the sidewalk. I kept them in view as I crossed the street. Standing there, nose-to-nose, they were oblivious of me, consumed by wrath. It was unthinkable that love could sink to this kind of crude quarrel that didn't care if it made a public display of itself.

Once I was past them I didn't look back. It was, after all, none of my business.

Four

I ARRIVED HOME one afternoon to find Sophie squatting on the floor beside my stereo listening raptly to an old vinyl album. I knew she had a much better system of her own at home and that Frederick had amassed a collection of vintage records and tapes that was envied by collectors far and wide. So the idea that something of mine could hold any fascination for her was hard to comprehend. My recordings were at best a haphazard assortment I had picked up here and there of no particular genre. Jazz, modern popular music, ethnic and international recordings, folk music, big band, classical—they were all represented to a certain degree. I had been accumulating the stuff for many years and had never bothered to organize what I had, and so finding a specific album was always an adventure.

Not a methodical or even demanding lover of music, once I found a piece of music I enjoyed, such as a Beethoven symphony or a Verdi aria, one recording would serve me as well as any other. I would not be offended because this pianist held the pedal down longer than that other pianist, because this conductor preferred a slower tempo than another conductor, or because one singer employed more vibrato than the next.

"Hi," I said. I took off my coat and hung it up.

She made a shushing motion. Her expression was one of intense concentration. From where I stood I could hear nothing.

I crept into the living room. We were listening to piano—but the notes were played with the softest of steps, reluctantly, as if guarding a secret they were unwilling to surrender to the listener. The irregular rhythm was like a person walking, then turning, retracing his steps, then setting out again as if unsure of the destination. One note repeated throughout, with chords and other single notes introduced here and there, all laid atop the foundation note as if at random. The effect was hypnotic and eerie. I pictured dark alleyways and shadowy figures stalking one another. It made my neck tingle with an imaginary draft.

I stood over Sophie for a moment—she ignored me—and then lowered myself to the floor immediately behind her. I attempted to fold my arms around her.

She wriggled against my grasp.

"Joseph, I'm listening!"

"Well, let's listen together. Okay?"

She didn't say anything. She resumed her hunched posture and remained utterly still.

The music continued its creeping movements, slowly, cautiously. The chords became rapid and then slowed—rose and fell in pitch as well—but the foundation note persisted until the piece came to a close, all that remained was the one note, ticking like a clock.

"What are we listening to?" I asked. I could well imagine that I had never heard this piece of music in my life. But since it was in my collection (or so I presumed) there was a good chance I had listened to it at least once.

"Joseph, be quiet!"

She turned her head only slightly as she delivered this directive. At the same time, she retrieved the sleeve from the narrow gap between the record cabinet and the stereo cabinet and handed it over her shoulder.

The cover image was a photo of a youngish woman with flowing dark hair sitting at a piano. Eyes closed, head inclined to the side, she appeared completely immersed in the music she was playing. Her relaxed features were long and angular. Above her head was emblazoned the Deutsche Grammophon emblem and the title *Maurice Ravel. Gaspard de la Nuit. Sonatine. Valses nobles et sentimentales. Martha Argerich, Piano.*

This was not something I had purchased.

The next piece had begun. I turned the sleeve over and read *Gaspard de la Nuit: 3 poèmes pour piano d'après Aloysius Bertrand.*

It began with a series of low, rumbling chords which were repeated before racing up the keyboard and rattling the upper register. What followed was music that evoked frenzied activity, as if characters were chasing one another across a stage. It darted back and forth, up and down, pausing momentarily as if hiding, then quietly creeping, then chasing once again. As the piece proceeded, I glanced at some of the notes on the sleeve. "*Scarbo,*" I read, "is even more fearsome, as the goblin flits in and out of the texture. The emphasis here is on rhythmic drive and diabolic virtuosity." This, I was sure, was what we were listening to, not only because the description fit the music but because the previous piece—*Le Gibit*—was written to evoke a body swinging from a gallows.

Sophie's head was lowered. She didn't move, as if engaged in a sacred ritual of sorts, or in a trance. But as the music hit a succession of crescendos amidst more rumbling notes, I noticed her nodding. The gesture was almost imperceptible, yet each time the music leapt up the scale and halted, her head dipped, as if agreeing with something. This was undoubtedly the rhythm, the ebullient precision of the notes themselves. The music vibrated with mischievous energy, evoking an unsettled spirit. I tried to reproduce Sophie's focus but found the music elusive, without pattern or structure. I could envision the chase but when I tried to set this aside and just listen to the music, was left far behind as it raced along its twisty path.

When it ended—with a brief trill as if the goblin had vanished in a puff of smoke—Sophie slumped and released a long breath.

"Oh my God. Did you hear that?"

Presumably the question was rhetorical.

She shifted to look straight at me.

"Did you hear what she was doing?" she asked, strangely adamant. Then her eyes slipped from mine and she seemed to gaze at nothing. She bit her lip. "I can't do that."

"You can do that," I said. "You can do anything you want."

She smiled but kept her gaze to the floor.

"It's sweet of you to say that."

"Well, why can't you do that? What's stopping you?"

Now she looked at me.

"What's stopping me?" She smiled. "What's stopping me is that I'm not good enough. That's what's stopping me."

I tried to appear annoyed.

"You're good enough. Don't worry about that. What you need is more practice."

"I've been practising it for a month. I still can't play parts of it."

"Well, maybe it takes more than a month. Maybe it takes years to get it right. How long did it take ..."—I checked the cover—"... Martha Argerich to learn it?"

She shrugged.

"I don't know."

"Well, there you go. Maybe it took her years to get it right. You don't know and will never know unless you ask her."

"Maybe I will." She took the cover from me and studied its photograph. "She's beautiful," she said, as if in despair.

"You're beautiful," I said.

Her smile widened.

"Why are you here listening to records?" I asked. "Is your system broken?"

"The house is full of people. Uncle Leonard and Aunt Tamara and all their kids. Mom's feeding the whole crowd tonight. And I think there are more on the way. It's somebody's birthday or something and it was too noisy. I had to get out of there. This is one of Dad's records." She looked at me. "You don't mind, do you?"

"Mind?"

I laid my hand on her knee and let it ride up her leg. She was wearing jeans and a pink sweater with long sleeves.

"When do you have to get back?"

"Not for a while yet."

I leaned over and kissed her. It amazed me how natural it now felt to do this, to touch and enjoy her body. My desire for her had not diminished at all in the weeks we'd been sleeping together. If anything, it had intensified; I thought about her constantly. In the past I'd regarded such statements as reckless hyperbole. How could anyone have another person on his mind constantly? Now I knew it was possible. Waiting for sleep, I thought of her. During an office meeting, I thought of her. My fixation had affected my behaviour and performance at work. I was often distracted and worked more slowly than usual because I felt compelled to go back and inspect all my written work before submitting it. There were errors—spelling and grammatical mistakes, idiotic lapses in logic—that were inconceivable a month ago. Actions I'd never tolerate from any of my subordinates. Now I knew, first-hand, that people were not machines. I was not the first person to fall in love; I expected this phase of my infatuation to pass. In the meantime I seemed to exist from moment to moment at the whim of forces I couldn't understand.

She raised herself to her knees and pressed herself against me. I unbuttoned her jeans and drew them down. I lowered her underpants. Her buttocks were round and soft, the tuft of hair between her legs a wondrous gift. Everything about her excited me. I loved her for letting me undress her. It seemed utterly alien and unexpected, the idea that I could be this close to another human being. I was astounded every time it happened. Until our kiss in the churchyard I'd seemed destined for a sad, solitary life of the mind. But Sophie had changed me. A year ago, I'd never have dreamed I could generate the sexual energy necessary to satisfy a much younger woman.

Eyes closed, her body shuddered as I ran my hand along her skin, from her small breasts down to her toes. She was beautiful, there was no other word for it. Her skin was milky white and so pale that it exposed the mauve lines of veins in her arms and neck and though her hair was light blonde her pubic hair was black. I would be satisfied to sit, to simply bask in her glow like a dark, parched planet drawing sustenance from a distant star. I knew now that I became a different person when I was around her. My natural timidity vanished and I became someone with an appetite, with riotous urges.

I carefully laid myself on top of her. She stroked me with a spirited, adventurous touch, without fear or inhibition. I had embarked on this affair conscious of my body's every flaw, its age, softness and paunchiness and unwholesome pallor. I did a great deal of walking but had never exercised seriously in my life and it showed. My muscles were concealed by a layer of fat that had spread everywhere beneath my skin. I was not corpulent but had about me a bloated quality that I attributed to my lifestyle. I sat all day in an airless office. I smoked only occasionally but too much, just the same. I was an unapologetic meat-eater always drawn to the richest foods on the menu. I tended to drink too much when I was alone and depressed. All this took a toll and was no doubt itself evident in my husky physique. If it were not for the walking—and I sometimes walked great distances—I'm sure I would have been too grossly out of shape for any but the most forgiving of lovers. As it was, Sophie seemed to enjoy me as I enjoyed her, as someone she could talk to and whose body was a source of pleasure.

I kissed her breasts and let my tongue caress her nipples. We had done this only a few days before, but she seemed ferocious with desire today. Her body quivered and writhed beneath my fingers, her mouth hung open in a slack expression. I heard her say something but it may only have been a whimper. I kissed her and she returned the kiss with a demented urgency that was almost violent. She clutched me to her and I could feel her fingernails marking my back. When I entered her, she emitted a series of throaty noises, almost a crooning. She pushed herself against me and I felt myself moving inside her, felt the rise of liquid longing. We settled into a rhythm but her movements were more vigorous than usual. I felt my pores rupture with sweat. Then her eyes opened and she smiled. I had thought I couldn't possibly love her any more than I already did but at that moment I sensed my heart rekindle with adoration. I was awed by the sky-blue of her eyes, her small straight nose, the fullness of her lips. She was a fountain of delight for me, a continuing source of joy, of pleasure, of renewal. I could scarcely believe that she had lived all her life at the periphery of my vision. Of course I had loved her, but only as one admires that which is immaculate and unattainable. Now she was here in my bed and I could not conceive of the possibility of ever being deprived of her laugh, of her touch. Her physical presence was a miracle, an impossibility. Yet here she was though I did not deserve her, or this much happiness. Yet, deserving or not, I was fully prepared to sacrifice everything I possessed to keep her happy and to keep her mine. Yet I knew that I would never be called upon to sacrifice anything because she would never ask that of me.

We collapsed into each other. My breath came in clogged gasps. I rested my head on her chest and listened to her heart hammering as if it would explode. She had completely emptied me. My limbs fell limply and it was all I could do to roll over so she could get up for the bathroom. I drowsed, bathed in sweat, my body throbbing from the sudden release. I didn't even want a cigarette. The physical challenge of keeping my eyes open proved too much for me, and when Sophie returned I dimly sensed her climbing in and pulling the sheets up to cover us both and nestling into my side. I fell into a sleep so vacant it was like I had been annihilated.

Floating to the surface, I sensed the apartment was empty. Turning over with a sigh, I was face-to-face with a photograph of Frederick and Pauline in a gilt frame. These days I suffered a brief pang each time I looked at it but could not bring myself to remove it. Sophie's portrait stood next to it, a head shot in which she looked directly into the camera, a half-smile on her lips. Her hair was curled and much longer than it was today, and it reminded me of how quickly the time had passed, and how overnight she seemed to become a woman.

Next to this was an old photo of my parents. Dressed in the garb of the forties, they stood side by side with their arms around each other. A blazing sun made it a poor photograph, bleaching their features into vaguely discernible shapes. But what made this photo unique—the reason why I kept it out—was that they actually appeared happy. One could tell their smiles were not feigned for the camera. At that moment, they really believed they had something to smile about. The arc of a Ferris wheel rose behind them but there were no clues as to when or where it was taken, or by whom. But it seemed to record a moment when their pleasure in each other and in being alive was manifest and real. It was how I preferred to remember them.

I heard a distant tinkle, music.

In the living room Sophie sat cross-legged on the floor by the stereo, her back to me, her head bowed. Her clothes lay where we had left them. She was naked. Ravel's music played. The sombre foundation note of *Le Gibit* was reiterated, and this time I could envision the body hanging by the neck, swaying in the still air, arms and legs stiffened in death.

Five

ON SATURDAY—THIS was May the eleventh—Sophie began attending sessions with her quintet. These sessions would continue until the end of the summer. She was meeting with them in a small auditorium in the basement of the Dalhousie Arts Centre. The quintet's existence seemed to be based on a casual interest from the participants, all students in the music program. But I know she was curious about the chamber music repertoire, which as a soloist she had not yet had an opportunity to explore. I suppose it offered her another way to cultivate her musicianship and represented an opportunity too good to pass up.

For the last couple of years she had been working in almost complete isolation with only her father to direct her rehearsals and advise her on repertoire. Selma Kraus had until her death lingered in the background as the ultimate authority on technique. But neither was involved with Sophie on a day-to-day basis. Frederick was an excellent musician in his own right but his expertise was more theoretical than practical. He could read a score and interpret the composer's instructions as well as anyone. But his studies in this arena had ended some years ago and he had no time to keep up with current scholarship.

In most cases Sophie embarked upon a new piece with only the written score to guide her and recordings if any could be found by artists she respected. And so her involvement with a group of musicians who shared her aims and interests could only be enriching.

I had resolved that at some point this summer I would find out where the sessions were taking place and sneak in to listen. Not today though, as they were only just getting started. And as great as the temptation was for me to follow her wherever she went, especially on a day like today when I had no obligations, I suspected she would feel I was intruding if I were to show up, as if I couldn't bear to let her out of my sight, just as she was trying to forge a bond with others of her own ilk.

The morning dawned clear, with a honeyed freshness in the air. True summer was not far away. I had made plans for this morning, for I wanted to be busy and not have to think about Sophie spending her time with these other, unknown people. Not that I was jealous, or even anxious. It made perfect sense for her to preserve a life apart from our relationship, particularly since we were keeping it to ourselves. I think we both knew we couldn't keep our secret forever and that a time would come when we wouldn't want to. By concealing our love, we were ensuring it would never grow into something worth sharing with the rest of the world. Like a plant shielded from light, it would always be stunted and brittle no matter how much we fed it in private. It would also continue to bear traces of moral ambiguity, and we would never be free to demonstrate our affection for one another openly. We weren't doing anything shameful. Most people would understand this. The only shameful part was that we had to conceal our happiness and pretend that nothing between us had changed.

And in many respects, things hadn't changed. When I looked at her I could still see the innocent girl I had known for nearly twenty years. Our physical union had not destroyed that image in my mind. But she was an adult now and she had made her decision. Eventually her parents would be facing the reality of that decision. They would have to accept the fact that it was not unusual for second cousins to marry.

Today, however, was not the day to break the news.

I had not been to visit Frederick and Pauline since my illness and had only spoken to Pauline a couple of times in the intervening weeks. I wasn't avoiding them but considering all that had occurred felt it wise to maintain a discreet distance. Given my altered perspective on the entire family, my manner would undoubtedly signal that something was different even if it was not clear to anyone but Sophie and myself what the nature of those differences were. I also knew that if Sophie were home at the time of my visit, her presence would affect my behaviour; I would not be able to help it. I decided that, if I was ever to resume my custom of dropping in whenever the mood hit me, then, initially at any rate, I would want to do so at a time when I could be certain that Sophie was elsewhere.

This morning seemed to present a perfect opportunity to resume that part of my old life. I did not phone anyone. I left the flat and walked downtown to the weekend market where I bought some fresh vegetables. I continued south along the waterfront, pausing for a cigarette in the small park outside the train station. I sat on a bench for a minute and watched people go by. Then I bought a cup of coffee and a croissant at the hotel cafe. I suppose I was dawdling, trying not to think about Sophie. The morning would have been much more enjoyable had she been with me. But this was not within my control and I tried not to brood over it. She was a professional musician and there were things she had to do. Like any working individual, her time was often not her own. She made enough demands on herself and didn't need mine. We had spent many blissful hours in each other's company. I was happier than I'd ever been. If our relationship ended tomorrow, I would still have my memories of our time together.

So why was I being pestered by doubts? Why was I struggling against a sense of despondency so leaden I could barely hold my head up? Ordinarily I'd feel blessed by an entire day free of appointments and obligations. Why did this freedom look like idleness, empty hours to kill with pointless errands? I had always been able to appreciate basic pleasures: a child smiling, sitting on a bench watching birds forage for seeds, or sipping coffee and reading a newspaper in a diner. Distractions abounded to help me past the difficult moments. But this morning every act seemed futile. As I left the café, I fought the desire to return home and bury my head under a pillow and await Sophie's light step on the porch, the only thing that would rekindle my spirit.

I took a breath and pressed forward. Eventually I found myself rounding the corner on to Young Avenue. The dwellings gracing this street were among the most exclusive properties in the city. Some were absurdly proportioned houses, constructed from the same materials and with the same values in mind as the houses in any poorer neighbourhood, only bigger and grander. Others had sprung from the imaginations of architects unfettered by fiscal limitations. Turrets and archways were common. One building resembled a medieval castle. Another presented the street with a visage that was three floors high, every inch of which was rose-tinted glass. Some were new and others almost a hundred years old. The first families to build along here had made their money in shipping or banking and then passed the family home to their offspring.

Only a few of these families remained. The majority of residents on the street were doctors, lawyers and other professionals who had purchased their homes within the last ten or fifteen years. 1220 Young Avenue was one of the least ostentatious of these residences, its dignified countenance made somewhat imposing by twin pillars on either side of the entryway. To the left, hidden from the street behind a row of beech trees, was an addition: a large octagonal room with three sides made up of windows. This was Sophie's rehearsal space and it easily accommodated her two pianos. To the right was a double garage. The slightly inclined driveway was constructed of oddly-shaped interlocking bricks that fit together like puzzle pieces, at the centre of which was a mosaic of coloured stones fashioned into a crest—the caprice of some previous owner. This morning no cars were in evidence. Looking up, I could see the curtains had been drawn back from the window in my own room, which was at the far right. Sophie's bedroom was in the back and, as luck would have it, at the other end of the house from mine.

There was no answer to my knock. I didn't bother ringing the bell since I disliked the idea of making either owner or hired help run for the door from some far-off corner of so large a house. Instead, I followed the path through the wooden gate around to the back, pausing for only a moment to peer into the music room as I went.

In the spacious yard a large stone patio had been constructed at ground level, a couple of steps down from the main dining room and Sophie's music room, both of which exited into the back through sliding glass doors. To one side a door opened on to a porch and just beyond that to the kitchen. Beyond the patio was a perfectly flat expanse of lawn, which eventually sloped downward into the trees and bush that hid the adjacent properties. Huge oaks and maples stood sentinel all around the perimeter. Frederick and Pauline had been attracted to the house by the degree of privacy the yard afforded, especially during the summer months when the trees provided a dense cover. Without even closing your eyes, you could easily imagine you were living a life of splendid seclusion somewhere in the English irregular countryside, far out of town with no neighbours for miles.

Pauline was at work in her garden, which was situated next to the wall. Flower beds dotted the yard, front and back, and at the height of the season these would be crowded with the pinks, purples and whites of the petunias and geraniums that Pauline loved. Also by then the rhododendrons would have achieved full, dramatic bloom. My foliage of preference was a cluster of tall flowers trembling on their stalks, mostly irises and tiger lilies, that filled an oval-shaped mossy patch near the rear of the yard. These were surrounded by hunched, leafy things that looked somewhat like lettuce but which Pauline had informed me were named hosta. Nearby were several beds of low grassy plants that for most of the year looked weedy and spiky but which toward the end of July erupted into hundreds of pink and white blossoms that permeated the yard with a sweet spicy fragrance like cloves steeped in honey. A landscaping company tended the flowers. Pauline also grew vegetables, of which she was quite proud, in her little rectangular plot.

"Good morning," I called as I approached.

She looked up from her tilling and shielded her eyes.

"Joseph!"

She laid her implement on the ground, pulled off her gardening gloves, which were as white and clean as any gloves I'd seen in my life, and came toward me. We met at the centre of the yard.

"My lord, you've been a stranger."

She kissed me lightly on the cheek and threaded her arm through mine.

"Yes," I said. "I'm sorry about not being around. There's been a lot going on."

"What's this? A present?"

Happily, she tugged on the corner of the bag and peeked inside.

"Just vegetables," I said, slightly embarrassed now by the meagreness of my purchase. "From the market. Some radishes, a few zucchini, leeks for soup."

She wrinkled her nose.

"Sounds delightful."

She rested her head lightly against my shoulder and we began strolling in the general direction of her patch of freshly tilled earth.

"So, tell me what you've been doing."

I cleared my throat.

"Keeping to myself mostly, I'm afraid. I've not been going out much. I must be still recovering from whatever that bug was."

"Yes. Frederick was saying it's not an easy one to shake off. If you don't watch out it comes back and you're starting all over again."

"I'm feeling all right now. I'm trying to get out and do more walking. At least the weather's turning nice."

"I hope you're not overdoing it."

"Well," I said, laughing, "you know me."

"I can't believe you've nothing to tell me after all this time. No news at all? No new love in your life?"

I released an inward groan. She knew nothing, of course, but I tensed just the same.

"Sorry to be so boring. Sometimes I think I should invent a social life just so I'll have something to talk about."

She squeezed my arm.

"Everyone is healthy I take it?" I asked, hoping to steer the conversation away from myself.

"As always, knock on wood. We've been lucky this year."

"How are your Mom and Dad doing?" Pauline's mother, my aunt Adele, had had a cancer scare the previous summer. They lived an hour away in the famed port town of Lunenburg.

"They're well. As a matter of fact, they're planning a trip."

"Oh, yes?"

"To England. Dad's brother is there, you know, and there's lots of other family to visit."

I nodded. For some reason this morning the idea of delving into family matters made me anxious, as if it might take me places I didn't want to go. We reached the patch of recently-disturbed earth. In past years Pauline had harvested substantial quantities of tomatoes, squash, cucumbers, peas and carrots. Most of it she gave away to friends, the local food bank and Hope Cottage, which serves hundreds of free meals daily and where she sometimes volunteered in the kitchen. But some she kept for her own table.

This morning she showed me where the various crops were going to be planted and explained about pests and how she intended to keep her vegetables free of them. Her hands glided back and forth over the earth in broad sweeping movements, as if she were conceptualizing a blueprint for thousands of acres of farmland instead of planting vegetables in about a hundred square feet of earth in her back yard. I watched her and listened.

She wore a blue paisley kerchief on her head, a denim shirt with the sleeves rolled up, olive-green work trousers, and lace-up boots on her tiny feet. She had put on weight these last few years, but in the pleasing manner of those who seem to fill out existing spaces without creating new ones. Approaching forty, she still possessed the girlish charm that had left me smitten years ago and which continued to shine through whenever she opened her brown eyes wide and laughed. I suffered a pang of regret now, though I struggled to keep it beneath the surface. I was interested in what she was saying and as always looked forward to sampling the fruits of her efforts.

But I was all too aware of the grotesque charade I was enacting simply by being here and behaving as if nothing was different. I was a charlatan and she deserved to be treated with greater respect.

I was about to confess everything when she asked: "Would you like some tea?"

"Yes. Please."

She was looking at me oddly. I turned and we headed toward the house.

"What?"

"You're so funny, Joseph." She hurried up beside me. "Where were you just now?"

"I was just ... thinking."

"About what?"

I was safe, for now. The urge to confess had fled. I decided I was happy I'd come.

"About you. About us. I don't get to see you much anymore and I'm sorry it's turned out that way."

"Well, you know ... Real life intrudes, and all that. There's plenty of time. We're still young. Nothing is forever. There are lots of ways to say it."

"I guess I wish we had a chance to say it more often."

"You can come over anytime you like. You know that. We'd love to have you. Come and stay for a week, or a month. The room is always there for you."

It's not the same, I was going to say. Instead I said: "I just might take you up on it."

She smiled and plugged in the kettle.

I placed my vegetables on the granite counter. The plastic shopping bag rustled, emphasizing the silence. Pauline had had the old kitchen gutted a few years back. The new cabinets were white with a matte finish, the walls a deep forest green. I sat at the island unit in the middle of the room and watched her remove the kerchief and loosen her hair with a shake of her head.

"Where's Frederick this morning?"

"Oh, another meeting. This board he's on. It never ends, even on Saturday. It's a good thing he loves it."

I thought it proper to add: "And Sophie?"

"She's meeting with some students at Dalhousie about forming a chamber group. It's beyond me why she's bothering. She'll never have time to practice those pieces as well as her own. But it's like talking to that chair. She makes up her mind and you're wasting your breath if you argue with her."

"It might be good for her, actually," I said, for this is what I'd told myself. "Working with other musicians. The give and take. She's always worked alone. Maybe she'll learn something."

"Maybe," she said. "But she's so … oh, I shouldn't say this because she's trying. She really is. But I can't talk to her about her concert career. She refuses to hear what I have to say. Sometimes I think she does things just because I've advised against them."

"Children," I said. "We were all like that."

She glanced at me and smiled.

"Were we?"

"Well, maybe not you," I said. "You actually did do everything you were told."

"I did not."

"Oh, I think so," I said, teasing her now. "You were the only teenager I know of who never went through a rebellious phase."

She poured the water then dropped two tea-bags into the pot.

"We did some pretty risqué things when we were young, if I remember correctly."

"Like the time we set fire to the barn," I said. This was back when my parents still socialized. Pauline's family had a summer cottage on the south shore and my parents often visited on the weekends. Nearby was an abandoned farm where Pauline and I used to sneak off to play. To get to it, we had to cross a busy highway, trek up a grassy hill and navigate a patch of trees and bramble. Going there was forbidden. It was a dangerous spot because the house was falling down, in fact the roof had already collapsed. We could easily have cut ourselves on broken glass, or stepped on a rusty nail, ruptured a rotten floorboard or drowned in the nearby bog.

The barn smelled like the animals that used to live there. Ropes hanging from the rafters were perfect for swinging over the remnants of hay bales scattered across the floor. One day we discovered an opening into the space under the barn. Of course we had to explore it, so Pauline stole some matches to light our way. But all we found were rusted cans and smashed beer bottles and we soon gave up. But we must have left one of the matches to smoulder. That evening the adults were kept on alert by the spectacle of smoke trailing skyward from the direction of the farm. Later a neighbour came by to tell us the barn had burned to the ground. It was a while before Pauline and I went back to check out the damage we'd done.

"Oh, yes." She laughed and shook her head. "I'd almost forgotten about that. You know, I told Mum later on that you and I had done it but she wouldn't believe me. Or at least she pretended she didn't believe me. I guess it amounts to the same thing."

"You told her?"

"Well, yes. I was trying to be good. I always tried to take responsibility, didn't I?" She mused silently for a moment, then shook her head. "I cried and cried, hysterical with guilt. But when I told Mum what had happened she said I must have dreamed it."

Pauline lifted the top off the teapot and prodded the bags with a spoon, swirling them around.

"You took responsibility for me enough times," I said, even though it was a difficult thing to admit. She was always being asked to take me along when she went to the museum or the park. I was a piece of baggage she had to lug around everywhere she went.

"I don't look at it that way," she said. "I was older and you were younger. Your parents didn't have time for you, or even know what to do with you."

"That's true enough."

"After they got sick ... Well, how could anyone expect them to keep up with a six-year-old boy?"

"They could have tried," I said, surprised at the force with which my resentment returned once the old wound had been pricked.

"You know Joseph, I didn't mind having you with me. It was fun. I missed not having any brothers or sisters. It's lonely growing up like that ..."

She didn't finish this thought. Instead she poured the tea into two china mugs glazed with images of pink roses over a soft yellow background.

"You stayed with us a lot that first year. It really was like having a little brother."

"I remember being in the hospital," I said, recalling stark white walls, a bag of clear fluid hanging from a pole, anxious faces peering down at me.

"It was blood poisoning," she said, arranging half a dozen of her chocolate chip cookies on a plate. "It wasn't spotted until it was almost too late. Mum told me you almost died."

"No wonder I don't remember much about it," I said, though some impressions had stayed with me over the years. I was released from the hospital and returned home to find it transformed from the sparkling place where I'd grown up to a mausoleum where the lifeless inhabitants sat motionless for hours, following the shadows from room to room. Even in spring, all the windows were shut and the curtains drawn. My parents had developed heavy circles under hollow eyes and a slow creeping manner of moving, as if they'd aged a hundred years overnight.

I followed Pauline into the living room and we settled ourselves on the chesterfield before the coffee table. The room was spacious and rectangular, with high ceilings and walls of creamy eggshell trimmed in white. Paintings—landscapes, a still-life or two—were hung here and there. On the table in the corner was the portrait gallery that Sophie had complained about: photographs of her from the age of three to about nine in a variety of poses—seated, standing, wearing a wide-brimmed straw hat, at the piano, at the cottage. The broad window overlooked the street. At one end, the fireplace and mantel nearly filled the entire wall. At the other a set of French doors opened to the front hallway where an antique grandfather clock ticked loudly.

"It wasn't too long after you left the hospital that you moved in with us. I remember being so pleased because we'd always had so much fun together. But you were still getting your strength back. I probably would have killed you if Mum and Dad hadn't made me leave you alone sometimes. It wasn't so much you tagging along as it was me dragging you. I couldn't understand why you had to stay in bed and why I couldn't make any noise. It was like having a new toy and not being allowed to play with it. Here you were, probably homesick, and I was always making you do things."

We sipped our tea.

"I'm sure you didn't do me any harm. The distraction probably did me good."

"My lord, Joseph. I used to drag you everywhere. I even showed you off to my friends, like you were a new bicycle or something." She laughed. "My father got so mad once that he locked the door to your room when you were sleeping, so I couldn't get in."

"I don't remember that," I said.

"Well, you wouldn't. You were asleep."

We were both laughing now.

"Do you remember how I used to get into bed with you?" She glanced at me over her teacup, her eyebrows arched.

The cup and saucer rattled softly in my hand.

"No," I said.

"After you were with us for a couple of months I got into the habit of going into your room at night and getting into bed with you. Maybe you don't remember because I don't think you woke up even once. I never told you this before?"

I shook my head. She sipped her tea and looked straight at me.

"Mum was talking about how you were getting better and saying that you'd be going home soon. I didn't want you to go, of course. It seemed you'd only just arrived. Summer was coming. I was pretty much in love, either with you or with the idea of having you around, I suppose. At that age—what were we, seven and nine?—

it's not important. All I know is that I didn't want you to go and so I used to wait until the middle of the night and then sneak into your room and crawl into your bed. You kept right on sleeping."

She shook her head and gazed at the floor. At that moment—with her face angled away and the light catching her hair—the resemblance to Sophie stopped my breath. I sat very still trying not to gasp, hoping she wouldn't notice my discomfort. In the hallway the clock's ticking seemed to swell and fill the room.

"I only did it a few times. Then you went home anyway. I cried for days. I took all my things into the room where you'd stayed and pretended you were still there. I almost made myself sick. God, it was pathetic."

"Poor thing," I said, my clenched throat keeping my voice steady. Watching closely to see if she noticed the tremble as I placed the empty teacup on the table, I said the first thing that came to mind. "Um, no, you never told me this before."

"Well, it is kind of embarrassing. I don't know why I'm telling you now. It's not important or anything." She smiled and sighed dramatically. "Just one of those childhood secrets."

"But it seems to me from that point on we were together almost all the time."

"Yes. Your parents ... I don't know what it was. They just didn't seem able to cope anymore. I might have seen them a dozen times after that. Maybe not even that. I asked Mum what was wrong and all she ever said was that one or the other was sick." She looked at me. "So you don't know what was going on."

I shook my head.

"No. All I remember are closed doors and everything being dark all the time. My father would tell me in the morning, 'your mother's not feeling well today' which meant I had to go to your place after school. But then other times it was her saying that he wasn't feeling well. It was like they'd contracted some disease and then spent the rest of their lives trading it back and forth."

But of course I knew it was not a disease, as in a bug being passed from one to the other. If it was as simple as that, why didn't I catch it? And where was the cure? No. Though I was young and confused and didn't want to face it, I could not escape the tension between them. I saw them silently pass in the hallway, not giving each other so much as a glance. I watched them lock eyes across the kitchen table and then look away. My mother with her glass of whiskey, my father with his cigarettes. As I grew older I realized that I had a front-row seat to a loveless marriage. And more, that they were doing this to each other deliberately.

Without asking, Pauline refilled my cup. The tilt of her head, her calmly expectant expression softened further by a contented half-smile, made me think of Sophie again.

"I guess I'm still confused about why they let themselves get like that and why they didn't try to do something about it. Maybe they were sick, but I didn't see any reason for them to be so miserable day in and day out. I remember being afraid I was going to catch it from them, whatever this was, and end up just as morose and boring as they were. I'd look at the food on my plate and want to throw up. I was only a kid and I was afraid, and they were so wrapped up in whatever their problem was they didn't care."

"They must have cared."

"Well, if they did they didn't show it." Pauline's glance over her teacup was a mild rebuke. "I don't know. I suppose they were good to me in their way. There was no shortage of food. We had a house so we weren't freezing in winter. But it wasn't like being a family any more. We never did anything or went anywhere together. I was never allowed to make any noise. I didn't dare invite friends home from school. You were the only one who ever came over and even that wasn't often."

"I think Mum used to visit sometimes. But I know it upset her."

"I should probably talk to her about it again. She might be able to fill in a few of the blanks. I wouldn't be surprised if she knows more than she thinks she does."

"She never talks about them, you know. Never. I can remember when she came home from your Dad's funeral, all she said was that it was a mercy it was over."

I laughed.

"Well, the funerals were kind of anti-climactic. They'd been dead for years anyway. Putting them in the ground seemed redundant."

"Joseph, that's not a very nice thing to say."

"I'm sorry. But it's closer to the truth than you might think. You don't know what it was like to live with them and see them getting worse every day."

"I'm sorry I brought it up."

"No, don't be. Please." I leaned forward and touched her hand. "I'm sure it's healthy for me to talk about this. It's been hanging over my head as a kind of unfinished business. I know there's nothing I can do about it, but it would help if I could come to terms with it. Talking helps."

"It still bothers you?"

"Only in the sense that I avoid thinking about it. About them. I can accept that they were miserable all those years. But wondering if I was the cause … that's hard to deal with."

"Oh, I'm sure you weren't the cause. How could you be?"

I shrugged.

"Well, that's just it, isn't it? How could I be? How would I know?"

I took another sip but the tea was tepid.

I stood. "I'm sorry. You were gardening. I didn't mean to stay this long."

She rose and loaded our tea clutter on the tray. "There's no hurry, Joseph. Really. I was about to suggest that as long as you're here you might as well stay for lunch."

She lifted the tray. Flustered by the thought of Sophie walking in and thinking I was checking up on her, I guiltily realized I'd neglected to perform this simple task for Pauline.

"Oh, thank you but I couldn't do that."

"Why on earth not?" She laughed. I followed her into the kitchen. "There's no shortage of food, if that's what's worrying you."

"Ha, ha," I said. "No, I've just got some things I have to do. That's all. But thanks anyway. I'll stay next time. I promise."

"See? Now this is what makes me think you have a woman hidden somewhere. You were never so busy before."

I could actually feel the blood drain from my face as I struggled to convey calm; it left a coolness in my head that emphasized my body's surging heat and sweat.

Pauline instantly turned solemn. "I'm only teasing, Joseph." Then she laughed. "You look like you've seen a ghost."

The clock in the front hall whirled its gears before tolling eleven times. We watched each other as the notes chimed, leaving in their wake a trembling echo.

She took my hand.

"Joseph, if there's something wrong you can tell me. You do realize that."

I smiled and hoped it did not appear forced.

"I'm just tired. I haven't been sleeping well lately."

"There are ways to fix that," she said, an amused glint in her eye.

She knew I was brushing off her concerns. Was I really so transparent that a glance told her everything she needed to know?

"I'm sorry I brought up that business with your parents. I really am."

"I told you, I'm not sorry. It's there and I should face it. Like I said, talking helps."

We embraced lightly.

"Talking, maybe," she said as we drew apart, "but not having to answer question after question." She searched my eyes. "You're sure you can't stay?"

"I'm sure."

"Where have all the years gone?" she asked. "It doesn't seem possible that it's twenty years since we were kids and you used to come and stay with us."

"More than that," I said. "You and Frederick have been married that long."

"Yes. Twenty years this fall."

The silence that descended was a presence, as palpable as if someone had stepped into the space between us. Rooted to the spot by my fear, I was only dimly aware of Pauline leaving the room. Staring out the window I saw the leaden skies and thought of Sophie, who I suspected would be completely unprepared for rain.

I was roused from my reverie by the touch of Pauline's hand as she lifted one of mine and placed a plastic bag in it.

"What's this?"

"Your shirt. It's been washed and pressed, so try not to get it mussed up."

"My ..."

Panic forced my heart into a mad hopping dance. I felt like I was the victim of a gigantic practical joke.

"Honestly, Joseph. You must remember lending it to Sophie that day she got caught in the rain. I think it's wonderful of you to let her use your place. Of course, she'll leave a mess behind. I tell her to clean up after herself, but you know how much good that does. I hope you'll let me know if it gets out of hand."

My head swam as if I were drunk. How much had Sophie told her?

"No," I said.

"What?"

"I'm sorry." I made myself look at her. "I have to go."

Three familiar vertical ridges appeared between her eyebrows. I backed away and almost fell over my own feet as I fled toward the front hall.

"Joseph?"

She followed and took me by the arm as I twisted the doorknob.

"What?"

"It's locked," she said. "Here."

She flipped the lever, releasing the bolt from its socket.

"Now you can go."

I stood at the door, ready to pull it open and make my escape. But I felt her behind me and sensed her bewilderment, her injury, sensed her drawing me back inside—into the house, into our friendship, where there were no secrets. I was no good at deception; I'd never been able to hide my feelings. So why had I imagined that, with everything depending on it, the false face I'd hoped to present to the world would work? I realized now that what I wanted was next to impossible. It required a more elaborate pretence than I was able to devise.

I turned and faced her. Tears glistened on her cheek.

"I'm sorry," I said. I reached out my free hand and let it come to rest on her shoulder. Then I moved it up to her face where I rubbed the tears away with my thumb. "I'm not myself these days. I hope you can forgive me."

"Anything, Joseph."

Unexpectedly, the words stung.

"I'll explain it all to you one of these days," I said, my voice almost a whisper.

She nodded and smiled through her tears.

"And we'll all have a good laugh, right?"

"Yes, we'll all be laughing by then."

She held out the bag of vegetables I'd brought with me and almost left behind.

In a few seconds I was out the door and down the front walk. I heard the door close behind me. I didn't look back. The clouds had turned a bright day full of promise into something grey and sombre.

Six

⟨ ～～～⟩

I HAD NOT for a single moment imagined it would be like this. I hadn't foreseen the pulverizing guilt or the irresistible pull of the truth: the urgent desire to blurt out a confession. Above all else, I had wanted to avoid hurting Pauline and I'd done precisely that with my clumsy efforts to make everything appear normal.

Where had the notion come from that loving Sophie was the right thing, the only thing I could do? I was happy, yes. But the cost of happiness need not be so high, surely. Again, it came to me that I'd fallen in love with a young woman who presented singular hurdles to that love, simply because of who she was.

For a start, I could never allow one word of this relationship to be uttered in Pauline's presence. It would kill her. And it was not even a question of approval or disapproval; I knew she would simply regard my actions as an utter betrayal of our friendship. There was something deeply special between us, a bond stronger than I could ever fathom. It went far beyond us being the next thing to siblings. There was never any rivalry or jostling for attention that seems to tarnish relationships between siblings. We were allies in every particular, unquestioning supporters of each other's goals and aspirations. Her kindness and gentle encouragement over the years had helped me succeed. At every step, I had her to fall back on. Early on we took up residence within each other's heart.

When I was young I had fantasized many times about the possibility of marriage. At a certain point in my life, starting a family together had seemed logical, perhaps even inevitable. I could not imagine spending the remainder of my time on this planet with anyone else and was certain she felt the same way. That this did not come to pass is perhaps further confirmation of the strength of our attachment. I watched, as if on a movie screen, as she strolled casually away and into the arms of another man—someone I eventually learned to love and respect as well—and did nothing about it because I could see it was what she wanted. My love for her was sturdy enough to support the burden of my disappointment as I accepted that I did not own her. Granted, for a short time I felt betrayed. But I recovered and carried on with my life, my feelings for her intact.

Now, I can see no indication that Pauline shared my feelings. I was a lonely child. She was a gracious and obliging constant in my life, a focus for my affections and confidences. It was natural that I would fixate on her to the degree that I did. Girls that age are more pragmatic and in tune with their emotions than are boys. I'm certain Pauline was aware of how I felt but she disengaged from me and took up with Frederick with such tender diplomacy that her transformation from my teenage companion to Frederick's wife took place, to my eyes, almost overnight. I was barely eighteen on their wedding day and stood in the church smouldering in my suit, hoping that someone would step forward to voice the objection to the match that I so keenly felt but was too timid to express. After that I stayed away from her for a long time, for months sullen and resentful even at family functions. But then my life took a turn I could not have anticipated.

After a year in a general arts program at Dalhousie I had reached the decision that I should leave to pursue my academic career elsewhere. I was accepted into the business program at the University of Toronto. While shopping for new clothes, I ran into Pauline in a downtown department store. The moment I met her eyes, I saw my recent behaviour for what it was: the peevish, jealous tantrum of a bored adolescent. We embraced and cried. I must have apologized a hundred times that day. I couldn't understand why she was so eager to take me back but chose to count myself lucky. We chose a restaurant and ordered lunch. I wanted to know everything about her because she was a new person for me now. She told me she was pregnant. It was one of the most wonderful moments of my life. For more than two hours I gazed at her across the table, grinning like an imbecile. It was like discovering, in an obvious place, a treasured object thought forever lost.

As the solitary life I would lead began to take shape, I came to depend more and more on Pauline and Frederick for a connection to the world of practical concerns. Without their aid and encouragement there's no telling what I might have become.

A car horn blared. I raised my head to find myself on a street far from home. I began to backtrack. Drops of rain struck my face. At one point I became aware of the two plastic bags, one in each hand, and it occurred to me that I must have presented a ridiculous figure, tramping in circles, clinging to these bags as if they contained the essentials of my life. I was about to fling them into a bush when I spotted one of the homeless who frequented the neighbourhood settling himself into a bus-stop shelter and lighting up a stubby cigarette. As I went by I dropped the bags into his lap.

My pleasure at getting away to attend university in Toronto was tempered by the fact that I was leaving Pauline just as I was getting to know her again. I didn't anticipate returning for quite some time. There was nothing for me at home, for this was the period of decline that would end with both parents in their graves.

My father had for many years worked as a stock clerk at a lumber supply yard. He was paid well and unionization provided numerous benefits but his job was not his life. Before the illness that almost finished me, we enjoyed many hours doing father-son things. We would go to movies or visit his sister, my Aunt Adele, Pauline's mother. We played catch, he took me fishing. He was also a romantic sort and frequently surprised my mother with presents, or came home to announce that for no particular reason we were all going out to dinner. Often, we took long drives into the country. He would stop at some farm to buy fresh produce and the farmer, who seemed to be a friend, would take me around to visit the animals.

Sometimes he stopped by Aunt Adele's on the way out of town to pick up Pauline. He was impulsive, witty, a bit reckless. He wanted me to have opportunities that he'd never had and perhaps went overboard signing me up for piano lessons and swimming lessons and God only knows what else. He seemed to take enormous pride in having a son. He was maybe forty when I was born, forty-five when I got ill. A few years younger, my mother was beautiful and energetic, sociable and very bright. Not that I believe she possessed a profound intellect or a serious, inquiring mind. She was smart without being overly curious, perceptive in a genuine, unexceptional, practical sense. Her brilliance was there in her eyes for anyone to see. She, who filled my early years with characters and scenes from books she loved. She read to me almost every night of my life.

Her favourite was Kipling because of his fanciful characters, vivid imagery and stories that never quit. But she also read from C.S. Lewis, Beatrix Potter, Kenneth Graham among many others. My father loved listening as well, often sitting in my room or standing in the doorway so he could hear. Occasionally we asked her to read to us in front of the fireplace, and my father and I would settle into the chesterfield, me on his lap, and listen as the fire crackled and her voice painted a whole other world for us.

It's clear that for the first few years of my life I experienced the kind of enchanted childhood of fairy tales or movies; I was spoiled. My parents coddled me and Pauline entertained me. Laughter and light filled the house. One of my earliest memories is of my mother flinging back the curtain, letting the sunlight pour into the room where I was sleeping and telling me to get up up up up because it was another day and I didn't want to miss it! We ate breakfast together every morning and I can remember a table laden with jars of orange marmalade and blueberry jam and honey, mountains of toast, eggs poached and fried. The aroma of fresh coffee permeated the house, along with the smokiness of sizzling bacon. I didn't want to miss any of it. But most of all, I didn't want to miss being with them. My parents were reason enough to get out of bed in the morning.

The contrast with my later childhood could not have been more stark. I can hardly explain the transformation. It was like we were living under quarantine, tainted by something that for the good of humanity we had to contain within the walls of our house. I realize that the metaphor I keep returning to is one of sickness and contagion. That was certainly the atmosphere I remember. However, I was certain neither of my parents suffered from a physical ailment, even while knowing that nothing so mundane could possibly explain their behaviour.

Our retreat from the world of simple pleasures was absolute. In the place of amusement or diversion, my parents sought out charitable works separately, serving these causes almost in opposition to one another. My father found a group that removed mentally handicapped children from institutions and placed them in the community. My mother was attracted to the church. My father remained at the lumber yard but only until he qualified for the minimum pension that would keep the family afloat. When I was about fifteen he left with no fanfare the company he had served for thirty years, returning home that day and hanging up his coat like any other day. He smoked cigarettes and drank coffee. My mother preferred liquor.

When not busy with their philanthropy, they spent long evenings in various rooms of the house, mostly in the kitchen where, if I happened to venture in quest of food once I'd finished my homework for the night, I might encounter them seated across the table from one another, often in total darkness. Sometimes I noticed a deck of cards on the table. If there was any conversation it was conducted in murmurs and whispers. They seemed reluctant to speak to me at all, my father especially. My mother confined her comments mainly to practical matters: Did I want another serving at supper? Did I have clean clothes to see me through to the end of the week. But my father rarely said anything and the look on his face— an expression of immeasurable sorrow and humble contrition that made me think I was looking at a man with a broken heart—prevented me from opening my mouth unless I absolutely had to.

I did not, however, want for anything. They kept their shared malaise to themselves. I was provided for, sometimes lavishly. If I got sick, they waited on me with an almost embarrassing slavishness. When I enrolled in university they took care of my tuition. But it was as if they had used up all their love in the first five years of my life and after that were utterly depleted and could provide for my physical needs and nothing more.

In the years between the childhood illness that marked a turning point and the day I left for Toronto at nineteen, they nursed these eccentricities and abdicated control over their own lives, always yielding joylessly to the demands of the charity of the day. "Duty" was a tyrant that held us prisoner. Deriving a moderate degree of satisfaction from my achievements in school, they consistently fell short of praising me for my accomplishments, as if to come first meant nothing to them and to pretend otherwise would be hypocritical. My father took me aside after I'd won a medal for academic achievement in grade six and lectured me on the dangers of pride. No matter how much I, or others, might cherish the results of my labour, I was always to remember that it was worthless. Only by bearing in mind this simple fact would I grow up selfless and therefore a valuable member of society. It was no good to set my sights on some goal if the only reason I was doing so was for personal glory. Human beings are by nature corrupt and I was never going to rise above this no matter how many medals I won.

Then he patted me on the head and favoured me with one of his doleful smiles, as if the beneficial effects of this little speech were already making themselves apparent in my conduct. I was crushed. Did he really mean there was no point in doing anything? On the one hand, he likely was correct to say that personal glory was not sufficient reason for striving to achieve a goal. There has to be some evidence that completing the task will serve the general good, or we might as well not bother. On the other hand, it seemed to me that gaining the admiration—or avoiding the disdain—of friends and neighbours was a good enough reason for doing something, especially if the job was a useful but distasteful one.

At any rate, this philosophy of pessimism did exert a profound influence on my academic pursuits from that day forward even though I was too young to realize it at the time. I held back in everything I did. Even when I knew I could do better, I deliberately sabotaged test results by leaving questions unanswered or inserting errors, just to avoid first place. I came to associate success with shame. It might be a stretch but I believe my father's defeatism crept into my life and made it difficult for me to relate to people. I held back. If I sensed triumph or romantic love lurking around the corner, I abandoned the enterprise. I had the same needs and appetites as any adolescent, I wanted to participate and excel. I wanted people to like me but felt ashamed if they did. My teachers were perplexed because they saw my potential and couldn't understand why I appeared to have difficulty taking my marks to the next level. A chemistry teacher in grade twelve went to great trouble to inform me, in a pantomime of disgust, that I was a lazy bugger and that I could easily raise my marks if I only bothered to try. But I wasn't about to be swayed. By anyone else's standards I was doing just fine.

Because many of my early years were spent beneath the mantle of gloom that enveloped my parents and touched everything they did, there were times when I began to perceive it as a normal condition. The only thing that saved me from growing up into some sort of moralizing self-flagellant was my exposure to Pauline and her side of the family. My mother drank heavily and was often "indisposed" or "under the weather" and, on these days, I would thankfully go to my Aunt Adele and Uncle Willard's house after school. If my mother's confinement was to be a lengthy one, my father would come by with the clothes and other things I would need during my time away, which could stretch into weeks but was more often only a few days. The spare bedroom was always mine when I required it. Although not large, it had a high window facing the street and adequate closet space. Also, by some quirk of design, it had its own bathroom. So while Pauline and her parents shared the main bathroom down the hall, I could take my own bath or shower in privacy. I especially appreciated this when I grew older and more self-conscious about my body.

I remember, too, there came a time when, after I started junior high school and began to see my parents as the peculiar individuals they had become, I would phone Pauline and ask if I could come over and stay for a few days. I might be working on an assignment or studying for an important exam, or maybe I did so out of a craving for normal human contact. Pauline never turned me away.

In this way we were together often and for long periods, and Pauline was both my balm and my inquisitor. She never allowed me to sink into despondency or spread the gloom from my house to hers, for if I spent more than a minute feeling sorry for myself she didn't hesitate to twist my arm or attack me in a pillow fight or entice me outside to a movie or a visit to one of her other friends. She asked me plenty of questions, which I did my best to answer but we didn't actually begin talking about what was going on in my house until much later, when we were both well into our teens.

When I was ten, it was confusing and embarrassing to have parents like mine, and anyway I didn't know how to express my feelings on the topic. No doubt other children my age had parents who were eccentric and antisocial, who were alcoholics or abusers or worse. But at that age you can't catch even the slightest glimpse of the light of day beyond your own agony. So I held it in and spoke very little about my mother and father. I also did not want to expose myself to ridicule by making my problem generally known, for at school there are always bullies who seek out weaknesses in others. My parents were my weakness. By not talking about them, I was shielding myself from the kind of schoolyard torment I watched others endure, like the three Mulcahy sisters whose mother had abandoned them and moved to the United States with a juggler, or Timmy Ryan whose father was dismissed from his job at the Royal Bank and eventually went to jail for stealing. I also did not want to have to say anything unkind about my parents, for even though I was resentful and sometimes bore this resentment as a smouldering fire in my gut, I remained loyal to them as only a son can who has nothing else to cling to. It's difficult for a child to examine his life with an adult's hard-hearted detachment. I was not capable of this until much later. And when the time came to talk about it, Pauline was there to listen.

Approaching my flat, I wondered why the people I passed weren't recoiling from a despicable phony who'd just lied to the person he trusted most in the world and to whom he would lie repeatedly in the future. The tears on Pauline's cheeks still haunted me, but I didn't want to think about the end of my liaison with Sophie.

What had I been thinking when I allowed her to kiss me in the churchyard? Where had my reason fled when I brought her back to my flat and undressed her and took her for a lover? How could I have made my life so complicated? I realized that it was a permanent condition for me, this need to conceal and to lie, to add layers of complexity. Even if there came a time when we were no longer lovers, our secret would remain. Its shadow would follow us, colouring every word, gesture and glance. Only death would allow us to escape it.

What saddened me even more than this was the wariness that had crept into my soul and become a crucial part of my nature. Granted, Pauline had caught me off guard when she related how she'd joined me in bed when we were children. Though certain her actions had been nothing more than childish mischief, when she'd let her secret out into the light I'd sensed danger. The sudden tension in my muscles and constriction in my throat told me she was watching my reaction, looking for a weak point. She had told me her tale in all innocence—she had not spent the last thirty years in agony over it I'm sure—but because I was hiding something from her, I suspected her of hiding something from me, something of greater consequence than her words seemed to admit. I suppose my panicky, guilt-ridden response to her confession was in part a response to my own self-imposed burden. I had projected my vice upon her and sullied her even more profoundly than I had at first thought.

I shook my head and kept walking. How could I go on thinking this way and not want to put a bullet through my brain?

I had not yet considered what I was going to say to Sophie. There was evidence that she'd revealed aspects of our relationship to her mother. I was not pleased about this and had no intention of concealing my displeasure. If we were to continue seeing one another, I was now determined that it be done in absolute secrecy. Sophie's mother would not suffer as a result of our actions. I had, earlier, considered revealing everything to Pauline and Frederick and making our attachment public. Getting married. I saw now that, blinded by euphoria, I believed others would share our happiness. My graceless, stupefied response at the mere sight of my shirt in Pauline's hand was ample enough evidence to prevent me from revealing the contents of my heart, to anyone. Sophie and I were not the sort of couple one expected to encounter in polite society. People were bound to whisper. She was well known in musical circles; her father had achieved a degree of renown within the medical community. The family was affluent. We were bound to attract attention. People crave excitement, the more sordid the better.

Even though my fingers had grown clumsy with dread I managed to unlock the door without dropping the key. I wasn't sure when or even if Sophie was coming today but was relieved to see I was alone.

I didn't know what to think. I sat down and stood up again. I plugged the kettle in for tea and forgot about it until I heard the water bubbling. Looking for my bag of vegetables I tore the kitchen apart in panic until, eventually, I recalled giving them to a homeless man. I was becoming incapable of rational thought. What did Pauline know, after all? That Sophie had been here and that I'd loaned her a shirt. That I'd given her a key so she could eat lunch at my table if she so pleased. Pauline saw no problem with this and had, in fact, appreciated the small kindness I had bestowed upon her daughter. She'd looked at me with bright eyes and declared me "wonderful."

Staring uncomprehendingly out at the winter-ravaged branches of a maple tree, breath rasping in my lungs, a sudden realization so simple, so powerful it resembled an electric shock, left me light-headed and trembling. My secret was safe. And it was very likely to remain so.

Pauline would never suspect improper conduct between her own daughter and her beloved cousin. Even if concrete evidence—my shirt in Sophie's closet—bellowed its guilty presence, Pauline would not, could not, believe it. A wholesome woman like Pauline did not dwell upon the vulgar indiscretions of others. If she had a flaw, it was in thinking too highly of people, myself included. In my mind I heard Sophie on the day of the Kraus funeral complaining that her mother treated her like a six-year-old child. Pauline would readily admit that her daughter was attracting male attention and within my hearing had expressed her concern. But in her mind, she clung to an image of Sophie from sixteen years ago, the scampering tod-dler seated at the piano, perched on Frederick's lap, gleefully bang-ing random keys and giggling at her own antics.

Relief flooded my tired brain and buoyed my heart. It is a meas-ure of the severity of my moral drift that I felt exultation instead of sorrow. I was prepared, now, not only to continue violating the spe-cial trust that Pauline had reserved for me but to exploit it without mercy. My liaison with Sophie could carry on without fear of dis-covery. I could count on an especially fierce Pauline to conceal our secret—not just from the world but from herself as well.

Part Four

One

I NOW REGARD this period of my life with stupefaction. Finally facing the fact that I was capable of such vile disloyalty and— even worse— that I stole such intense pleasure from it, leaves me bewildered. It was partly to be expected since I had acquired a beautiful and intelligent woman for a lover and was drawing a degree of fulfilment from her devotion I'd never have suspected possible in a simple affair of the heart. I swear to you, I glowed with happiness. Every waking moment I could feel elation and barely suppressed mirth bubbling under my skin. People at work observed me—I could feel their curious eyes staring—as if they suspected I was losing my mind. But I was not just happy—the word falls absurdly short of what I was feeling. No, I was ecstatic, I was delirious, I was insane. My customary morbid expectation that things not only could but would go wrong—vanished. I was finally living the life I was meant to live, that all I'd done and seen and felt in the past was merely a prelude to what I was doing and seeing and feeling now. The dubiousness of my behaviour escaped me. All I thought of was Sophie; her smile, her touch, the promise of her continued presence in my life. I truly believed I could make her happy, that I was making her happy every moment I was with her. And, as I often asked myself, what harm can possibly come of happiness? I was barely capable of seeing beyond our clandestine liaison to the other people it affected, such as Pauline and Frederick, their sphere of friends and relatives. I tried to think of those others. But my vision had become so clouded that I convinced myself that our happiness meant everyone's happiness. I had overcome the horror I'd suffered at the sight of my shirt in Pauline's hand. Nothing had come of it; the ready-made explanation was appallingly plausible. Surely this meant that anything could happen.

Our warm season peaked in late July. The purity of the summer air in our Maritime city often takes visitors by surprise. Yet we who've breathed it all our lives know that summer also brings with it a still, moist warmth that is inescapable, like exquisite longing. Many evenings Sophie and I made hot, slow, sticky love and afterwards washed each other clean in the shower. Then we would go somewhere to eat, maybe to a movie and when we emerged from the cinema it was still light out, the air just beginning to cool. On Saturdays, following her session with the chamber group, we would stroll downtown and indulge in a late breakfast or perhaps coffee and dessert at one of the outdoor cafés along Spring Garden Road.

We lived very much as man and wife, except that she still resided at home with her parents. We chose not to meddle with this for the present. The subject that for a while had occupied all of us and caused Pauline no small amount of anxiety—of Sophie moving into a studio or apartment of her own—had died away of its own accord, for the simple reason, so I believed, that having found a lover and a living space where she could spend time alone if she wanted to, Sophie had also for the time being satisfied her craving for independence.

Two

D ESPITE MY EUPHORIC state, I was increasingly aware, often painfully so, of what I was doing and the damage it was likely to cause. These days, looking back, my poor guilty conscience returns me to one evening from this period, the dizzying pinnacle of both summer and the love that Sophie and I all too briefly shared.

My memory is vivid because a random conjunction of events gave the four of us—myself, Sophie, Pauline, Frederick—separate causes to celebrate.

It was July 28, a Friday.

Sophie and I had not made plans for that evening and I had woken in the morning expecting an ordinary day. But when I arrived at work just after 8:30, the place was already buzzing with the news. I hadn't even picked up my pen when Miss Pindar scurried into my office and shut the door. Eyes wide and suppressing a smile, she informed me that Ty Burgess was taking early retirement. She said the news would become official later that morning when Mr. Barrow, the VP of Finance, called everyone together for a formal announcement. What's more, that very day—Friday, July 28—was to be his final day at work.

To this point I have not mentioned Ty Burgess. He and his overbearing self-regard are of little consequence to my story. However, if you are at all familiar with office politics, it will come as no surprise that one person with a domineering personality, loud opinions on every topic imaginable and a constant need for approval can sow disorder and unease among co-workers. Younger staff and new hires were overwhelmed by his pushy, all-knowing demeanour, a situation Ty encouraged and exploited, letting them believe that, by doing what he asked of them, their way forward would be smooth. But Ty had no supervisory duties and even less influence over career trajectories. His seniority was in years only; as Director of Bookkeeping I outranked him. However, he had been with the firm for so long that he took it as a given that his views counted for more than anyone else's.

Not to belabour, but his officious way of expressing himself in any situation—as though his words were golden—held everyone hostage. If you tried to interject he would simply raise his voice. You could be sure that any meeting he attended would last thirty minutes longer than necessary. Perhaps his most annoying habit was to dream up projects and assignments, which not only created extra work but work that invariably landed on someone else's desk. And he was smart. His suggestions were framed rationally and came off sounding perfectly sensible. And no matter what duty or task he recommended, never once was he heard to say: "Oh, don't worry, I'll take care of it myself!"

It was no surprise to see that news of his departure was greeted with dry eyes all around. As of July 28, for everyone at Murchie's the load would be that much lighter.

After work that day, when I arrived unannounced on the doorstep of 1220 Young Avenue, it was with a bottle of wine in my hand and an unaccustomed bounce in my step. The prospect of the office minus an irritant of long-standing had started me thinking that other improvements might occur sooner than I could have hoped. It was, as someone had wryly observed, addition by subtraction.

Even though the reason for my celebratory mood was not one that anyone in the Gebhardt household was likely to appreciate, I didn't want to spend Friday evening alone. I knocked and entered. I called out, "Hello!" From the depths of the house Pauline responded, "Hello!" It was almost six. I found her in the kitchen, spoon in hand, leaning over a pot simmering on the stove. The radio was on, a late-afternoon news report from the local station.

"Joseph! What a pleasant surprise! I hope you'll stay for some of Mrs. Radcliffe's fish chowder?"

"Of course," I said.

She was beaming, bubbling over with good cheer. Switching off the radio she gestured that I sit at the table so she could tell me her own news.

For some years Pauline had served on the Board of the Public Gardens and for her entire tenure the primary issue facing the Board had been the poor condition of the wrought-iron fence encircling the Gardens. Upkeep of the Gardens is the city's responsibility; it's included in the municipal budget. Over many years a number of bequests have also been made; money that's needed to keep the Gardens operating year to year. Fundraising and other efforts to set aside a reserve to cover a major project had been largely unsuccessful. In the meantime, while board chairs have come and gone and city councillors have used the Gardens to get elected and then gone silent, its fence has deteriorated further until, now, sections were being reinforced with chicken wire and propped up with planks of lumber.

"Last week," she said, "we went to City Council and made a presentation. Did you know the Public Gardens was the first city park in the country and it's been declared a site of national significance? Yes, I thought so. They all know this too. But what's new is a federal program that covers significant sites and our application was successful!"

She leaned forward.

"But it depends on the municipality matching the federal funds. Today we found out that the city is willing to do this. They voted to give us fifty thousand dollars. Can you believe it?"

"That's wonderful!" I said. "Congratulations. I'm so proud of you."

I took her hand and squeezed it. It was very warm.

"This Council is notoriously tight-fisted," she said, rising quickly to her feet. "I was shocked when I learned of the decision. I wouldn't dare to speculate what their real agenda is. All I care about is that we got our money." She pulled open a drawer and retrieved a corkscrew. "Why don't you open the wine?"

We poured and clinked glasses. We chatted about next steps, when the money would be made available, when the repairs were likely to take place. I quizzed her for details and she had an answer for everything. Typically with Pauline, nothing would be left to chance.

"You seem happy," she said, her hand resting lightly on my arm. She was studying and assessing me—looking for tell-tale signs that would reveal the reason behind my jovial mood. It was a remnant from our childhood, this private, wordless means of communication. When I was young I could not keep anything from her. The signals she saw were beyond my control. She'd expect full disclosure from me, anyway. Nothing less would satisfy. If I didn't tell her everything she would pout, or pretend to and I couldn't have that. But recently I had become very good at dissembling, even guarding myself at times. I was wary of her, a circumstance I found thoroughly depressing. But it couldn't be helped. Today, I had not stopped smiling since entering the house and probably this had muddied the signals. My glee was evident but not necessarily attributable to any one thing. Retreating to the stove she gave the chowder a stir. "Is there something you want to tell me?" Pauline seemed to be concentrating on the soup, so I couldn't see her face.

My elation had not cooled but when I compared my petty and somewhat mean-spirited news with hers, it did not seem worth sharing. I may have, at some point, mentioned Ty Burgess in her presence, part of a general complaint about the miseries of office life. But she had no reason to remember the name. Bringing him up now and launching into an account of years of bullying and manipulation would only spoil the evening.

"Just that I'm happy," I said. "And happier now because of your news." I raised my glass.

She gave me a quizzical glance and not for the first time I couldn't read the expression on her face.

When Frederick arrived a short while later, we learned he had received approval from Health Administration Services to begin developing an art therapy program at the Children's Hospital. It would be modelled on a successful program at Sick Kids in Toronto and would be the only art therapy program in the east. In a few weeks he would go to Toronto, meet with some people and "get the ball rolling."

He then produced a bottle of 20-year-old Highland Park, which he'd picked up on the drive home, and though I was already on my second glass of wine, I decided to sample the scotch and found its honey-tinged smokiness most gratifying.

Sophie, as it turned out, had been upstairs the whole time on a conference call with her booking agency, squaring up the final details of her concert schedule for the coming year. It was nearing seven when, without warning, she appeared in the kitchen doorway, somehow dazzling in a plain white t-shirt and jeans, her feet bare. My heart set off at a gallop at the sight of her. Instantly, my imagination went to work undressing her, summoning up the curves and contours of that willowy body I knew so well.

Still, I wanted to take her in my arms. I wanted to smother her with kisses.

She didn't look at me when she spoke. This was for her parents.

"Mom. Dad. You'll never guess! Never in a million years will you guess!"

Pauline jumped to her feet. "Don't make us guess, Sophie! Please!"

It was a coup, plain and simple. Sophie had already been booked into a half-dozen venues in small towns throughout the New England states. So far the larger, more prestigious venues had been beyond her reach. But Grace Cabot, at the agency, kept her ear to the ground and had learned that the Boston Symphony Orchestra was looking for someone to fill in for a pianist who had backed out of a concert scheduled for October. The featured piece was Mozart's 23rd Piano Concerto, well within Sophie's established repertoire. The opportunity had come up suddenly, but the negotiations had been protracted. Among other things, Grace had had to submit a recording of Sophie playing the piano part unaccompanied. Sophie had mentioned Boston, I recalled, but without the details, just as a date that might or might not be added to her New England itinerary. Today the decision had been made to add Sophie's name to the list of performers in the Orchestra's fall schedule. Her publicity info would be distributed as an insert, included with the Orchestra's concert brochure, which had already been printed and was being readied to send to subscribers.

"I'm going to play Boston Symphony Hall!"

"Bravo!"

Pauline squealed and clapped her hands.

"Say you'll come. Please say you'll be there."

We were on our feet, embracing Sophie as a group. I fought to catch my breath, to keep my emotions in check, but my eyes ran with tears. I was gasping. The liquor had gone straight to my head. I was so proud of them, this family of which I was lucky enough to count myself a member. They were absurdly accomplished. They got things done, they scaled the heights. My paltry achievements hardly merited a footnote next to theirs.

"Yes. Yes. Don't you worry. Of course, we'll be there my dear girl! Of course, we will! Boston here we come!"

I excused myself and went to the bathroom where I splashed my face with water. I stood for a moment over the sink, staring at the mirror. My gaze was steady, my thoughts clear. Surprisingly, despite the booze and wine, I was not in a bad state. Beneath me, my legs were two sturdy supports. My good humour was holding. I was hungry and dinner would soon be on the table. The sound of excited voices reached me from the kitchen, Sophie's rising above those of her parents. Frederick made a comment that reached me as a low rumble. Pauline burst out laughing. I did not want to analyse the moment, I wanted to enjoy it. Wiping my eyes I spoke to myself in the mirror. "We deserve this," I said. "We are good people. Don't be such a damn fool."

Pauline and Frederick both looked up at me as I entered the kitchen. Sophie did not. There was more whisky in my glass. I drank it down without hesitation. Sophie's withheld gaze was part of the game we were playing behind her parents' backs. I could not help but be aroused. I sat next to her at the table and did not look at her.

But the evening was slipping by. Pauline clapped her hands and said: "Sophie, please set the table."

"I'll help," I said.

We set the dining room table with exacting care, as if expecting royalty, taking our time while Pauline warmed some rolls in the oven. Our conversation was bland, inconsequential. "What did you do to-day?" "Oh, went to work, came here. Nothing special. Congratulations on Boston. That's very exciting." "Thank you." I passed close behind her, breathing in her fresh rose-petal scent, not touching her. We fell silent. I passed behind her again, brushed against her and blew lightly on her neck. She shuddered and her body tensed. The faintest of exclamations escaped from her throat, "Oh!" We both reached to straighten a knife and when our fingers touched the spark of desire quickened my breath. Then we were done. Sophie returned to the kitchen to help her mother serve the chowder. I joined Frederick beside the stereo cabinet. And while I feigned interest in the Chet Baker album he'd selected, my heart gradually slowed to its regular rhythm.

It was anything but a normal evening, though in many respects it was completely normal, even ordinary, with the four of us sharing yet another meal, enjoying each other's company as we had so many times in the past. Fish chowder on a warm summer night may seem counter-intuitive, but it is eminently agreeable and satisfying. You eat, sweat, drink some wine, sweat some more. The gaiety around the table never diminished. Pauline, Frederick and Sophie spoke about the day's triumphs and what it all meant. Frederick—always serious, occasionally morose—laughed as much as I had ever seen him, dropping his reserve and delighting openly in his brilliant wife and beautiful daughter. And, yes, I was eventually persuaded to report my pleasure at the departure of a troublesome individual from Murchie's, thus giving me good reason to raise a glass with the people I loved the most.

I banished all thoughts of deception and betrayal from my mind.

But I was alert to the danger of letting things get out of hand and when the evening started to seem like a logical turning point, the perfect chance to reveal to Pauline and Frederick the truth— Sophie and I were in love (that's how I imagined framing it)—I knew I'd had more than enough to drink and that it was time to leave. It was late and I was tired. Frederick was putting on another record. Pauline and Sophie were seated close together on the settee, earnestly discussing formal wear and outfits for her concert tour. While no one was watching, I slipped into the kitchen and phoned for a taxi.

When I returned to the living room, it hit me what was wrong, with me, with the whole predicament in which I found myself. I had been reminded again and again—before, during, and after the meal we had just shared—of the sublime pleasure that Frederick, Pauline and Sophie drew from each other's presence. They were a family and they loved each other. But they were also friends: even if they hadn't been related, they would spend time together and champion each other's causes. The evidence of this was clear in what I had witnessed only this evening: Sophie and Pauline side by side at the kitchen counter, laughing like sisters. Sophie at the piano, Frederick stationed behind her, eyes closed, entranced by the slow movement of a Schubert sonata, embracing her afterward. Pauline and Frederick holding hands like young lovers. I was a part of it too. Over the years I had contributed to the trove of affection and trust that we all drew on whenever we needed support or guidance. They had let me in, years ago, and they kept inviting me back. God knows why, I sometimes thought, but they seemed to enjoy having me around. I never questioned their loyalty; they never questioned mine. The last thing I needed to brood over at this moment was consequences: what would be lost when the truth came out, what my actions would cost them, who would be hurt, and how badly.

But there we are. Naming it makes it real.

"Joseph, you're leaving?"

Pauline approached me in the entryway.

"You're not having fun?"

"It's late," I said. "And tomorrow's another day, etcetera. Thank you, once again, for a lovely meal."

She tilted her head. Again, that searching look in her eyes. "Is something the matter?"

Sophie had come up behind her mother. With a gentle nudge, she sidled past her and now stood where Pauline had been just a second before. She raised herself on her toes and wrapped her arms around my neck.

Softly: "Will I see you tomorrow?"

"Count on it," I said, thinking: This is it. She's going to kiss me. "Goodnight, then."

She gave me a chaste peck on the cheek. Smiling, she moved off, nonchalant, toward the kitchen, where Pauline was hastily packing up some leftovers to take home. I watched her, following the sway of her hips. I could not move my eyes away.

Outside, I lit a cigarette. Frederick joined me while I waited for the taxi. We smoked without speaking. It was well past sunset, but the underside of a dense cloud cover captured the radiance of the city and reflected it back to us. The album he had put on the turntable—tranquil piano jazz with languorous saxophone accompaniment—ended while we stood there. I was unprepared for the silence, which descended with no warning and seemed to pull everything into it.

The urge to put the truth out there crept up on me again. I resisted, but in a few seconds, it swelled to an almost overpowering sensation of weightlessness, like the swoon that in my imagination would precede stepping from solid ground into the abyss. Ignorant of my struggle, Frederick stood beside me. He was humming something comically out-of-tune—jazz or Mozart, it was impossible to tell. Then Pauline came out and delivered into my hands a sturdy two-handled canvas bag containing tomorrow's lunch: a plastic tub of chowder, a few rolls, some salad.

"Be careful Joseph. The chowder's still warm."

I nodded.

"There was no need," I said. "But thank you all the same."

"Well, there's too much for us and you have to eat."

I could feel her eyes on me again, searching my face for a hint of what she thought I was keeping from her. Mercifully, the taxi was just pulling up.

"We're so very lucky," Frederick said. "Blessed, I think."

I didn't say anything. Neither did Pauline. There was no point agreeing with such a statement. We all knew it was true.

I turned and looked back. They were standing together now, Pauline's arm looped through her husband's. The top of her head barely reached Frederick's shoulder (later, at odd times, this image would bring a smile to my face). The house loomed above them, somewhat of a hulking monstrosity, but nurturing and protective just the same. Central in my view was the window of Sophie's bedroom. The light was on and she was moving about inside, throwing shadows. But she was still playing the game. She refused to show herself.

I grew anxious on the way home, unable to fathom my mood. The taxi driver—a young man of Mediterranean extraction—wanted to chat, "to improve his English." But I was only half-listening. I mustered a couple of monosyllables in response to his comments but was not much help to him and eventually he gave up.

The evening had been enjoyable and festive—I could even say momentous—but I could not ignore the chasm that now existed between myself and Pauline and Frederick. No longer were our interests unquestionably aligned, and that was hardly a cause for celebration.

Three

~~~~~~~~~~~

ITH SOME VACATION days coming, I wanted us to leave the city for a while so we could be alone together. Now that Sophie's schedule was set, her responsibilities were at a low ebb. There was no reason why we had to confine ourselves to the city. Over dinner one evening—I had made a pasta dish with tarragon, penne and smoked salmon in a cream sauce—I proposed we rent a car and take a room for a few days or a week at a bed-and-breakfast somewhere. We needn't stay in one place the whole time. We could drift about as the spirit moved us. There were plenty of towns and villages to choose from, plenty of places to stay where nobody knew or cared who we were.

I waited for her to answer. For one moment my heart sank because her expression seemed to cloud over and I thought she was trying to conjure up reasons for refusal. She took a sip of wine.

"I'd love to—but how? How can we both just go off like that?"

"And not raise suspicions," I said, completing her thought.

She took up her fork. "It doesn't seem practical ... or wise. Not that I'm a big fan of wisdom or anything." She smiled. "You know what I mean."

"Yes. I've thought of that. But if we go about it the right way, will anyone really care? Will anyone even notice?"

She looked at me.

"It just seems like asking for trouble, is all I'm saying."

The candlelight played in her hair but her eyes looked uneasy. It seemed to make her sad to think how difficult everything was. We couldn't even enjoy a spontaneous kiss in a public place. I reached across the table and stroked her cheek. Her skin was like silk. She closed her eyes and kissed my hand.

"I know," I said after a moment, reluctantly removing my hand from her face. "And you've got to practice, and you've got this group and everything. But so far, we've done all right. You have to admit that."

"Yes," she said and sighed gloomily. "Joseph, where are we going with this? How long can it go on? When I think about what's ahead, it makes me tired. I feel exhausted all the time, like I'm carrying this weight around with me everywhere I go."

I drew a deep breath. I didn't want her to be sad. I didn't want her to have any doubts about us.

"I know it's difficult sometimes. But can you really say you're not happy? I can tell you are. It's in your eyes. There's a light there. We will have to make a decision. I know that. But we have to plan carefully. We can't rush."

"My parents are the problem, aren't they?"

She stated this bluntly, as if Frederick and Pauline had deliberately placed themselves between her and the emotional fulfilment that our affair represented.

"Not a problem," I said. "Not necessarily."

"What then?" she asked. "I can't see them being pleased with this. I'm not sure what they want for me but a love affair with my own cousin probably isn't it."

"What do you want?" I asked carefully. I placed my fork on the table and lifted my glass.

"I don't know," she said. Tears slid down her cheeks. "I am happy. I am. Happier than I've ever been. But it seems like the whole world is against us. If we have to keep this a secret forever, then what's the point? I want us to be together but I don't want people sneering and pointing. I want to live my life and not have to worry about what other people think. It's all so confusing, sometimes I don't know what to do. I want to tell my parents; I want to share my happiness with them. But I can't. I can't talk to anyone. When you're not there I feel lost, like I've woken up alone in the forest. I know people don't always get everything they want. I'm realistic, I don't want you to think I'm not. Either we'll stay together or we won't. I understand that things can change. Feelings change. People grow apart. We can't always know what's coming. But I guess I feel like I'm not really in control. It's like I'm waiting for something to happen, and I don't know what it is."

She looked up and for a moment she seemed like a child, just a child. My heart clenched.

"Maybe that's what you can do for me," she said. "Tell me what it is I'm waiting for."

I took her into my arms and cradled her, rocked her back and forth exactly as I had done many years ago, when she was so much smaller. I wanted to comfort and protect her from all these uncertainties. I wanted her to know that I would never change, that I would always be there for her. But why, if my intentions were so noble, did I feel numb with guilt as I considered all that had transpired since those days when she fit more easily into my embrace?

The question I had put to her a moment ago now preyed upon me. What did I want? How far was I prepared to go to keep her by my side? Maybe it would be best for everyone if we ended this now, tonight. Why not spare ourselves the painful decisions that were waiting for us down the road? Why not spare her parents the agony of my betrayal? But when I thought of what my life would become if I gave her up, I grew afraid. I couldn't live with the image of myself that sprang into my mind. There I was again, the confirmed bachelor sitting alone in his cluttered flat, sipping brandy, reading the evening paper by lamplight, watching the dust settle on his miserable array of belongings. Strolling downtown on a cloudy afternoon to pick up a few things, bringing them back. It was like a poem or a song I'd once heard, at the end of which the unassuming hero, to everyone's shock and dismay, strings himself up from the rafters.

Until a few months ago I'd been content with that life, a lonely one for sure but nothing about it had struck me as pathetic. But I couldn't go back. Not now. I would rather die than revert to what I had been. I had no respect for that person, no desire to become him again. And as I hugged Sophie more tightly and felt her arms grip me just as tightly, I realized that through each of my actions since the day of Selma Kraus's funeral I had forfeited all of those simple, solitary pleasures that had given me comfort and provided amusement, and that the task that lay ahead of me, if I was to get through this alive, was to convince this beautiful, gifted, spirited young woman that the only place she belonged was in my arms.

Four

⌒

WE WENT AWAY together. I reserved rooms for us at the Inniskillen Inn in the town of Wolfville, some forty miles outside of town. It was a sprawling Victorian house, capriciously converted to separate guest rooms, each sporting a distinct ambience or flavour and reached by means of intricate passageways and odd sets of stairs. There was the Golf room and the Yacht room, the Bronte and the Dickens, Gothic and Renaissance. You get the idea. I had never been to this establishment before, and had only once or twice been to Wolfville. But I had heard some talk of the Inniskillen at the office and gathered it was held in high regard.

Recently I'd read about the Inniskillen dining room in a tourism magazine I'd found. The praise heaped upon both the food and the presentation was lavish and I recalled a photograph of a benevolent-looking couple in their sixties, the owners, beaming with pride as they posed in their starched outfits before a well-stocked bar.

You might ask how Sophie and I managed to arrange this little excursion, how we put it to her parents and obtained their permission. I admit that we did it through subterfuge.

It may seem to the reader that Sophie and I had grown complacent, relying upon the gods or chance to conceal our affair. It was true that Sophie spent a great deal of time in my flat; true as well that our routine was make love late in the afternoon and then walk downtown to a restaurant, returning to the flat at dusk to make love once more before I walked her home or saw that she took a taxi. It was also true that people might have observed us together, again and again. However, the pattern of our activities was not quite so regular as it might seem.

For instance, there were days when I did not see her at all. Sometimes I ate alone and she appeared later in the evening. Sometimes we met downtown for dinner and she returned home directly afterward. On several occasions she came to the office and we went to lunch together. At one point we had a disagreement over something and I didn't hear from or see her for three whole days. There was, as I say, sufficient variation in our schedule to ward off suspicion. I continued to see Pauline and Frederick more or less routinely as well, though admittedly less often than before. We were careful. We did not try to hide the fact that we enjoyed each other's company. But neither did we let on to a soul what we were doing when we were together in my flat with the shades drawn.

I don't believe Pauline's suspicions had been aroused. To her way of thinking, I had opened my door to Sophie as an act of kindness and generosity, in a free-wheeling spirit of avuncular big-heartedness. She was certain that her daughter would take shameless advantage; eat all my food and leave a clutter of dirty dishes in the sink; bring her friends over and have parties and break my furniture. Pauline told me over the phone and reminded me face to face that I should let her know if things got "out of hand."

She seemed to be expecting Sophie to behave scandalously, like an undisciplined teenager with no respect for other people's property. I don't know what she based this on. To be sure, Sophie had a wilful streak and was no stranger to sulky moods and occasional fits of temper. Once, years ago, I'd watched her smash a plate when she failed to get her way. People don't live together in the same house without clashing from time to time. Pauline's caveat was no doubt intended to provide me with an escape route should the arrangement grow troublesome or onerous. And I appreciated it, for at all times Pauline had everyone's well-being on her mind.

But Pauline was unaware of the true situation and this, in combination with other factors, allowed Sophie and me a degree of latitude in our behaviour that I'm certain we would not otherwise have permitted ourselves. The fact of the matter was that Pauline did not want Sophie moving out on her own, and since this whole issue seemed to vanish overnight the moment Sophie obtained a key to my flat, Pauline expressed her gratitude often and at length. It was as if I had plucked her daughter from the grip of some depraved compulsion that would have consumed her as surely as if she had begun selling herself on the street.

So the proposition of a brief trip out of town did not seem untoward. I needed a vacation and Sophie wanted to get away from things, if only briefly. It seemed ideal for us to take rooms at an inn and go up together in a rented car. Sophie could drive. Once we got there we could do as we liked. I could read and take in the sights, Sophie could find a tennis partner, or go swimming. We would have our meals together but only if we wanted to. Nothing was compelling us to spend every moment in each other's company.

I remember sitting in the front room of 1220 Young Avenue with Sophie and Pauline one afternoon a week before we left for Wolfville. The reservations had already been made but here we were, presenting it as a fresh notion materializing out of the air. I cursed the gnawing in my stomach and entered into the spirit of the lie with conviction. I pretended to be slightly put out and said I'd have to think about it. Sophie pouted and complained that nobody ever wanted to do anything around here. Pauline reiterated her daughter's proposal and declared that it would be good for me to get away and even offered to make the arrangements herself. I needn't lift a finger, she said, the two of them would take care of everything. I glanced at Sophie who, stationed behind her mother and a better actress than I would have given her credit for, made a face and stuck out her tongue at me.

Our success in this game of deceit was instant and complete. Within minutes of the subject being brought up, I was agreeing with Pauline that it would do me no harm to breathe the country air, offering as an afterthought that I'd heard of a place and would make a few phone calls.

We arrived early in the afternoon on a Saturday. Wolfville is a charming little community, crowded with examples of nineteenth-century architecture, bustling with the commotion of roadside markets that brim over with fresh farm produce. But it's a university town as well and plays host to a theatre festival. Nestled out of the way on an otherwise unimpressive side street was one of the best second-hand bookstores in the province. The single cinema on the main street (actually called Main Street) was showing French black-and-white films from the 1950s. There was, in short, no lack of cultural diversions with which to amuse ourselves should we become bored with each other.

Since nothing was being done under a cloak of secrecy, we signed in using our real names. Each room had a radio, television and a phone with the capacity to record messages.

I had the Hunt Room, with its wallpaper depicting hounds chasing foxes through the forest, followed by red-jacketed masters on horseback. An ancient shotgun was mounted above the bed and a set of antlers graced the wall over the fireplace.

Completely by chance Sophie got the Music Room, with wallpaper showing musical staves, a plaster bust of Beethoven glowering on the mantle and a set of portraits of composers who had died young—Mozart, Mendelssohn, Schumann, and Schubert. To complete this quaint and absolutely delightful scene, a violin and bow hung above the bed.

All settled in, we stood side-by-side and it occurred to me that we hadn't discussed whether we were going to continue our charade, or if we were prepared to reveal ourselves as lovers to an unsuspecting public. I'd chosen this place for the freedom to be lovers because nobody would know us or care what we did. But now I was confronted by our age difference. I was thirty-seven, Sophie was nineteen. Weren't people going to notice and remark? Would there be whispers and furtive glances when our backs were turned? Taking two rooms now seemed idiotic. What were we trying to hide if we were going to pretend to occupy two rooms at night only to make it plain during the day that we were desperately in love with one another? Maybe people aren't as easily shocked, nowadays, but someone was sure to notice we weren't sleeping apart. I felt sadness wash over me, as if all our efforts had come to nothing. But then something else rose up within me, a raw sense of unfairness that brought anger bubbling to the surface. Why should I care what people said, these people who might glance and whisper? What we were doing here was nobody's business but our own. These people I was so worried about had every right to an opinion but no right to speak it out loud. If there were glances and whispers, so be it. It was 1971. The world was changing. Maybe Sophie and I should just get married and have done with it. What, after all, were we waiting for? People might voice objections, shun us or force us into exile. Should we make each other happy and live our lives to the fullest, or should we observe antiquated social norms so that a few people wouldn't be scandalized? Surely the strength of our passion would convince others that we were following the only course available to us.

"Oww ... Joseph!" I was clenching Sophie's hand in mine and I felt her trying to wriggle free.

"Oh, my God, Sophie. I'm sorry."

I took her hand and kissed it, watching her watch me. She was smiling. Her gaze had become dreamy but her expression remained earnest and full of intent. I leaned over and kissed her on the mouth, then on the neck. A gentle whimper floated from deep in her throat, followed by a breathy sigh. Normally I initiated the process of undressing her but today she stepped back and began to unbutton her blouse. She let it slide to the floor and then slowly loosened her skirt and let it slip from her fingers. My eyes didn't leave hers. She hadn't worn any undergarments and when she pressed her length against mine, I regretted being so slow to disrobe. I wanted to kiss every inch of her. But she laid her hands on my chest, moving me backward until I bumped the edge of the bed and sat down. I started to unbuckle my belt, but she pushed my hands away.

"I'll do it."

In two swift moves trousers were around my feet. She caressed me for a moment and climbed into my lap, facing me with her legs around my waist. Then she guided me inside and began a slow rocking motion. Lying flat, I tried to respond to her movement by stroking her breasts and stomach, her legs and thighs. I touched her mouth and her tongue sought my fingers. Her gaze remained steady and I met it, absorbing her beauty, her lush lips, the slender neck, the small mound of belly, her sex. Then she closed her eyes and raised her head. Her mouth fell open. She emitted a series of moans. And I felt myself rising to meet her in that private place where we went as deep as we could go, where it was just her and me and the gift of pleasure we gave to each other. For a few sweet moments my mind was obliterated. Gone were the anxieties and the awkward and terrifying questions stalking me through all my waking hours. But none of that mattered because I knew where I was and with whom. And I knew what had to be done.

Five

I HAD TAKEN the rooms for a week and we spent the next couple of days in languid contemplation of the world around us, watching without concern as the minutes and hours slipped by. We must have been exhausted by our daily routines at home, for we spent a great deal of time curled up in each other's arms, napping, or drowsy and yawning while trying to read. My state of mind improved greatly, however, especially on the first morning after our arrival when I awoke to find Sophie beside me in bed. I glanced at the clock and saw that it was almost nine. But the time didn't matter. I turned over and observed her sleeping, thinking how fortunate I was to have her there and how indebted I was to whatever force or being had sent her to me. She was even more beautiful with the lines of her face relaxed in sleep. Her lips were slightly parted and I could hear the soft cadence of her breathing. She was having her hair trimmed often now and I could see her whole face and her small ears. I was trying not to think too much about what it meant for her to be here with me. She was here and that's all that mattered. She was now an irrevocable part of my daily existence. Instead of endlessly questioning my good fortune, I decided to accept it. It didn't matter what other people thought. True happiness is hard to come by. Why was I wasting energy resisting it when it was right here in front of me?

A nearby church bell jolted me out of my deliberations. Sophie yawned and stretched, her childlike arms emerging from beneath the blankets. She was so thin. There was something unformed about her. And yet she was fully a woman, capable of making decisions, and not afraid of anything. She astounded me; more complete and sure of herself and where she stood in this world than I'd ever be. And I was probably right in thinking this whole affair had been her idea, that she had taken the lead at every juncture—that I was just a prop, an accessory she had picked up along the way because she liked the look of it. Of what possible use could I be to her? She was going to have a spectacular career as a concert pianist and I would sit waiting for her to return from her latest tour, envious and old. So much older. She could choose among many younger, attractive and interesting men. It was unfathomable that out of all the choices available she would have selected me. I was a relic, without a creative bone in my body. Dull and plodding, I was an ox to her butterfly. Perhaps it had been an impulse, a reckless voyage into the unknown. She had been bored, and I had appeared in all my temperance and finery: an amusing way to fill the hours until the next diversion came along. But surely thinking this way was unfair, to both of us. I had seen nothing to indicate that she loved me any less ardently than I loved her. She gave herself to me without hesitation, at the least touch, without me asking. She wanted to spend time with me, doing something or nothing, it didn't seem to matter. How could I doubt her sincerity?

I curled into her and felt my ardour rise when in response to my caress she rubbed herself against me. In an instant all doubt evaporated.

We were not alone. The Inniskillen Inn was popular and we shared the premises with some thirty other couples and families. We did not hide our affection for one another. We were obviously not married, nor engaged to be married, for we wore no rings. It is simply the nature of the world that some people would be inclined to take notice of our status from the clues we provided and that others would not. We were prepared to accept this as the price for being alone together.

We ate breakfast, lunch and dinner in the dining room at the Inn. There were other restaurants in town but the Inniskillen was clearly the best. Between the elaborate and generous meals we strolled around town, exploring shops and museums or enjoying a cup of coffee. The weather remained clear and warm the entire week. Some nearby farms offered tours. The university boasted a fine arts program and the art gallery was exhibiting works of "magical realism" by a few well-known artists from the region. The theatre festival was currently producing Chekhov's *Uncle Vanya*, for which I purchased tickets. The cinema was showing Tournier's *Claire Villard*. We had plenty to do and see.

But I couldn't help watching people around us, measuring their responses to the sight of Sophie and me, hand in hand. I don't know if I was relieved or disappointed that nobody seemed to remark upon us one way or another.

The incessant warm weather became somewhat enervating and so on Wednesday morning I asked Mr. Bonnard, our host, if the kitchen staff would prepare a basket lunch we could take to the beach, the best part of which was a short drive beyond Wolfville, through the Valley and along the Fundy coast. This presented no problem at all, and shortly after breakfast Sophie and I were on our way.

Sophie drove, the only option since I'd never sat behind the wheel of a car in my life. She certainly didn't seem to mind. But as I reclined into the plush upholstery and enjoyed the passing scenery, I had the nagging sense that I had reneged on a duty, one universally considered to be masculine in nature.

Following the innkeeper's directions, we found the beach, which was busy. The scene was a commotion of small children at intervals screaming, crying and shouting. I had never seen so many small people or heard so much random noise. It was obvious the place was raucous and beyond anyone's control and we continued driving. After another twenty minutes we came across a provincial park with only a few parked cars and some tents and trailers positioned beneath the trees; otherwise the place seemed deserted. The beach was pebbly with grass, dirt, big round boulders and the silvery saltwater-washed remains of trees. But there were stretches of clear pink sand, and this in combination with the near solitude was everything we could have desired.

After changing into our swimsuits in the flimsy little huts provided for that purpose, we found a place to set our towels and the umbrella we'd borrowed from the inn. Sophie ventured down to the water in her modest one-piece striped with thin bands of white.

I lay back intending to read my book—a light mystery—but could not take my eyes off her. The sun was high, the salt air fragrant. A breeze played around us and the beat of the surf lulled me into a torpid dream state. I had not been to a beach for many years and was wearing trunks I'd bought for this vacation. Outdoor swimming was not a leisure activity that had ever enticed my parents, even at their most active and sociable. My recollections took me back once again to Pauline, Aunt Adele and Uncle Willard and steamy summer afternoons when we would crowd into the car and visit a local beach. Pauline was mischievous in the water, pinching, splashing, pushing me over backward. I was a scrawny youth, ridiculous in an ill-fitting suit, all knees and elbows, mortified at the thought of having to demonstrate my prowess in the water, for I could not swim a single stroke.

Pauline would push me over and then drag me out, coughing and heaving, triumphant because she'd rescued me from certain death. I enjoyed getting wet but only as an antidote to the heat. Other than that, I found the whole exercise humiliating. I hated the sensation of damp mucky sand between my toes, of salt drying on my skin, of my nakedness on display. The only reason I went along was to be with Pauline, who always had a wonderful time and who could swim like a guppy. For her sake I pretended to enjoy myself. Many years after this, I took indoor swimming lessons at a club, learning the strokes and the value of water activities as a remedy for stress. But I'd lapsed in this, as I knew I would when I took it up. And today I was ill at ease, wondering if I'd have the nerve to say no if Sophie beckoned me into the water.

She strode forward, slowly, deliberately, into the sea. The water climbed to her knees, then her thighs. She lowered her hands and swished them about in the water. The sun lit her whole body, making it appear as if she were floating. The stripes on her swimsuit glimmered. Further out the waves lapped against her waist but the sea was as smooth and as placid as I've ever seen it. Cruising serenely along several hundred yards offshore were a few sailboats and just beyond lurked a larger vessel without sails, a fishing boat perhaps, that didn't seem to move the entire time I watched it. Sophie was up to her breasts now. Just then I heard a child cry out and turned my head toward the sound, which had come from the parking lot. I couldn't see anything but when I turned back, Sophie was gone. Panic leapt up my throat. I stood and scanned the water for movement.

"Sophie!" I headed toward where I'd last seen her, cupping my hands around my mouth as I called her name.

Her head burst through the surface. She stood and shook the water from her hair and waved, motioning me forward.

I waved back. The thudding in my chest subsided and I returned to my towel, adjusted the umbrella for maximum shade and sat down. I took up my book but felt so foolish that I couldn't concentrate long enough to read even a single sentence.

After a few minutes she joined me on the sand. I stood and rubbed her up and down with a towel.

"You're cold," I said.

"It's not bad."

She put on her sunglasses and stretched out on her stomach, resting her head on her arms.

"This is better," she said.

We didn't speak for several minutes and I watched a few seabirds foraging in the water. Two seemed to be arguing over something. One approached the other, pecking at the feathers on its nether end and the assaulted one emitted a squawk as it lifted itself into the air and came to rest a few feet away. They repeated the process, pecking at the other's feathers until it squawked and moved off. In this fashion they became separated from their companions by a good hundred yards.

"Joseph?"

"Ummm?"

"How come you never talk about your childhood?"

I shrugged, not entirely surprised that she'd asked. It had to come up sometime.

"What's there to tell?"

"I'm just curious. My mother's told me a few things. Not much."

"So you talk about me behind my back?"

She smiled.

"Of course we do."

"Should I be flattered?"

"I wouldn't let it go to my head if I were you."

I tried to think of what to say, or what she wanted to hear. There was nothing I wanted to hide from her. But something in me remained wary.

"I grew up mostly by myself. If it wasn't for your mother and her parents I probably would have gone mad."

I answered her gaze with one of my own.

"Mmm. Tell me more. I want to know everything."

"Well, I was born on a Saturday. It was raining." She was watching me, evidently waiting for more. "Sophie, this is really boring."

"No, it isn't."

"Okay. Well, we lived in a house on Jubilee Road, not far from where your mother grew up. The house isn't there anymore. Somebody pulled it down to put up an apartment building. I was happy for a while. We did things together, as families do. It was nothing special, but I remember having fun—and I remember a real feeling of being loved and appreciated. It was great, actually. I remember the house being full of light. People laughing all the time. My father was a great joker. He'd take me out and try to teach me things. He'd drive me out to the country and we'd go to a farm where he knew people and they'd take me down to the pig pen or out to the barn to look at the cows and the horses.

"He was mostly self-taught. He left school when he was really young but was curious about everything. I still remember one afternoon, driving home in the rain. He stopped the car by the side of the road and he pointed and there was a rainbow, probably the most perfect one I've ever seen. He explained to me all about how the water droplets refract the light, separating out the different colours. I can remember his big hands moving as he tried to make me see what was going on because he was convinced there was an explanation for everything and he didn't want me growing up with my head in the clouds.

"My mother liked poetry and she'd read to me and talk about art and the imagination and about how you can take an idea and turn it into anything you want. She loved stories and made-up things. But she also liked to tell me about the lives of writers and artists. I don't know where she got all this." I shrugged. "Somewhere. Anyway, it was like growing up in some sort of academy where ideas were always floating around in the air. They treated me like a miniature adult. It wasn't as if they expected me to learn all this and recite it back to them. They just wanted it out there so that if I ever needed it, then there it was."

I looked at her, expecting her to be asleep. Her face was turned toward me.

"This isn't boring," she said.

"Then I got sick."

"When did this happen?"

"I was almost seven. I don't remember the details because I was unconscious most of the time. They told me I'd become infected somehow and it went through my bloodstream and that I almost didn't survive. I had transfusions and was put on a special diet. It must have been traumatic for my parents, their only child that sick. Well I got through it all right, obviously. But when I got home everything had changed. My parents were never the same after that and the whole house became this dark, dingy place. It was like living underground because they kept the curtains drawn even during the day. For a long time, while I was getting better, I went to live at your mother's house. I'm not sure that I knew what was going on, though. I suppose, to a six-year-old, it seemed like my parents had disappeared. They were gone and in their place were these two ... I don't know what you'd call them. They just moped around, hardly saying a word to each other, or to me. It was the strangest thing."

"What did you do?"

"Well . . ." I paused, then forged ahead. "You'll think this is stupid, but I didn't do anything. I spent a lot of time with your mother. I went to school, did my homework. I guess I sort of accepted what had happened, even though I didn't understand it. What else could I do? I mean, I've thought about this a lot and the only thing that makes sense is that my parents chose to be that way. Maybe that's not it at all but they certainly didn't try to convince me otherwise. It was sad to watch them waste their lives.

"My father was still working at the lumber yard. And they had their community work—noble causes and all that—but the way they went about it, the joy was gone. It was like they were trying to bury themselves." I shook my head. "I could be wrong about them. But I had nothing else to go on. They never tried to explain it to me. I guess I could have asked. It's just that when you're young . . . you accept things. It left me wondering though—remember I was small and didn't know any better—if it was somehow my fault."

"It wasn't your fault, Joseph. It couldn't have been your fault."

"Your mother talked to you about it?"

"A little," she said. "Not much."

We were silent.

"When did they die?"

I looked at her.

"You don't have to tell me."

"Well . . . no, I mean, it's hardly a secret. It was while I was away at university. My mother went first. Liver disease. She drank herself to death, basically. I came home for that. A few people showed up at the funeral. Mostly your family. I tried to talk to my dad but he just waved me away. He told me, 'It's over now so don't worry about it.' I remember asking, 'What's over?' I assume he meant my mother's suffering, which was self-imposed as far as I could see. But he never gave me an answer. I stayed with your mom's family instead of going home. My dad said the house was too much of a mess. I saw what he meant when I visited.

"There was stuff everywhere. I was shocked because it had always been spotless. These days they call it hoarding. I would've helped clear the place out but he wasn't interested. I asked more than once but he always put me off. Finally I got sick of pestering him and gave up. Before going back to Toronto I went over to the house one more time but if he was in there he didn't come to the door. I could have let myself in, but I didn't. I phoned him from Toronto. I tried to make the calls a regular thing—a scheduled event—because I was determined to make the effort. I wanted a connection. But he hardly spoke to me.

"It was like, 'How are you?' 'Oh, fine. How are you?' 'Oh, fine.' And that was it. He told me not to bother coming home for Christmas. I never saw him again because he died the next year. I came back and settled the estate. Put the house up for sale; got rid of all the junk; burned lots of papers, old bills, photographs. I went through boxes and boxes of that kind of thing looking for a clue to their behaviour. I spoke to his sister, Aunt Adele, your grandmother. She couldn't tell me anything. Or wouldn't. I don't know. It was strange. Very strange."

Sophie reached across the sand and took my hand.

"Joseph, I'm sorry. I'm so sorry."

Well, no ..." I answered her grip with a squeeze. "It's not anything to be sorry about. It's just the way things were. It's unfortunate, but hardly a tragedy."

"But you had to live like that."

"Some people have it worse. Some people don't even have parents, or a house to grow up in. At least I had that."

She was shaking her head.

"I wonder what happened to them."

I looked at her, at my reflection in her dark glasses.

"I guess we'll never know." I didn't like to dwell on this aspect of my past, which was beginning to take on maudlin overtones, and

Sophie sensed my reluctance to continue. She left me to take another swim and shortly after that we ate our lunch. We fell asleep, stretched out on our towels. By this time another couple had arrived and laid claim to part of our strip of beach. They'd brought a radio, which they kept tuned low, but not low enough in my opinion, its percussive murmur infiltrating my consciousness and subverting my dreams. I glanced in their direction from time to time, as a demonstration of annoyance I suppose, though I didn't really expect them to turn it off. And they didn't.

Eventually Sophie stirred and suggested we go for a walk. The sun was at a lower angle and some clouds had moved in front of it. Nonetheless, I put on a shirt to protect my arms and shoulders, which had grown red despite the shade thrown by the umbrella.

We deposited our supplies in the car and then, hand in hand, set out in the opposite direction from where we'd spent the morning.

It was a good beach for walking as long as you had the right footwear. Despite my sedentary lifestyle, I did own a pair of running shoes and Sophie had her canvas lace-ups. A path had been worn into the hard clay, but we still had to climb over dirt and loose stones, avoiding pools of water as we went. On this stretch there was no sand to speak of; the edge of the forest reached all the way down to rocks exposed by the tides. We made our way with care, holding hands the entire time. I was not going to allow Sophie to slip and fall.

We climbed over a stony outcrop. After a few minutes the rocks levelled off and we found ourselves on a shallow stretch of sandy beach. There was nobody around and we headed toward the water. Sophie took off her shoes and let the sea wash over her bare feet.

I was conscious of the day, and the week, coming to an end. Sadness welled up at the thought. What was next? Sophie would soon begin practising in earnest for the new concert season and soon she'd be on tour. I wouldn't see her for weeks at a time. The more I tried to push these concerns aside, the more difficult it was to escape them. What would I do with myself? And how on earth would we ever contrive to be alone together?

Neither of us had said much since we started walking, immersed as we were in our own thoughts.

Then Sophie released a sigh.

"Yes?" I said.

"Oh, I keep thinking of your poor parents and how sad they must have been to shut themselves up in that house. What a terrible way to live. I can't imagine what would make anyone do that to themselves."

"Neither can I and I've been thinking about it for almost twenty years."

She gripped my arm and rested her head on my shoulder.

"But I'm glad you told me about it. I want to know everything about you. I don't think there should be any secrets between us."

"It wasn't exactly a secret," I said.

"I know. But there aren't any, are there?"

"Any what?" I looked at her. "Secrets? Don't be ridiculous."

"No? Really?"

"You mean, like do I have another girlfriend hidden away somewhere or am I really a Russian spy or did I have an affair with my high school gym teacher? Things like that?"

"Sort of, I guess."

"Well, I don't. And I'm not. And I didn't. What I haven't told you though was that I was voted 'Most Boring' in grade twelve."

"I'm happy to hear that."

"What about you? Anything you're not telling me?"

"Oh, Joseph, you probably know more about me than I do. I can't believe the life I've lived. Nothing ever happens."

"Be thankful. And anyway, I wouldn't say that this"—I gave her hand a light squeeze—"is nothing. It's pretty exciting to fall in love."

"I guess. But, you know, it's kind of dull in its own way. Ordinary, I mean. People fall in love all the time."

"Yes, but we don't fall in love—you don't fall in love—all the time."

I looked at her, awaiting a response. But she kept her head tilted down and remained silent. We'd reached the end of the beach.

Ahead of us jagged rocks loomed up to form a cliff face. We turned to go back.

After a few steps she seemed to stumble.

"Ow!" she said, and lifted her right foot. At first there appeared to be nothing. But as we looked on, a bead of blood appeared on her skin, at the edge of her foot near the smallest toe. It grew until a drop formed, which fell to the sand. Then another bead appeared in its place.

"Wouldn't you know it," she said, sighing.

I helped her over to a rock where she could sit. Then I examined her foot.

"It doesn't look serious," I said. The break in her skin was a curved slice about half the size of a pea; so small, in fact, that I could hardly see it. But the blood kept coming just the same. I wiped it away with my finger.

"Does it hurt?" I asked.

She shook her head. But I could see she was a little shaken. She shivered.

"It's just ... blood scares me. That's all." She forced a smile.

I held her foot in my hand, feeling its warmth and her living pulse moving through it, carried along by the blood that scared her. The cut was a small thing, insignificant. But the possibility of infection was there. I tried to brush away the damp sand, but it clung to her skin and wouldn't be moved.

Despite the cut, she put her canvas shoes on and we walked back to the car. By the time we got there the blood had clotted and the bleeding had stopped on its own.

"God, this is so silly," she said as she got in behind the wheel. She laughed and shook her head. There was a first-aid packet in the glove compartment and after drying her foot with a towel I covered the cut with a small bandage.

"No sense taking chances," I said, which was true enough. And anyway, it was time to head back to the inn.

* * *

A young couple had arrived early Sunday evening and over the course of several days residing under the same roof our exchanges had become more personal than the polite hallway greetings customary in such circumstances. The couple—Brian and Alicia Skinner—were not much older than Sophie, perhaps in their mid-twenties. On a few occasions we saw them at breakfast, sometimes on the veranda in the afternoons and also in town, passing time in much the same manner as Sophie and me. From my conversations with Brian I gathered they had both recently graduated from Western University in Ontario, were recently married and were looking for jobs. The vacation was a gift from his parents.

Brian was tall and darkly handsome, with a slight build, sharp features and short brown hair, which he had a habit of touching and shaping at intervals during conversation. By contrast, Alicia was short and rather broad in the hips, with a pale, pretty face and black hair falling in thick curls to her shoulders and which provided a charming frame for her features. Sophie seemed comfortable with both of them and I saw no harm in striking up an acquaintance as they'd soon be returning to Ontario. To tell the truth, spending time in their company was pleasantly distracting. They took us out of ourselves, so to speak. They were interesting. The conversation was always lively. They recommended some local sights that Sophie and I later enjoyed. Any inquiries they made into our affairs were casual, in the manner of people simply trying to fill a social void. At no point did they press for information or pursue an inappropriate degree of familiarity.

In short, they gained our trust, so much so that on our next to last evening at the Inn, we arranged to dine with them.

I can forgive myself the occasional innocent mistake. We all make them. But in this instance I allowed a mistaken first impression to ruin what could have been a pleasurable evening alone with the person I loved most in the world, and that I can neither forgive nor forget. From what I had seen of Brian and Alicia Skinner, I believed them to be very much devoted to one another. But not long after we were seated and had ordered wine I began to suspect that Brian was taken with Sophie to an immoderate degree. As we sat waiting for the wine and as the evening took on its sorry shape, I envisioned a life of nothing but misery and heartache for poor Alicia.

I was seated across from Sophie, the Skinners opposite each other. Immediately upon taking his seat, Brian adjusted its position, ever so slightly—but noticeably—in Sophie's direction. He then took advantage of this shift to lean over and whisper into Sophie's ear. The moment his lips brushed her flesh, I felt something tighten in my chest, for his action implied a degree of intimacy that to my knowledge did not exist. I glanced at Alicia, hoping to meet her eye. But her head was down, eyes resolutely focused on the menu before her. I'm ashamed to say my gaze lingered on the flecks of dandruff revealed by the part in her hair and collected loosely at each temple.

Sophie's face bore a somewhat startled expression. However, she smiled at his message and avoided my eye for at least a minute. Then Skinner erupted in a torrent of chatter he maintained all evening without seeming to take a breath.

His discourse took two distinct forms: quizzing either Sophie or me, but chiefly Sophie, about our life together at home, habits, likes and dislikes and pontificating at length upon topics of evident consequence to himself but surely devoid of interest to the rest of humanity.

I don't enjoy maligning people and will not bore my reader by repeating any of Brian Skinner's oration. But allow me to state that I found the man not only tedious, but vain, vulgar and officious, and wondered if he had been drinking. Sophie, in her innocence, was no match for his relentless scrutiny and from her he learned that we were not married, that we had taken two rooms, that she was nineteen, that her parents were well off and that for the time being we were keeping our relationship from the rest of our respective families (to her credit she did not divulge our common blood). Each time one of these pieces of information slipped out, she cast me an anguished glance, as if to say: Please save me from this. I interrupted him frequently and brusquely and more frequently as the evening wore on, quite rudely. But my efforts did little to staunch the flow.

I did not tell him my age when he asked me, I simply smiled and remained silent, to which response he sniggered in a suggestive manner. At that point Alicia chimed in with a comment about the weather and how fortunate we'd all been but it was too late to salvage any part of the evening. And besides, her husband ignored her and turned once again to Sophie, who as I could clearly see by her sluggish response, had long since wearied of Brian Skinner, even if she'd been (as she confessed later) flattered when he initially fixed her with that sly, seductive gaze and began his interrogation.

But the evening was about to take one more turn, for better or for worse, I'm hardly in a position now to say. One of my purposes in planning this holiday was to spend a few days in intimate seclusion with this girl whom I cherished so dearly; a few days free of the attention of family and friends. I wanted us to leave behind our responsibilities and public identities and spend this short time together as two anonymous lovers. Above all, I wanted to avoid attracting the notice of anyone in a position to deduce who we were simply from appearances or behaviour.

I was not prepared when Mr. Bonnard approached our table and took me aside. I was puzzled and he seemed embarrassed. I'm not sure what he understood, or assumed, of my relationship with Sophie but at least he had the decency not to ask. What he finally said was that a table of young ladies at the other end of the dining room had inquired if the young lady at this table was Sophie Gebhardt and if so would she play something for them. Sophie and I had noticed the upright piano in the sitting room across the hall from where we were eating. Sophie had lifted the lid and fingered the keys upon our arrival but had not touched it since. Now, however, for whatever reason, the connection had been made. I was going to tell him to convey Ms. Gebhardt's regrets to the other table when Sophie, who'd overheard the question during a lull in the general noise level of the room, stood and offered to play. I understood at once that she saw this as an opportunity to escape from Brian Skinner but I couldn't have been more disappointed by her response had she offered to sing and dance as well.

I gave her a tight smile as squeals of delight erupted at the table of young ladies. In truth I was almost in tears, because it seemed to me that the edifice of secrecy we'd taken such elaborate pains to construct had been destroyed in one careless stroke.

A smiling Sophie was led to the piano followed by a gaggle of worshipful youngsters and several adults as well. Brian and Alicia Skinner made no move to go, so I resumed my seat and ordered a double brandy. Mr. Bonnard appeared at our table as Sophie teased the first notes of a Chopin waltz out of the thunderous old instrument, apologized for the inconvenience and offered us our dinner and drinks on the house. Brian raised his glass to me and I understood that there was not and never will be any justice in this world.

Looking over what I have written, I see that I have inadvertently emphasized the farcical elements of that evening. Quite possibly, it was both more and less pleasant than I have characterized it. Sophie said afterward that she always enjoyed being recognized, as it happened so rarely. The girl who instigated the event told her that she remembered Sophie coming to her school a year or two earlier to lead a workshop and that she'd been inspired to take up the piano. The incident with the Skinners I put down to bad luck. They had never represented themselves as anything but a young couple in search of a diversion and so I cannot in all fairness claim to have been misled. However, they were not what I thought them to be. The inn itself was fine; the Bonnards were impeccable hosts. So why do I look back on that evening as a turning point? Why does it seem that our relationship was diminished by what occurred? I loved Sophie just as deeply as before. Her feelings for me, from what I could tell, were unchanged. Why did I begin to suspect, as I followed her up the stairs after this spontaneous and much-appreciated recital, that we had deceived ourselves and that what we were trying to do was impossible?

Six

W E RESUMED OUR places in the world and life went on as before. There was, however, a change in the pattern of our lovemaking. Without any warning we found ourselves—or at least I did and Sophie did nothing to discourage me—tormented by an appetite for sex and a craving for physical intimacy that bordered on the insatiable. We took chances that would have seemed foolhardy even just a few weeks ago. Perhaps the warm August weather was to blame. Or maybe it was the realization that Sophie would soon be performing in cities I would never visit that turned longing into lust.

I visited Pauline and Frederick often, joining them for meals and for drinks in the garden. I often found myself in the midst of a group that Pauline had assembled; neighbours or friends or visitors of some other sort; colleagues of Frederick; people they knew from church. Sophie was always there and our glances were always colliding, across rooms and across tables, across whatever was separating us at the moment. She sometimes gave informal recitals after these meals and as she did this I would steal away from her parents and their guests, who were gathered in the back yard or in the parlour or spread through the house. I would join her in the music room if she was alone and would massage her shoulders and rub her neck and kiss her, leaving the doors wide open. A palpable, addictive thrill was part of the risk. Once, a man blundered in just as I wrapped my arms around her and kissed her on the cheek. I still remember the burly silhouette, drink in hand, frozen in the doorway. I couldn't see his face but was sure it was nobody I knew. No doubt he'd followed the music meaning to discover its source. From her position at the piano, Sophie couldn't see him. And so she continued to play—a Schubert sonata if I remember correctly—and he stood there indecisively, half in and half out of the room, shuffling his feet, considering his options, until he retreated, tottering down the hall, likely uncertain about what he'd just witnessed.

On another of these summer evenings as August was coming to an end, I excused myself from a dull conversation with an Austrian doctor in town for a conference and followed Sophie. The hallway was dark but I knew the way well and slipping off my shoes, crept toward her room, keeping close to the wall as people do in movies. Perhaps I had in mind a brief embrace, some kisses. The house was full of people and any number of reasons could have prompted someone to come in search of one or both of us. But the risk of being discovered was as exciting as the thought of having Sophie to myself. I came to her room and let myself in. She was lying on her bed. She'd removed her clothes. She watched me slip the bolt in the door.

Neither of us said a word. The room was dim, lit by a single lamp and by the failing daylight. As I moved toward her, my shadow seemed to leap across the room to her bed. It was a teenaged girl's room, messy, with posters on the walls and socks on the floor and a menagerie of stuffed toys posed on shelves and atop dressers. Fragmentary sounds—voices, laughter, the clink of glass, footfalls on the brick steps—mingled and drifted upward through the open window. I began to undress, folding my pants over the back of a chair, ensuring first that the creases lined up. As she watched me Sophie bent one leg, raising her knee. A woman spoke very loudly for a moment, praising the flowers at a wedding she'd recently attended before turning her attention to Pauline's garden. I heard Pauline respond in a subdued voice, her words blurred by other voices, other sounds. I had laid all my clothes neatly on the chair. Sophie reached out her arms to me and I went to her. The bed groaned softly as I rested my weight full upon it and we paused, because at the same moment it seemed that all conversation and noise had ceased, as if the entire world had stopped to turn its attention to our next act. The sensation of being observed or heard sent a brisk chill along my spine. I held myself rigid as I strained to hear. But the din of conversation and movement resumed, floating through the window as if it had never paused. Sophie eyed me quizzically, concerned I suppose that I'd heard a sound outside her door. I smiled, whispered that it was nothing, kissed her, and we continued as if all that mattered was our two bodies locked in embrace.

Seven

THERE'S NO DEFENCE for our behaviour. The idea of risking our secret, recklessly exposing it to the light of day, waving it under people's noses, was an intoxicating power. I'm not saying we sought opportunities for exposure. We were simply less discreet than we'd been in the spring and early summer, at times dangerously impulsive.

For instance, in the first week of September Sophie travelled to Toronto for meetings at a recording company. The day she returned she met me leaving my office and in plain view on the front steps of the building I lifted her off the ground and kissed her what felt like a hundred times. When I reflect upon our actions I have difficulty believing that anyone observing us could have failed to guess what was going on. Perhaps people knew and were waiting for us to come to our senses. Perhaps they were too appalled to accept what appeared to be happening. It does strike me that we were very lucky, that on more than one occasion the slimmest of margins—perhaps seconds—was all that saved our secret from falling into the hands of those individuals from whom we wished to keep it.

I find it especially difficult to believe that Pauline—one of the most perceptive people I know—did not have suspicions. All through this period I avoided being alone with her, too often I was reminded of our years growing up together, of my huge debt to her and her family and of my enormous betrayal. I was afraid that, if she asked, I would confess everything. I've provided ample evidence of her generous and loving nature but she also possesses the sort of emotional insight that—having set out to deceive her—left me in terror. I could easily recall many instances when through guile or an emotional gambit involving tears or smiling promises, she persuaded me to reveal something I had intended to keep to myself. Adept at reading people, she could probably guess what was in another person's mind, if she knew them well enough. At some level of consciousness I was aware of the pain she would suffer if we were discovered. I loved her dearly and sought, always, to protect her from distress if I could.

Whenever, however feebly, I tried to reconcile my actions with my intentions, it was clear I had no idea where it was all going to lead. Could Sophie and I keep up our ruse for years? Decades? Would she even want to? How on earth could we maintain this level of duplicity without going mad? How unpleasant would it be if we just went to her parents and declared our love for each other? I hate lies and selfishness; I wanted to be fair. I wanted a conclusion that would satisfy everyone. But lurking behind these notions of fairness and happiness was a vision of Pauline struggling to contend with passions and circumstances that nobody, let alone a conscientious mother and a good person, should ever have to face.

I also wanted to avoid guilt and was racked by doubts and the unalterable realities of our situation. Chief among these were the twin demons that had plagued me from the start: our blood relationship and the yawning fissure between our ages.

I was eighteen years older than Sophie and yet she seemed untroubled by this. I admit that, when we were together, in bed or in public, it was not something to which I gave much thought. When we were making love, it was irrelevant. When we were enjoying one another's company and talking about things that interested us, it never intruded. When one of us introduced a topic unfamiliar to the other, because of being too young or too old, it was a cause for hilarity, not embarrassment. Yet when Sophie was not with me those eighteen years loomed in my vision as an unbridgeable gulf. Not only did I conclude that my age would prevent her from ever really loving me—she had only deceived herself thus far into believing she loved me, poor girl—it would be the cause of great future suffering when she finally understood the root cause of her dissatisfaction.

There was a further aspect to the age issue that caused me concern. Sophie was beautiful in every conceivable way. No woman I have met before or since can match her for radiance, or that easeful grace that comes from being completely at home in one's body. Her stride had a casual and sensual swing, her every gesture informed by music only she could hear. In conversation she projected a self-effacing quality that put people at ease. She didn't try to win points with her celebrity or beauty and wasn't interested in trumpeting her accomplishments. Nothing offended her more than someone fawning over her. Of course, people immediately noticed her obvious attributes, even when they had no idea who she was. And then they would see me and I almost always noted a subtle realignment of their features. How can this be? they seemed to be asking. Who does he think he is? And, worst of all: What's wrong with her? There is a species of humanity forever on the lookout for the worst in others. They applaud when others fail, cheer when a rival falls on his face, all the while sniffing out possible weaknesses. These are the bloodsuckers one seeks all one's life to avoid.

Occasionally, at a restaurant or the theatre, we would fall into conversation with other couples, as was the case with the Skinners. It sometimes happened that I would be left on my own with a husband or a lone male out for an evening while Sophie retired to the ladies' room. What transpired in her absence could sometimes make me regret my membership in the order of mammals to which I belong. I remember a theatre intermission during which a lascivious banker—a wizened creature with a droopy eyelid—didn't stop ogling her the entire night. When we were alone he fixed me with his loathsome gaze and suggested, using his cigar as a prop, that Sophie's role in my life was restricted to a single activity. Other instances were more subtle—a knowing wink from a middle-aged waiter, the detestable insinuation lurking behind Brian Skinner's smirk—but no less disturbing. I sometimes felt that because I was older and Sophie much younger, the corrupt male element that circulates among us presumed I was a like-minded ally. It added a disheartening aspect to our romance from which I did my best to shield her.

Our common blood, though not apparent to those around us, was nonetheless fundamental to my attitude toward the entire relationship. It was like the colour of one's eyes or skin: a fact that could neither be denied nor circumvented. Since we didn't know how people would respond, why risk censure on this basis alone? Granted, we were only second cousins and I seem to recall a widespread assumption, on the rare occasion when such a topic came up, that taboos regarding sex and marriage between relatives ended with first cousins. But there was always a reminder, either in the news or drifting about in general discussion, that any sexual relations between relatives was frowned upon. A notorious case of incest, in which a father and mother had sex with all their children, and encouraged the children to have sex with each other, had just come to a wretched conclusion in the courts. And though I knew what we were doing was altogether different, this had less to do with our own feelings on the matter and much more to do with trying to anticipate how her parents would react.

And the fact was that neither of us knew what to expect. At times, I imagined various scenarios. Sophie and me on the sofa across from Frederick and Pauline. In one of these, our confession of love and intention to marry elicited howls of joy and hugs and kisses all around. In another, the expression that registered on Pauline's face was one of horror and I was subjected to torrents of abuse before being summarily ejected from the house never to return. I also saw myself making a lunch engagement with Frederick and discussing my feelings for Sophie in the neutral surroundings of the hospital cafeteria. I regard Frederick as a friend as well as one of the wisest people I know. But when I placed us together in this setting, I could not imagine the conversation. Often, I told myself it wasn't the right time. Or I suddenly realized that having Sophie as a lover was the one aspect of my life that made the rest tolerable.

In this state of befuddlement, I watched the weeks go by and did nothing at all.

Eight

I TRUST YOU will understand that by making this confession I
am not trying to excuse my actions or temper your disgust.
Absolution is much more than I can hope for. I wish only to
set the record straight. Please bear with me.

I had noticed, when we were unpacking our clothes that first
day in Wolfville, that Sophie drew from her suitcase a small notebook covered in blue narrow-ribbed corduroy and tied with a red
ribbon. A few nights later I awoke alone in bed and as I lay waiting
for her to return I grew conscious of the faint scraping sound of pen
on paper. I turned my head and drew down the bed sheets. She was
on the window seat and writing in the notebook, which rested on
her raised legs. Her face in profile, lit by the silver lamplight from
the street, was so sweetly angelic—so calm and contemplative—that
I did not disturb her. I did not see the notebook again until the first
time we made love in her room at her home. I have described one of
these occasions, but to my everlasting shame it was not the only time.
We did it at every opportunity because it was exciting, because it
seemed to take us into new realms of intimacy. It was easy to pretend that we were each occupied with our own business or interests
in different parts of the house or else outside wandering the grounds.
With her parents, or maybe a party of visitors, or sometimes only the
domestic help downstairs, we would disrobe and move quickly into
one another. Normally we had intercourse.

At other times, with the silent efficiency of the skilled hedonist I'd encouraged her to become, she performed acts on my body—with her fingers, with her lips, with her tongue—that I shudder now to recall, and this within the chaste environs of her girlhood bedroom. On several of these occasions I noticed the notebook resting on her desk, where I imagined her recording our every act as soon as I was gone. Once, when she was in the bathroom while I was getting dressed, I picked it up. The ribbon I mentioned earlier was actually a strap equipped with a Velcro fastener. Afraid of the noise opening it would make, I returned it to the desk.

I had no reason to regard the notebook as a threat. I knew Sophie was not going to leave it on the coffee table in the living room. I had no evidence that she had recorded anything of a compromising nature. But once I'd learned of its existence I could not ignore it. For many weeks after the tragedy that ended our affair it occupied an ignoble corner of my mind where the mere thought of it falling into the wrong hands gave me the sweats.

Nine

SOPHIE KEPT HER commitment to the chamber group until the end of the summer. They were scheduled to perform pieces by Mozart and Haydn in the Art Gallery on campus sometime in early September. I had not sat in on any of their weekly sessions, even though I knew the time and location of each. Part of my reasoning for staying away was that I thought of myself as serious and dour. I felt that Sophie should be able to enjoy a few hours away from my sobering influence. I knew also that she was working with musicians who were less experienced than herself, and that they might not appreciate me staring at them, possibly judging them, as they tried to prepare for a public performance. For her part, she neither encouraged nor discouraged my attendance.

I made a habit of asking Sophie how the sessions were going; I wanted her to understand that I was interested and that she had my support. I was not trying to pry; my interest was natural. However, she didn't want to talk about the pieces they were rehearsing or the other musicians in the group. While never once expressing regret at having joined the ensemble, she never appeared particularly excited about it either. She may have been apprehensive at having linked, to a certain extent, her own reputation to the competence of four un-known amateur musicians. If the performance went well, they would all benefit; if it went poorly, the blame would likely be hers. I tried not to dwell on it. I asked the obligatory questions, but when it became clear she didn't want to discuss it, I did not press her for answers.

Thus far I have avoided the painful topic of jealousy. My love for Sophie was unconditional. I had opened myself up to her, exposing my physical as well as my psychological flaws. Enchanted by her beauty, charmed by her disposition, in awe of her talents, I wanted only to make her happy. Whatever shortcomings she may have possessed, these appeared to my dazzled eyes simply as evidence of her humanity, which endeared her to me even more. I was utterly besotted.

But there is another side of love that is not commendable. I was an insecure lover, unsure of my skills in bed and doubtful that I was attractive or virile enough for her. I was convinced she would eventually grow weary of my attentions and embark upon a more gratifying and vital relationship with a younger man. In fact, I expected that any day she would refuse to let me touch her, that she would sit me down and explain, patiently and tearfully, that it was over. Furthermore, the multitude of obstacles preventing us from making our relationship public was a compelling and sensible reason for her to want to back out of it. As long as we hid behind closed doors, we were placing the future on hold. Why should she want to do this for my sake?

As much as I understood that she had every right and more than sufficient cause to want to leave me behind, I could not find the courage to urge her out the door. I clung to her ever more tenaciously as the arguments in favour of us going our separate ways accumulated in my mind. Sophie, who in addition to the chamber rehearsals was spending hours alone in her studio practicing new works for her fall concerts, seemed unaware of my anxieties. I began inventing reasons to take greater advantage of Pauline and Frederick's hospitality. My stove was on the blink or there was a noisy construction project nearby creating a ruckus at all hours. Soon I was turning up on their doorstep several times a week, even on days when Sophie and I had already seen each other. And still, she gave no indication that my near constant presence irritated her. When Frederick left town for a conference, I stayed over, using the excuse that having a man in the house would make everyone feel more secure. I was both selfish and weak. I told myself that I needed her simply in order to survive. I also convinced myself that in this matter I had no will of my own; I had allowed my entire existence to become subsumed by hers.

If I had raised these concerns with her I'm sure she would have said I was crazy. Whether or not she perceived the extent of my devotion, she did not once push me to do something I did not want to do. Had she behaved in the petulant and conniving manner of a child of privilege, or had she not displayed a sober and reflective side to match my own, I would doubtless have grown weary of her.

The reason why I did not attend any of the rehearsals of her chamber group was not that I was selflessly observing her need for privacy but that I was jealous of the male musicians she was working with who were close to her age, at least one of whom was bound to possess the physical and mental attributes she would desire in a lover. I did not want to see her sitting next to this person, see him leaning over her shoulder as they discussed the tempo of a troublesome measure, or watch her smile at him as he made an astute or witty observation. My insecurities held me prisoner. The slightest hint that she might direct her affections elsewhere was sure to send me spiralling into despondency. I was also terrified that over-possessive behaviour on my part would anger her.

You will understand, therefore, what an extraordinary act of will it required to make myself attend her rehearsal on the first Saturday in September. I didn't want to, but with my fears growing more acute, it seemed, by the hour, I had to see for myself if this group of musicians harboured a potential rival. I arose that morning determined to set my doubts to rest once and for all. I took my time over the morning newspaper. I chose casual dress and walked to the Arts Centre. The building comprised several performance spaces, large and small, as well as classrooms and offices. They were in the basement. I followed a set of concrete stairs down two or three flights but when I tried the door at the bottom it was locked. I listened for music but all was silent. I went back up and wandered across the lobby and down a hallway past a range of vending machines to another stairwell. This took me down into a little vestibule that led on one side into a cavernous performance space. On the other side was a set of security doors that opened to my touch. It was through here that I heard the sounds I had been seeking.

I immediately recognized Sophie's signature on the music. Her understated lyricism filled the empty hallway, which was bare and dusty under harsh fluorescent lights. After Sophie had played another bar or two, the strings joined in, giving shape to the main theme. The entrance to the room they occupied was through double yellow doors with brass rectangles affixed where one would normally press to open them. I wasn't about to do this because I didn't want to create a disturbance. And I soon understood that I was not going to enter the room at all. In my imagination I'd envisioned a miniature auditorium, dimly lit and with rows of plush seating arranged in a bowl, into which I could quietly slink and settle unnoticed. But the rehearsal was happening in a large, brightly-illuminated practice space. I would be sitting in their midst, impossible to ignore.

The music continued, building an irrepressible momentum the way some of Haydn's compositions do. The five instruments were engaged in creating an intricate mosaic of sound, all contributing equally to the final product, which echoed the length of the empty hallway, its terse rhythms and melodic sequences delivered with astonishing precision. At one point the movement breaks, and the music continues after a single beat of silence with a lone note played by the cello, which is drawn out for a full measure. The melodic line is then re-introduced by the first violin, which is joined after a moment by the second violin and then the viola. The last to return is the piano, which initially enters the dialogue with a few tinkling high notes. Over the course of several measures the strings recede into a secondary role and the piano takes over its lead position.

I was listening intently, mesmerized, anticipating the approaching climax of the movement, when the music abruptly halted. At that instant Sophie's laugh rang out, filling the hallway with its familiar sweetness. I felt a spasm go through me, as if I'd been startled out of a deep sleep. All at once the hallway lights seemed far too bright and I felt an urge to flee, as if I were in imminent danger of being discovered lurking where I had no legitimate business. Sophie let her fingers fall on the piano keys apparently at random, producing a discordant racket. This was followed by the murmur of voices as the musicians discussed what they had just played, or so I presumed. I peered through the separation between the two yellow doors just as Sophie laughed again. She sat at the keyboard, in profile, her head raised and her neck exposed as the laugh shook her entire body. The other musicians were arranged in a semi-circle around the piano, seated with their instruments at their sides or on their laps. There were two males and two females. Everyone appeared to be enjoying the joke. The two girls, one of whom was the cello player, leaned their heads together. The two men, or boys (from my vantage point I couldn't be certain of ages) held their instruments steady in their laps but said nothing. I couldn't see their faces. Sophie was clearly the focus of attention. Their eyes rarely strayed from her and as the jesting passed they seemed to await a signal from her before going further.

Sophie flipped a page of her score.

Someone said: "Do it again."

"Yeah, Sophie, do it again."

Sophie cast them a mischievous glance. Her face radiated an impish charm, a childish delight in the attention she was receiving mixed with a swaggering self-possession that was purely adult. Her clothing strengthened this impression for me. I am always shocked when I hear music such as the Haydn being played by musicians wearing casual clothing instead of the formal attire the music seems to call for. This incongruity makes painfully obvious the absence of gravitas that is due such superior levels of composition and musicianship.

This morning Sophie was wearing a red-checked shirt, tight jeans and leather boots which, combined, called attention to the slim lines of her body. To what degree she wished to incite erotic musings in her male companions I cannot say. But when she shifted herself on the stool or stretched out her arm, their eyes followed her every move.

After the general call for an encore, she performed a mock curtsy, sat down and lowered her head over the keyboard. She straightened her back and drew a deep breath. A beat. Then she spread her shapely fingers above the keys.

What erupted from the piano were the familiar opening trills of Chopin's *Minute Waltz*. The music danced as it always did when she played it but something unusual was going on, something I caught after hearing a few more notes. She was playing it very fast, as if pursued by demons, or as if the building were burning and she couldn't leave until she'd finished. Chopin's little masterpiece has become somewhat of a cliché in the concert world but in the proper hands it displays considerable charm. It's also devilishly difficult to play, as I can attest from miserable experience. Sophie was racing through it, her hands covering the keyboard faster than I could follow them. The break, where the trilling ends and a more sober progression assumes its place, she treated as a dance step as well, slowing her tempo only slightly. Then the trills began, faster and faster, carried forward by her remarkable musicianship and agile fingers. Impossible as it may seem, she did not miss a note as she reached the crescendo, rocketing through the finale as if the world around her were on fire. But before her companions could even begin their applause or cheers, she returned to the beginning and this time played it through even faster, the individual notes like water cascading down a steep slope. Again she managed to give each note its due, so that neither the waltz nor the melody was obscured by her manic display. She reached the end this time with a deliberate flourish, raising her hands in a gesture of triumph as the last chord tumbled out of the instrument.

She stood, laughing as loudly as I'd ever heard her, and bowed.

As I looked helplessly on, one of her male companions jumped from his chair and embraced her, wrapping his strong arms around her and lifting her off the floor. They were all laughing at this point and none of them seemed the least bit surprised by this embrace, least of all Sophie, who had her arms around him as well. I felt some relief to see they didn't kiss and that Sophie turned away from him the moment he set her down. But my face burned and my body stiffened as rage flared in my gut. They had done nothing shameful and for all I knew Sophie may have been mortified by what little had occurred, nevertheless my anger took root. Trembling, struggling for breath, I pressed my face against the door, determined that nothing would escape my notice. One of the girls said something to him as the young man resumed his seat, and I distinctly heard the word "Taylor," the name of the boyfriend Sophie had earlier discouraged but who had resisted giving her up. It seemed reasonable now to assume that this was the same person and that he'd joined this group in order to be close to Sophie.

I wanted to take my bitterness outside and fling it at the world. But I could not tear myself away, for Sophie had resumed her place at the piano and was beginning another piece.

Chopin was of course one of her favourite composers and she'd chosen from another of his waltzes; one with a serene, almost regal tempo. It begins in the low register with a ponderous chord followed closely by three triplets. A fourth triplet begins, but this is interrupted by a series of trembling notes that lift the melody into a higher octave. Then the initial theme is repeated, and the higher notes round out the theme for a second time. All the while, the left hand maintains the rhythm, very softly, with minor chords. Then the second theme takes up, and though it is much more intricate and dance-like—evoking a willowy figure rhythmically stretching and bending in an empty room—it retains the mournful inflection of the opening. The music progresses through a series of variations on the triplets, becoming stately and warm, just beginning to sing, and then closing grimly in on itself as if pausing to reflect, then opening again as if awakening to the heat of the sun. It is most effective when played with restraint, for it contains within its brief span passages that approach despair and passages that can move the listener near to rapture. Sophie's rendition effortlessly captured these conflicting passions, sketching them with confidence and subtlety and also conveying her own love for the music. The waltz closes with a repeat of the triplets. The composer's directions stipulate that they be executed with such muted tranquillity that the listener is not always aware until after a few measures of silence have elapsed that it has ended. As the music faded she remained hunched above the keyboard, as still as a photograph. Neither did the other musicians move, so deeply were they in her thrall.

She lifted her arms and, to my surprise, buried her face in her hands. She appeared to be weeping, though when she raised her head, she seemed instead to be laughing. I strained for a better look but the others were on their feet milling about. All at once the clatter of a chair being pushed aside broke the calm. I jumped away from the door and stepped quickly down the hallway just before one of the girls emerged from the room. Lighting a cigarette, she strode purposefully in the opposite direction. I heard voices, laughter and loud discussion. I heard Sophie's lilting voice. While relieved she was not crying, I wondered what had happened in there and what all the theatrics meant.

I had to get out before I was seen and hurried down a corridor I guessed would take me toward the front of the building and possibly up some stairs and out. But I was not familiar with these passageways and arrived instead at a storage area for theatre equipment. I saw parts of sets, dismembered stairways, a portion of papier-mâché stone wall and a huge vase of wilted sunflowers. I pushed open another door and was startled by a congregation of wide-eyed mannequins standing between me and a set of metal stairs. I pushed my way through the throng, knocking some to the floor, bumping the limbs off others. The stairs led up to a trap door. Panic mounting, I felt if I didn't escape soon I'd either begin screaming or crumple to a heap on the floor. Inhaling a lungful of dusty air, I pushed hard and waited for my eyes to adjust to the dark. My head was sticking up in the middle of the stage of the main auditorium. I looked out at the bowl of nine hundred seats, where I'd sat many times. Aside from watching a ballet or listening to a symphony concert, I'd also seen Sophie perform on this stage, the first time a mere eleven years ago. Her piano would have stood on my head. But I was sweaty and mortified and didn't feel like indulging in memories. Instinct and the last remaining scrap of my sense of direction made me climb onto the stage and turn left, where I found a door that opened to the lobby, which, thankfully, was empty. From here it was easy to escape to the street, but before I could make a move I heard voices. Emerging from the same stairwell I'd descended twenty minutes ago was the cigarette-smoking cello player followed by a boy with a violin and another girl carrying a viola. Last in the procession were Sophie and the one I assumed was Taylor Bradford.

They couldn't see me so I stayed still and observed them. I wasn't listening carefully for although curious I was also apprehensive about what I might overhear, having seen and heard enough. But these last moments caused me agony of a very specific nature. What I noticed was how Sophie carried herself amidst her contemporaries and, as even I had to admit, her natural companions. She spoke loudly as one of a group trying to be heard. She laughed in an uninhibited, vivacious manner that I had witnessed before, though not in the last several months or, at least, not when we were together.

She had about her today a free-spiritedness, as if she'd shaken off an illness and discovered new reserves of energy. She appeared transformed, a different species from the woman who was my lover. Here was someone who was having the time of her life simply being herself and spending a few hours in the company of people she liked. Here was a young woman who knew she could arouse passion in others simply by doing what she did best. Here was someone who enjoyed innocent fun. There was nothing of a sexual nature going on; nothing lewd or suggestive in anything I'd seen since arriving. There was nothing to warrant the fury that burned within, nothing to justify the agitation that had gripped me at the sight of her in a younger man's arms. I was trembling, not because I'd gotten lost in the meandering passageways of a labyrinthine building. My distress arose from the recognition that Sophie belonged to these people much more than to me. My love was a millstone around her neck. My passions were so twisted and my longings so corrupt that I saw danger everywhere, in every pair of eyes that lit on her, every hand that touched her. I was so covetous and fearful and lonely that I could not trust her to be out of my sight. I had not come here to enjoy the music, as I'd convinced myself was the case, but to see that she was behaving.

Only when the front door of the building clattered shut did I awaken from my musing. For a moment I thought I was going to be ill. But I managed to quell the nausea and took a step forward, then another. Feebly, I nudged myself across the stone walkway and down toward the street.

It was a beautiful bright clear day. My face blazing with confusion and shame, head down, I walked home.

Ten

THE NEXT SEVERAL days I spent alone. Leaving my flat only for a change of scenery at the library or the military museum, I found myself in the company of other aimless mortals with time to fill and nothing to fill it with. At home, I did not answer the door or the telephone. My only contact with people known to me came when I called the office to say I wasn't going in.

I needed to make some decisions and this meant avoiding anyone who could sway my thinking or tempt me from the path I hoped to follow.

I tried to avoid self-condemnation. That my behaviour had been reprehensible was beyond doubt. I wanted to consider my actions from different angles in order to understand what I now had to do.

I could take some comfort from the fact that the damage I'd inflicted was limited. Sophie had been sexually active prior to our first time in bed together. I had not robbed her of her virginity or awakened something in her that was not already astir. Quite possibly she would have been making love to someone else if not to me. All I did was allow myself to fall under the spell of her desire and her beauty and take her to bed. A failing on my part to be sure, but hardly a criminal offence. I had made love to someone society had deemed out of bounds and enjoyed myself. I was able to bring her pleasure as well.

But what is the difference between making love once and making love fifty times? The same act, the same immorality over and over. Multiplied—but by number, not by degree. I was not like the thief who, emboldened by success, progresses to assault and then to murder.

Nor was I a rapist, on the hunt for new victims. I had but one "victim" and she was a willing participant—more willing, in fact, than I had been at the beginning. She initiated the contact; she found ways for us to be together; she had accommodated herself to my schedule and my life style. At any point she could have ended our affair simply by saying it was over.

What was my crime? I had reneged on a tacit agreement made many years ago with Pauline and Frederick that I would look out for Sophie and defend her from harm. And herein lay the truly heinous aspect of what I'd done, for they trusted me as only a close and sympathetic relative or friend can be trusted. I had taken that trust and used it as a shield to protect myself even as I violated it. Pauline and Frederick were as much victims in this affair as Sophie was, as much a victim as I was. Even if they couldn't have me arrested, they would be justified in banishing me if they discovered what I'd done with their daughter.

How could I have imagined myself contented on those warm summer evenings when Sophie lay beside me, both of us happily satiated by the exertions of sex? How had I blinded myself to the moral quagmire into which I'd ventured? How could I have been so naïve as to envision a future together for Sophie and myself? The magnitude of my folly was indeed so great that mere words can't describe it.

It was a week of steady rain and I spent it alone with my thoughts. Sophie was busy with her practising, rehearsing and general preparations for her New England concerts. She may have tried to call me. She may even have come over when I wasn't at home but, if so, left no note. I was thankful for being spared the ordeal of deciding whether or not to reply.

One way I kept busy during this week was a wholesale cleaning of my flat. This is not something I do often or gladly but because I was taking this time for myself I saw no reason why my body shouldn't benefit from some honest exertion while my mind was engaged. Some of these chores, such as moving the stove and refrigerator and cleaning behind them, I'd been postponing for years. I dusted everywhere I could reach. I removed the glass panels and shades from ceiling light fixtures, soaked them in warm soapy water and laid them on towels to dry. I scoured the top of the kitchen cabinets. I went through my closets and threw away several bags of outdated clothing. I sold a box of books to a second-hand dealer and made enough money to take myself to lunch.

During this time I came across some of Sophie's belongings, items I'd put aside meaning to return them: books, jewellery, bathroom accessories. I discovered a pair of her socks and an earring under the bed. Shoes, a sweater, other clothes that had replaced my own on hangers in the bedroom closet. Her hairbrush on the dresser beside the mirror, its tines still gripping strands of her hair. I marvelled at how quickly and deeply our lives, symbolized by these objects, had become intertwined. We had indeed been living as husband and wife in almost every respect, the single exclusion being a marriage bed we could share night after night. She bought and stored food in my refrigerator; made and received calls on my phone. She came and went freely—it was not my flat alone any more. It was ours and, to a significant extent, hers.

Pauline had warned me that Sophie would move in and take over, and though the nature of the occupation that had occurred was obviously not what Pauline had in mind, her prescience in this matter came as no surprise. A mother knows her daughter and Pauline and Sophie were very much alike. But then something else happened. As I drifted about at my own pace, establishing a personal rhythm and not worrying about anyone else's needs or desires, I discovered, as if for the first time, that I enjoyed being on my own. I enjoyed the act of preparing a simple meal for one, of leafing through the newspaper and deciding on a whim to walk downtown to a movie. I even enjoyed my own company, odd as that may seem. The melancholy that descended at the thought of life without Sophie was still strong, as was the threat of scandal. But with my emotions more or less under control and my mind inclined toward ending the affair, I believe I was in a healthy position from which to view a future with Sophie not as my lover but as my friend.

And what I saw did not necessarily displease me. I could easily retreat to bachelorhood but Sophie had shown me that I was capable of sustaining a meaningful relationship with a woman. I was not, after all, an emotional invalid whose relations with the opposite sex would always be limited to arms-length conversations at the work-place or chaste exchanges with bank tellers. Thanks to Sophie, I had discovered emotional resources sufficient to initiate a liaison and the depth of character necessary to keep it going. I need not spend the rest of my days in a prison of my own making. I was as free as the next person to take my life in a direction of my choosing.

This level of self-awareness emerged after days of silent reflection punctuated by intervals of strenuous physical labour and serene idle-ness. Helped by the luxury of free time and a spell of bad weather, I was able to reassess my recent actions and my life in general. Though I had certainly strayed, I had recognized my thoughtless stupidity before any irreparable damage had been done and could now plan a course of action that would set things right. If I was lucky, every-thing would revert to the way it had been before Sophie and I had become lovers. If I was not, I would likely be required to make a sacrifice. Hopefully, not a distressing one.

Congratulating myself on my clear-headedness and my willing-ness to relinquish selfish pleasures to safeguard the family and serve the greater good—and looking forward to getting the whole busi-ness over with—I found Sophie's letter in the Friday post.

Eleven

Dear Joseph:

> *I have been thinking about our relationship, as I'm sure you have too. I believe we must come to a decision. I hope it will not be too painful, for either of us. Please come and see me this weekend. My parents are gone to the country so we will be alone.*
> *I've missed you.*

Love,
Sophie

SHE HAD DRAWN a little heart beside her signature. The note was hand-written on scented lavender paper. Early on we agreed to avoid expressing our feelings in written form and to immediately destroy any notes or letters. But this one survived and every time I take it from its hiding place I am struck by the childish quality of the handwriting—the fat round letters and decorative loops and tails—as if the author were nine instead of nineteen. After more than a year the scent has faded and the folds are becoming brittle from excessive handling. I should get rid of it, simply out of caution, but can't bring myself to do so.

The letter was not a cause for alarm. Sophie had probably been unable to reach me. It was perhaps unfair of me to sequester myself as I had done, without letting her know what my plans were. But I don't see how I could have acted differently. It probably seemed to her as if I'd dropped from the face of the earth, or else was purposely avoiding her. I certainly didn't mean to cause her anxiety or suffering, but knowing my weakness where she was concerned, had I encountered her during my deliberations, I would very likely have reached a different conclusion.

I took my cue from her written note and did not reply. I would simply arrive at her front door.

A churning cloudbank hung over the city, soaking everything with a persistent drizzle. I took my umbrella and, at the last second, tucked Sophie's letter into my coat pocket. I don't know why. In retrospect it seems an unnecessary gesture, akin to preserving a grocery list after the purchases have been made. Perhaps I had a premonition of what was to come and wished to keep this vestige of her close to my heart.

When I rounded the corner onto Young Avenue and saw the tree-lined length of the street, I felt as if I were about to enter a long, dark tunnel. At that moment I realized I'd spent the entire walk in a mental fog. The drizzle had stopped, an eerie stillness enveloped me. I walked by a small curly-haired dog in the front yard of a house, whimpering and digging beneath a hedge; it didn't look up. A woman pushing an old-fashioned pram passed me going in the other direction. She didn't look at me. I was invisible. A sensation of weightlessness, as if my entire body was made of air, left me disoriented. A car crawled by, tires hissing on the asphalt, headlights lit. Was the driver searching for an address? When I looked up it had vanished. I stood still. The only sound was a distant swishing, like the roar of the sea from miles away. The ocean's salty aroma was powerful, as if I were standing at the end of a pier. When I began to walk, my steps sounded hollow in the empty street. I reached for a handkerchief and found instead Sophie's letter. Putting it back, I saw my hand sheathed in a black leather glove I did not recall putting on. I shook my head and laughed.

When I came to the house, I made my way around to the back. My shoes were wet from the grass by the time I reached the brick patio off the music room, where Sophie was at the piano, her back to me. Faintly through the glass came the sombre opening movement of Ravel's *Gaspard de la Nuit*, the single foundation note tolling heavily, evoking the lazy back and forth motion of a pendulum. I remembered her frustration with this piece as she struggled to learn it and how we had discussed it late into the night. But she appeared to be having no trouble now. Her playing was poised and confident. When the slow movement ended she launched into the skittish tumult of the next, her hands racing the length of the keyboard with the same devilish abandon she'd displayed with Chopin's *Minute Waltz*.

At the next break in the music I tapped on the door with the wooden handle of the umbrella. When she turned and saw me her expression was not one of delight. It was shock.

"Joseph, I didn't know you were coming. Why didn't you call?"

I stepped inside.

"I got your letter," I said, stupidly holding it up.

She gave it a dismissive glance.

"Yes, well. You should have called." She seemed distracted, as if she'd misplaced something. "I'm sorry. You surprised me." She raised herself on her toes and kissed my cheek. The room was cold. She was wearing a heavy green sweater, jeans and thick socks.

"Do you want me to go?"

But I had already laid the umbrella on a chair and was shedding my coat and then my gloves, which I also laid neatly on the chair.

"No," she said. "Of course not."

She went to make tea and I heard the clatter of utensils as I wandered around the room. I laid my hand on the keyboard, allowing a finger to press down and sound a feeble note. The instrument did not resonate the way it did when she touched it.

I followed her to the kitchen.

"I'm glad you've come, actually," she said. I pulled a chair out and sat down. "We really have to talk."

"Yes, I realize that." I crossed my legs and tried to appear at ease. "I'm sorry I wasn't around this week. I should have called. We could have got this over with sooner."

When she looked at me her expression was pained.

"I was waiting for you to call. I wanted to see you. But there's so much to do. And I had to practice the Ravel."

She pressed her hands together and massaged them. I wanted to go to her and warm them with mine. But I was immobilized by a strange dread that numbed my extremities and lulled me into a dream state. I felt oddly absent, observing Sophie from a distance as she struggled for the right words. I had no sensation of immediacy, or intimacy. I had no sensation of anything.

"I only sent that letter because I was too busy to come myself. I hope you can understand that."

"Sophie, I understand." The letter, somehow, had found its way to the kitchen table. I picked it up and began reading it. It was like I'd never seen it before. I was reading it a second time, trying to make sense of it, when she spoke again.

"It's over, Joseph. I've been thinking about this all week. It's not that I want us to be apart but I don't see how we can go on." She looked at me and her eyes were moist and her voice anguished. "But I guess you know this."

I nodded.

But did I know this? I matched her gaze and felt my eyes fill. Where had my strength gone? Where was my resolve? Hadn't I spent a week alone and reached the same conclusion? Hadn't I come to break the news and offer comfort? I couldn't understand what was happening. When I looked into her eyes all I felt was betrayal. Then came bitterness and mounting anger. She might just as well have said she'd taken up with a younger man and that, as far as she was concerned, the last few months had never happened. I shifted in my chair. I didn't want to be here. Just looking at her was a taunt because all I saw was what I was losing. I couldn't bear to see her watching me cry. I was not thinking how much I loved her or how desperately I wanted to retain her friendship after this was over. No. I was thinking how humiliating it was to be spurned by a nineteen-year-old girl.

"Joseph?"

The letter was in my hand. I almost tore it up but instead tapped the edge of the envelope against the table and laid it flat.

"Joseph, say something. Please look at me."

I got up and left the room. My intention was to speedily put on my coat and escape from the house but I did not return to the music room to gather my belongings. Instead I found myself on the stairs leading to the second floor. I don't think I knew what I was doing or what I was looking for, if anything. I just wanted to put distance between myself and her huge sad eyes and her adolescent pity and her reasons for ending our affair. I took the steps two at a time, launching myself upward as if trying to fly. I marched down the hall to Sophie's room and paused. I felt a wave of spiteful disappointment when I stepped inside and saw there was no naked young man scampering under the bed or into the closet. The bed was unmade; rumpled clothes littered the floor. I kicked a flimsy garment out of the way as I looked around. I stopped at the foot of the bed.

"Joseph, I think you should leave."

Sophie was at the door. She came toward me with her arm extended, as if she meant to take custody of me. Tears streaked her face.

"Joseph, come. We can talk later."

At her touch, I grabbed her by the arm and pushed her down on the bed. Instantly the tender expression on her face vanished. Her mouth dropped open in astonishment. A crude sense of triumph swept over me. When she tried to get up I pushed her down again. For a brief moment we looked into each other's eyes.

Then she was on her feet and running. I wanted to let her go but it was as if pursuit was the only option. I tried to say her name as I ran but in seconds I was winded and gasping. Her thick socks made it hard to control her footing on the glossy hardwood floor. At the top of the stairs I reached out to grasp her but my fingers caught only her sweater. I closed my hand on the loose material and swung her around. In her eyes was a mixture of shock and grief. She lost her balance ... no, I threw her off balance.

That's what happened. I threw her off balance and she fell away from me and tumbled backwards. Her head struck the wall with a sickening thud. She didn't cry out. The only sounds were the thumps of her body colliding with the wooden stairs. Seconds later she lay in a twisted heap at the bottom, head resting on her left arm, right arm pinned awkwardly beneath her body. I could not for the life of me understand what had happened. There was no question in my mind that in a minute she would stand up and brush herself off, smile and hold out her hand for me to take. It was a joke, surely, an elaborate charade. I sat waiting. I didn't cry. I didn't say her name. I sat, wheezing pathetically.

When I was finally able to move, I descended slowly and stood gazing down at her. I kneeled. I heard myself saying things like, "It will be all right, Sophie. I love you. Don't worry." I stroked her cheek. I may even have kissed her. Her eyes were open. I think she was awake though I'm not entirely sure. Her chest rose and fell in a rapid and regular rhythm but the sounds she made were laboured. I saw the blood. It formed a small uneven pool beneath her ear and was creeping outward in a slow rolling movement, like a tiny wave. Without thinking I arranged her body in a more comfortable position and brought a pillow from the living room, which I placed carefully beneath her head. My hand came away bloody but it didn't seem to matter. I was still talking, offering words of comfort. I couldn't stop. Slowly I grew aware of a high-pitched howl coming from another part of the house, which after some thought I determined to be the boiling kettle. I lingered with her for a long time before going to the kitchen, where I washed my hands and turned off the burner and then phoned for an ambulance. When I returned she was breathing in shallow gasps. Her eyes were still open and she hadn't moved. A minute or so later her lips parted just slightly and her body trembled. I smiled and told her again that everything would be all right. I may have even believed it to be true.

Twelve

COAT AND GLOVES on, I was waiting outside when the ambulance arrived. I had returned to the cupboard the cup and saucer that Sophie had taken down for my tea. I told people I had only just got there and that I'd found her at the bottom of the stairs. Her letter was back in my pocket.

My mind galloping, I watched as a young paramedic took charge.

"Did you do this?" she asked as she and her partner went to work. Panicked, I was unable to speak until I realized she was referring to Sophie's position on the floor, the pillow supporting her head.

"Yes." I nodded.

She stared at me, disapproval visible in the grim set of her jaw.

"And you are …?"

"Her cousin," I said. "Joseph Blanchard."

I tried to appear calm but had no idea what my face was telling her.

She asked for Sophie's name, age. She asked where her parents were and if I knew if she was allergic to any drugs. They fitted her with a neck brace and eased her on to a stretcher, handling her with practiced caution. She was not dead.

I thought: Thank God. Thank God. She's going to be all right.

Then there seemed to be some question of me accompanying her to the hospital. I acquiesced with a silent nod. By this point the numbness had faded and the implications of what I'd done grew enormous and vivid in my mind. My chest tightened and breathing became difficult. In the ambulance I listened and watched, trying to absorb what was happening. But my brain kept taking me back to that horrible moment on the stairs, the shock on Sophie's face as she slipped from my grasp. From the front desk in the Emergency Department I phoned the cottage to tell Frederick and Pauline about the accident. Frederick answered and quizzed me about Sophie's condition. But my responses were semi-coherent and certainly inadequate. I remember the frustrated silence at the other end and Frederick's terse "Thank you, Joseph. I'll phone ..." And he named somebody, no doubt a colleague at the hospital. I calculated it would take them about an hour to get back to the city and breathed easier, knowing Frederick was in direct contact with the people treating her injuries and taking charge of the situation. Next I went looking for Sophie but learned she had been moved to another part of the building for x-rays. There was concern about her neck and spine.

I wandered back to the waiting area and sat amidst the noise and chaos. Almost two hours later a nurse came and asked if I was Joseph. I wanted to say no. She escorted me to the desk and handed me the phone. It was Frederick. He and Pauline were upstairs. Sophie was in Intensive Care. She was unconscious but stable and being monitored.

I got directions and went up. The elevator opened on a broad, bright hallway. People moved about as they performed their duties but the entire ward seemed cloaked in a respectful hush. I felt a surge of panic as I approached the door. How could I face them and not confess the truth? I drew a breath and went in. Pauline stood immediately and embraced me. Frederick wrapped his arms around us and for a moment the three of us were joined in grief.

We spoke briefly and I repeated the story I had told, that I'd arrived at the house and found Sophie at the bottom of the stairs. Then we lapsed into a grim silence. Pauline resumed her seat next to the bed in the room's only chair. Frederick nodded as he looked down at his daughter. I'd avoided doing so but turned to Sophie now. She appeared serene with her head resting on the pillow and her eyes closed. But the tube in her mouth shattered the illusion. The pulsing I'd heard was the machine helping her breathe. Another machine monitored her heart. Here before my eyes was the full horror of what I'd done. I clenched my jaw and tried to order my thoughts. I'd entered the house through the studio, called her name, went looking and discovered her at the bottom of the stairs. I'd phoned for an ambulance. What happened next? I couldn't see it, couldn't think, couldn't remember what I'd told people. My heart thundered, but panic was out of the question. I refused to go to pieces in front of Frederick and Pauline. I was sweating and realized it was the room, which was unreasonably warm. I had to get out of here. But how? A minute later I was rescued when a nurse entered and informed us that there were too many people and that one of us would have to leave immediately. I said that's fine. I'd go home and clean up and see them in a little while. I kissed Pauline's cheek, briefly grasped Frederick's arm. I could not get out of there fast enough.

At home, I sat for hours. I may have fallen asleep but when I came to, it was the same day, but it was evening and the sky had turned murky. At some point I began packing Sophie's things in a suitcase, as if I were planning to take them to her at the hospital. But the suitcase never left my flat. The next day I discovered it, gaping open and half-filled, on the bedroom floor. Something must have interrupted me as I was packing, a phone call maybe. By this time, it was very late, in all likelihood past midnight. My addled state of mind was probably partly attributable to the fact that I'd had nothing to eat since the morning. I wasn't hungry. I desired nothing but Sophie's recovery, though even this remained largely unarticulated in my mind, for to do so would mean acknowledging yet again that she was lying in a hospital bed, gravely injured because of my treachery.

Early Sunday morning I was back at the house on Young Avenue. Pauline's eyes rimmed in red against the unearthly pallor of her skin come back to me easily now, as does her ardent embrace when she entered the living room to meet me. She held me for more than a minute but didn't say anything and later, after she had retired to the bedroom, Frederick explained that she was under sedation and therefore not entirely herself. Mrs. Radcliffe, the cook, was there, as was Deanna the maid, who lived upstairs and about whom

I'd forgotten utterly. But Frederick told me that Deanna had been visiting relatives the previous day and so couldn't tell them anything. I tried to mask my relief beneath a cough.

Deanna brought tea in on a tray. It was plain she'd been crying. I noticed Frederick watching me closely.

"How are you handling this, Joseph?" he asked, but his tone was conversational.

"I should be asking you that," I said. "I'm fine. It's a shock."

"I can imagine," he said, sighing. I began to gather from his languid manner that he'd been through a lengthy stretch without sleep, perhaps the entire night.

"How is she?"

He raised his eyes to the ceiling, and for a moment I thought he'd misinterpreted my question and was going to tell me about Pauline.

"The signs aren't good. Her neck wasn't broken. But there's a haematoma inside the skull. Bleeding. They've operated to relieve the pressure."

I nodded.

"You know," he said, "they told me that the accident happened very shortly before you found her. Perhaps as little as twenty minutes. If she'd been left lying there for even another ten or fifteen minutes she would not have survived." My expression must have told him I didn't understand. "They can tell these things. How long a person's been injured by the amount of blood they've lost. Coagulation. Science can be very precise."

I shook my head.

"If only I'd got there sooner."

"Yes. Well."

We both paused to sip our tea.

"You didn't see anyone else, did you?"

"No. Who?" When my hand began shaking I replaced my cup and saucer on the tray.

"There was a policeman here this morning," he said, and suddenly Frederick seemed very weary. He looked much older than I knew him to be. "When they were preparing her for the operation someone noticed bruising on her upper arm, just here." He startled me by reaching out and gripping my bicep very tightly up near my shoulder. He looked straight into my eyes. Then he let me go. "They were able to determine that it happened at roughly the same time as her other injuries. Maybe it's not significant. But if it is, it means there was someone here in the house with her, either at the time or shortly before it happened. It could mean someone pushed her down the stairs."

It was probably obvious to him by now that I found what he was telling me highly unsettling.

"I know. It seems inconceivable that someone could leave her like that and just walk away. Especially if it was someone she knew. If it was a stranger and she confronted him …" he shrugged. "… I can't say I sympathize but at least it's easier to understand how that could happen. Wrong place, wrong time."

He was hiding it but I could see he was distraught.

"Frederick, I'm so sorry."

"Yes, I know. I know. We're all sorry. Anyway, I just wanted to tell you this because the police will be questioning you."

"That's not a problem," I said, and managed to appear calm, though my mind was racing.

Frederick stated that he was off to the hospital in a few minutes. I said I would accompany him. This seemed reasonable. Seeing Sophie lying in the bed where my vile appetites had placed her was no less than I deserved. I felt, perhaps because of some twisted notion of fair play, that it was proper and fitting to subject myself to this ordeal once again and act the witness to what I had done.

Before leaving, we went upstairs to visit briefly with Pauline, who, as it turned out, was sleeping. Then, while Frederick used the upstairs bathroom and I went supposedly to use another one, I instead paid a visit to Sophie's room, which remained unchanged from the day before. I closed the door behind me. There was no sign of the notebook. The top of the desk had been rolled down and was locked into place. I forced a letter opener into the gap where the top met the flat surface and tried to pry them apart, but the lock held fast and I didn't want to make any noise. I went in search of Sophie's purse, which I found in a drawer in the bedside cabinet. I emptied the contents on the bed. Here were the keys. I tried one after another. Finally, the desk unlocked. I knew I was running short of time and that Frederick would be wondering what had become of me. Once I located the notebook, which was hidden beneath a sheaf of writing paper in a drawer, I put it back, closed the drawer and rolled the top into place but did not lock it, replaced the items in the purse, and put the purse back where I'd found it. I was in the front hallway in time to meet Frederick coming down the stairs.

My mind and energies were now utterly devoted to matters of concealment. I had been conscious, prior to the scene I've just described, of a profound lethargy affecting my limbs as well as my mental processes. Knowing that the police were involved brought me to a fever pitch of alertness. Frederick spoke to me in the car during the five-minute drive to the hospital but I heard little of what he said. I watched the streets pass by, people going about their business as if nothing momentous had occurred. And once more I found myself in a state of reverie. The world had receded and I felt cut adrift, watching as things happened but from a steadily increasing distance, as if from a train pulling out of the station.

We had been inside the building for only a few seconds when I noticed that everything—lights, colours, sounds—was hushed and muted. After waiting a minute we got into an elevator. We did not speak on the way up. In the ICU Frederick led the way down the hall, his grey coat flowing in the wake of his long strides. He paused outside the door and glanced back, I suppose to see if I was still there. Then the door was opened from within and we entered.

I allowed myself to look down.

The top of Sophie's head was swaddled in gauze. Her eyes were closed and her arms lay neatly at her sides. The smooth face showed no sign of fright or puzzlement. Absent too were the delight and laughter I had seen there so often. I saw a blank face—it could have been anyone.

I looked at Frederick. The man was not moving. He seemed so old. Nothing I could do or say was going to help him make sense of this.

We stood. The silence was like another person in the room.

Frederick expelled an unsteady breath from deep within his lungs and when he spoke his voice quavered.

"Ah, my beautiful girl," he said, and took her hand. The faintest trace of a smile played upon his lips and I imagined him thinking that no harm could come to her now.

I looked at her again and saw what I had been blind to only a moment ago: that one of her eyes was circled by a bruise, that her face was disfigured by a scattering of tiny gashes on her lips, her nose, her eyebrows, as if she'd been struck repeatedly. I did this to her, I thought. I articulated the words in my head again and then again, a dozen times. I did this to her. I did this to her. I tried to make myself feel it. I tried to bring the pain forward into my conscious thoughts and suffer the weight of guilt and responsibility bearing down on me. But I felt nothing as I looked at this blameless girl who had died because of my weakness and I think that's what sickens me most of all.

Thirteen

S HE HAD DIED as we were driving to the hospital. It happened
that quickly. A sudden haemorrhage in the brain and it was
over. A nurse had called the house and was told that Pauline
was sleeping and that Frederick was on his way.

The family came together and performed the necessary rituals
and duties. I helped Frederick compose and edit a lengthy obituary.
Pauline's parents, my Aunt Adele and Uncle Willard, were on hand
to help with funeral arrangements. The house was filled with relatives at all hours of the day and night. The prevailing mood was not
so much one of mourning as of communal reflection, of assessing
the past and looking toward a very different future. I sat down one
evening in the living room with some others, younger and older, male
and female and became immersed in a conversation that continued
until dawn. We opened some wine and talked about Sophie and
what she meant to us, about her talents, about our memories. But we
talked about other things too, topics unrelated to the tragedy that
had affected us all. It was a time of getting to know one another and
of seeing each other safely over to the other side of grief.

Throughout this period, I maintained a surface calm and a chill-
ing degree of emotional equilibrium. Reminders of Sophie were everywhere and they did not touch me. On numerous occasions I watched
Pauline consumed by uncontrollable tears, a paroxysm of grief that
left her fighting for breath. Roaming about the house one night unable to sleep, I wandered into the music room and found Frederick

seated at Sophie's piano. He had so far maintained a daytime demeanour of dignified restraint. But here he was in the middle of the
night, in a dark room, weeping with an abandon that should have cut
me to the pith of my being. I had never seen his tears before, much
less this utter helplessness. His strength had always been a source of
wonder and inspiration because here was someone who never let
himself go. I could not join him, could not even rest a comforting
hand on his shoulder. I retreated, placing distance between myself
and his pain. But his sighs filled the house. I could not escape them.

My mind was on the notebook and the risk in leaving it be. But with
the house full of people, I had to wait for an opportune moment to
take it. Sophie's room was quickly gaining the allure and significance of a shrine, at least among the younger members of the family.
The children of Frederick's relatives each made their solemn pilgrim-
age and stood gawking in the doorway. None had yet dared to cross
the threshold, but I could see a time coming when this would happen. Because the police had made a formal request, the room had
been left as it was on the day of the accident, with the bed unmade
and clothes on the floor. I understood their need for unsullied information but something about the fact that her socks and underwear
remained in plain view approached the level of obscenity.

Intending to stay for a few days, I had brought an overnight bag
and when the opportunity came it was a simple matter to remove
the notebook from the desk and tuck it in this bag. The next day a
young detective came to the house asking for me and he questioned
me about what I had seen on the previous Saturday. I repeated my
story verbatim but added a few things, like how I'd I thought it
strange that the house was so quiet and seemed deserted when the
door was not locked. Then I heard the squeal of the boiling kettle
and entered the kitchen to turn off the burner. I called Sophie's
name. There was no answer. I found her a moment later at the bottom of the stairs. I must have panicked (I said) because without
thinking I tried to make her comfortable. The next thing I could
recall was phoning the emergency number and then going outside

to wait for the ambulance. I didn't see or hear anything else. He wrote down portions of my narrative but his whole attitude was sulky and nonchalant, as if he had much more important matters awaiting his attention. At one point he yawned extravagantly. Then he thanked me and left. Evidently, he could see little benefit in pursuing the case of a teenaged girl who fell to her death down a flight of stairs because the inquiries went no further.

Sophie's funeral took place the following Monday, just over a week after her death. As one would expect, the sermon's theme was of potential that would now go unfulfilled. Common enough for an early death but the pastor's words could not even begin to delineate the massive talent or the enormity of what the world had lost. Against my advice, Frederick spoke briefly. I didn't think he should put himself through the ordeal of having to prepare a text and present it to a congregation. He was plainly exhausted and the watery light of early morning revealed cavernous shadows on his face. But he regarded it as a duty and brought it off rather well. Pauline also displayed an admirable degree of courage and resilience. I had been worried about her, we all were. She spent days sunk in despondency, gazing out windows or in the music room staring at the piano. Then one afternoon I'd thought I heard her coming along the hallway to join us in the living room, or to go upstairs. But when I heard nothing further after a few moments and she did not appear, I excused myself from a conversation and went looking for her. She was standing at the foot of the stairs looking at the floor, or so it seemed, her gaze fixed on the spot where Sophie had been found. She stood for several minutes without moving, except to lift her eyes toward the top of the flight, and then lower them. She did this several times. It was as if she were studying the trajectory of Sophie's fall and trying to determine how it could have happened. Then she sighed, shook her head and began climbing the stairs in her usual brisk manner. After that I did not worry about her quite so much.

The funeral left us deeply shaken but somehow everyone got through it. After everything was over, a limousine took us back to

Young Avenue. I had made this house my home for the past week but there was no reason to stay any longer. The three of us removed our wet things and stood silently in the hallway.

"I'll make some tea," Pauline said and rubbed her hands together. Frederick nodded.

We were alone in the house. Everyone had gone home. With a sorrowful smile, Frederick loosened his tie and went slowly upstairs. I held my breath and took in my surroundings. There is a moment following the death of a loved one when you look around and it is as if you have just that instant opened your eyes and are seeing the world for the first time. The smallest detail bristles with surreal clarity. It is also a moment of staggering emptiness, in which every object has been drained of significance, as if life itself has been robbed of meaning. I experienced this moment now.

The house was tidy, unnaturally so. Even though people had been coming and going all week, not a single item was out of place. The floor gleamed. But the huge spaces seemed oppressive, demanding that we somehow fill them. I realized it had been Sophie who so easily filled this house with her lively spirit and her superb artistry. For so long we had looked to her for this and she had shared with us energy, vision and an irrepressible life force. Without her to enliven its rooms and corridors, the house was a dead thing constructed from wood, glass and brick, held together with nails.

I followed Pauline into the kitchen, but when I saw her stooped over the sink, her shoulders convulsing and one hand shielding her face, I backed out of the room. I went upstairs in search of Frederick but the bedroom door was closed. Behind it I could hear him giving full, unrestrained voice to his anguish. I retraced my steps and stopped outside Sophie's room. I had not been in there since the day I took the notebook and when I tried the door, it was locked. I have no idea what I wanted or expected to find but felt disappointed nonetheless. I went slowly along to my own room and quietly shut the door behind me. I sat on the bed. It was time for me to return to my old life and I could not bear the thought of it. Even when my determination to break off the affair with Sophie was at its most steadfast, she always remained a presence in whatever future I envisioned for myself, as someone whose talents I could savour and in whose good fortune I could take vicarious delight. To think that I had destroyed the one thing in the world that was most dear to my heart was more than I could reasonably endure. That I would never escape this truth was only just. For the first time since her death I wept profusely.

Fourteen

AT HOME I finished packing the suitcase with Sophie's things. Unable to decide what to do with it, I put it in the closet. I still have this suitcase and have not touched it since that day.

A week passed before I could look at the notebook. In the meantime, I returned to the office and tried to behave as if all were well, or as well as could be expected. I performed my duties to the best of my ability and even managed to find some solace in the rhythms of the workplace, in other people's voices speaking of other things, in the stack of papers awaiting my signature. It was a welcome distraction and after a few days I phoned Pauline to ask how she and Frederick were doing and was not distressed by the answer I received.

In church on Sunday I found Sophie's folded letter in my coat pocket. Reading it was difficult—I could not believe how blind I'd been to its meaning and to her intention, which was clearly to end our affair. But she had taken care to say so in a way that would not leave me devastated. Upon first reading, I'd allowed myself an ambiguous interpretation that imagined she wanted us to continue. Wanted, of all things, to get married. I could see now that I had read my own desires into her words. Worse, despite spending an entire week settling on a course of action, I had been unable to carry it out because I was much too afraid of being left without her.

One night later in the week I opened a bottle of sherry and sat down with Sophie's notebook. There were pockets inside both covers and the three letters I wrote to her early in our relationship were tucked inside them. I set them aside.

The unlined pages of the notebook were cream-coloured with jottings and drawings scattered throughout. Some pages were blank. Nothing was dated. She also seems to have had no preference in writing implements, using ink, pencil and coloured ink. Some pages were filled with musical notations; others with sketches of trees, animals, people, houses. She was not a talented artist—the drawings were endearingly amateurish.

I went through the whole book in less than half an hour. She addresses much of what she is writing to someone unnamed but always speaks in general terms—of what has recently occurred in her life; of things she's heard; of music she would like to play or has played so often she never wants to hear it again. Her punctuation and spelling was eccentric. The following passage is typical:

> *You would never think that Bach's Toccata could be SO difficult—the notes roll away from me while I play and I can't find them again afterwards . . . so it's hard sometimes. I can get the notes but not the feelings—when I put on Gould and listen to him play Bach it makes me feel like I can do everything and nothing (He talks to himself when he plays, Gould not Bach.) I never want to be strange like him. He wore an overcoat: in the summer! and slept with lots of women, and Bach had 20 children! When did he write all that music?*

Since I planned to give the book to Pauline after reviewing its contents, I was relieved to find only a single reference to myself. This was most likely written during our week away, possibly the very night I saw her at the window gazing out at the town and writing in this volume. Because I must remove and destroy this page, along with the letters I'd written to Sophie, I will reproduce a section of the passage here.

> *Dear Joseph, you have made me so happy. I love you I really do, I feel all grown up now. I want you in my world forever, it is such a special thing. Please don't get tired of me like Lucien did. I told you a lie. I did not leave Lucien he left me because, he said, I was like a baby. I know he was right. I KNOW he was right. We were just playing but then I was mean to him. When we made love it was not like you and me—there was no music it was just something to do something to fill up boring old Saturday afternoon.*
> *But everything is different now. I'm different. I think you are too. How could we not be? I'll never tell anyone because it is so exciting. You sleep like a baby and I can watch you and it's like the moon and stars are here just for us, like the world is here just for us. Is this what being in Love is? I've always loved you, since before I was born and I'll never stop. I used to sing your name. Did you ever hear?*

For the rest of my life I will regard with awe the tenacity of the human spirit. I worried that Sophie's death would destroy Pauline and Frederick, but they found within themselves—and perhaps within each other—the strength to continue. Anyone could see they were suffering. But mostly they confined their grief to their private hearts and only rarely allowed anyone a glimpse of a wound that no one believed would ever heal. At stray moments you might catch Pauline gazing abstractedly at the large photo portrait of Sophie on the table in the living room. Or, as I noticed on occasion, Frederick would withdraw from company and seclude himself in his study. If you listened at the door carefully you could hear the clink of glass and the gurgle of liquid being poured. But if he was drinking heavily it did not show in his demeanour, which remained agreeable if somewhat more reserved than before.

In November, Pauline called to tell me that her mother, my Aunt Adele, wished to meet and discuss something with me. Our branch of the family is a slave to decorum and there is a respect for each other's privacy that borders on the fanatical. Nobody gossips, or speculates about "private affairs." Aunt Adele still behaves according to tradition, and it probably would not occur to her that she could contact me directly, even if we were the last two people on earth.

I was nervous about the meeting, but only because of fears that my secret would emerge before I was prepared. I had noticed that my health was not what it had been; I was suffering spells of dizziness and a pervasive languor, that a stiffness in my limbs was becoming more pronounced, that each day was more difficult to shake off than the day before. My thoughts had begun to veer in directions I did not want them to go and I was full of suspicions; that Sophie had left evidence other than the notebook, that she had told people about us, that somewhere a photograph existed that would reveal all.

Pauline invited her parents and me to dinner. I was prepared for a solemn occasion. We were all trying to ignore the prospect of Sophie's twentieth birthday in two weeks. Frederick and Pauline planned to be out of the country on that day. I had decided I would observe her birthday by getting drunk.

Because I wasn't feeling up to par I took a taxi. Pauline and my Uncle Willard were serving drinks. We were a subdued group, reflective but by no means morose. There was a fire on. The house was warm.

After dinner Pauline came and whispered that her mother was waiting for me in the music room. Evidently, the nature of this business was, of course, a secret. I had begun to perspire and my legs trembled but I was able to walk short distances without revealing how brittle I had become.

My aunt is not a small woman. She can cut an imposing figure when she wants to. When she speaks, people pay attention, and she knows how to get things done. A few years ago she launched a successful campaign to have a corrupt alderman driven from office. Somewhat afraid of her, I had always been cautious and polite in her presence. When I was quite young I once overheard her telling some-one that I was "a very nice boy," which I hardly regarded as a com-pliment. But I came to learn that this was as far with her praise as she would go with anyone and probably meant that I resided fairly high in her estimation.

The only light in the music room came from two small lamps. She was seated at the piano.

"Hello, Aunt," I said cordially.

She glanced up. Her expression was bright and open.

"Did you know I used to play the piano when I was a girl? And your father played too. He was better than I was."

She struck a major chord, a minor, then another major.

"But it's been so long," she said with a sigh, and abruptly lowered the lid over the keys.

I moved a chair over so I could sit next to her.

"Joseph, I want you to know that I'm sorry."

"For ... what?"

She had a letter in her hand. Familiar anxieties stirred to life. She was gazing at me, her hazel eyes glittering with intensity.

"Your father was a good man, Joseph. I want you to remem-ber that."

She held out the letter and I took it. She stood and began walk-ing around the room.

"With everything that's happened I felt I had to do something; clean the house, set things in order. I had been keeping some things for Sophie. But now ... anyway, there were boxes full of papers in the attic. I couldn't imagine why we were saving them and I got Willard to bring them down. Most of it was junk, ancient photo-graphs of people we didn't even know. Recipes. Letters. A lot of letters." She was staring at me again. "This was among them and as soon as I saw it I remembered." She gestured imperiously. "Look at it, Joseph. Look at it."

I lifted the envelope into the light and recognized the hand-writing as my father's. It was addressed to Adele. The paper was yellow and mottled with age.

"You won't remember, but after Henry died, Willard and I took a trip to Europe that lasted six weeks. This letter was waiting for me when we got back. You were in Toronto by that time doing your studies and I didn't want to trouble you with it, though I think maybe I should have. But I didn't. I put it away. Joseph, I really meant to give it to you long ago."

I opened the top edge of the envelope where it had been torn and brought out a folded piece of paper.

"Henry lived such a sad life. It was such a disappointment to him. He was confused and very angry. He had hopes for you. But then everything went wrong. He didn't know what to do with himself."

She clasped her hands together and released a fluttery sigh.

"Well, I won't say any more. I'll leave you alone to read it."

"Thank you," I said.

"You'll have questions, I'm sure. I'll do my best to answer them."

She stood in front of me and I smiled up at her. I felt as if I were a little boy again and that I was being cast adrift. She smiled weakly and left the room. I unfolded the paper, a scrap torn from a larger sheet. It was lined and filled on both sides with his unkempt writing. There was no date.

Adele,

> *I don't expect you to understand. I'm dying. I want to die. Believe me it's for the best. I've seen enough of what people can do to each other. The boy doesn't know any of this. You can tell him if you want. I don't care. God knows it's not his fault. But I can't stand to look at him.*

> *He's not my son. I don't know who the bugger was who fathered him. Someone Sally took up with at the church probably. She never told me. I asked, but I'm glad now I don't know. Wouldn't do me a damn bit of good.*

> *You remember when he got sick. Something in the blood they said. I went down to give them some of my own blood for the transfusion. Decent thing for a father to do. But it*

wasn't any good. Didn't match with his. Different as night and day. The doctor or whoever it was came to me and said, "You're not his father." No doubt. No doubt at all.

I asked Sally and she denied it. But you can't fool science. That's what I said to her. You can't fool science. The doctors, they know. She never admitted it. Not once. You always said she was a fool. But she was strong. We tried to wear each other down. Some will say it was a wasted life. But I know different. I'll stick by what I did. You think I'm crazy. Well, so be it. I'm not saying I'm sorry.

This is it for me. Toss my carcass on the scrap heap for all I care. Once I'm dead it won't make one damn bit of difference.

Henry

I read this through three times. My first thought, heated and bitter, was that she'd known for seventeen years and said nothing. Then I thought, it's all wrong, someone made a mistake. I read it again and stood up. My legs almost gave out. My knees ached, all my joints had stiffened while I was sitting. I placed one hand on the piano for support. But I was slipping. I could feel myself going down. I must have knocked something over, because Pauline was suddenly in the room. She looked distressed, and I could see her mouth moving but no sounds came out. Then the floor came up to meet my head and I don't remember anything after that.

Epilogue

A RECTANGLE OF sunlight has been crossing the surface of the table for most of the afternoon, and now, finally, it touches my fingers, then my palm. It is bright and warm. The library is cool and fragrant from the bouquet of red carnations and fresh white roses atop a walnut reading table. I like this room. I like the shelves of disorganized books that line the walls and extend ten feet from floor to ceiling. The ceiling is plaster, patterned with delicate *fleurs de lis* along with an ornate medallion at its centre from which hangs an ancient chandelier, its pendants graced with the dust of many years. Chairs and smaller tables are scattered about the room, but the large table is mine. Hardly anybody else comes in here for more than a minute or two.

If any of the older residents happen upon me reading or writing, they whisper apologetically and quietly retreat. They don't wish to disturb my "work." I am grateful for this.

It is now after five on an October afternoon and I have finished reading this account. Since the day I wrote the opening pages, my health has been in decline. Whether or not I live is immaterial now. Let it be said, however, that my suffering has not abated in the eleven months since I discovered that Sophie and I were not related, that our blood had sprung from separate genetic pools. For much of that time I was unable to write. I was confined to my bed and forced to undergo invasive procedures. What I originally imagined to be an allergic reaction has left me unable to digest solid foods. The stiffening in my limbs has advanced so that on a good day I can take only ten steps, with a cane, before sitting down to rest. On some days I cannot even hold a pen. I have quit smoking, though I resisted until a crisis made it necessary. I am still able to feed myself but for how much longer I don't know. I bear the scars of more than a dozen surgeries. The doctors mutter about immune systems and congenital disorders and have quizzed me about my family. But since I don't know who my real father is I can't help them. At thirty-nine, I inhabit the body of a septuagenarian.

I have left my job. The plan was to take a leave of absence until my condition improved but after months of treatments it was clear I was never going to return to the office. My resignation was accepted and shortly thereafter Miss Pindar delivered a box of my belongings to my flat. I was between treatments at that point and when she entered and saw me in my enfeebled state—the room in near darkness, myself hunched over in a chair and huddling for warmth beneath a blanket—her eyes immediately filled with tears. I have been obtuse about people all my life, and it was only at that moment, when nothing could be done, that I recognized Miss Pindar's feelings for me. She is a caring and solitary soul whose life, to my knowledge, has been singularly unrewarding. Her hair, which years ago had been a rich shade of cinnamon, and which in the years of our acquaintance has always been arranged in a severely bobbed style that delightfully accommodates her delicate features, has greyed in a precise and becoming manner. Her eyes—and I'm ashamed to admit I'd never noticed this before—are the dramatic dark brown of newly-turned earth. They seem sad, even when she smiles. She is one of those ageless women whose skin reveals no secrets.

As she regained her smile, I saw that she possesses an ethereal loveliness—not the sleek allure of someone much younger but a more profound beauty. She dazzled with the kind of splendour that, as with fine scotch, only deepens with age. We held hands as we reminisced on the years we had spent together at Murchie's and spoke of others who had come and gone. She told me that, since my departure, it had further deteriorated, that departments were at war with one another and that she was considering turning in her resignation. Then, our hands still joined, we were silent. Just before leaving she kissed me and promised to come back. I saw her to the door and watched her walk to her car and wondered how I had managed to be blind to such obvious charms for so long.

Through Frederick's kindness and influence I was able to secure a disability pension and a place in this nursing home. I still retain the flat and will return there if I am able. But I am in no position to say when that will be. I have been put on a regimen of medication; bottles of pills and vials of foul-smelling tinctures await me at all hours. Some of these regulate the severe pain in my joints. Some aid with digestion. Others work a sort of magic on my blood which does a poor job of carrying nutrients from one part of my body to another. There are drugs for my liver and for my intestinal tract, for my heart and my eyes and my bones. I am a wreck, a living cadaver. I let the doctors poke and prod me because what choice do I have? They don't know what's wrong but apparently that only deepens the mystery and adds to the allure.

The details of my condition have been distributed far and wide, in the expectation that someone somewhere will recognize the symptoms and recommend a fix. But I wouldn't be surprised if some of them think they're onto something new and maybe a way to make a name for themselves. Next week a couple of specialists who have been following my progress are coming from Toronto to take a closer look, news which I greeted with a shrug. I've resigned myself to whatever comes next. I'm a spectator in my own life, curious but detached. If this ordeal has taught me anything, it's that hope is infinitely more damaging than grief or anger.

There is a piano in the recreation room and one day while writing I paused as the unmistakable strains of Mozart's K. 333 B-flat major sonata began drifting down the hall to the library. The notes themselves seemed a rebuke: an unkind reminder of the past sent to torture me. I thought I must be growing delusional, that my brain—

which up until now seemed unaffected by my numerous ailments —was finally catching up with the rest of my body. I laid down my pen and listened and was relieved when I recognized flagrant deficiencies in the playing: numerous miscues and a halting approach to performance as of someone just learning. I continued to listen, following the progression of the music through the initial movement and into the second. Then, unaccountably, there was silence.

Curious, I pushed myself to my feet and took my cane from the back of the chair. It had been one of my better days and I made my way with only minor discomfort into the hall. By this time, I had been a resident of the Oak Valley Rest Home for almost two months. It is privately operated, a facility designed to serve the needs of individuals who, like myself, require low-level but long-term care. There are people here who have lived in this and similar institutions nearly all their lives, mentally and physically disabled men and women who, unsupervised, are incapable of working or navigating the outside world, but who are certainly able to perform basic tasks like feeding and washing themselves. There are elderly residents too; a few are bedridden or senile or confined to wheelchairs. But Oak Valley is not a hospice. Those who die do so unexpectedly. My companions are likely to continue drawing breath for many years to come.

The recreation room is in the newer wing of the building, which is largely constructed of steel and glass. But the original structure was a Victorian rooming house that still retains much of its charm even amidst countless renovations. At one time the library was a parlour. The fireplace still works. This is probably what attracts me. I'm reminded of houses I visited in my childhood, in particular the house where Pauline grew up.

The music resumed and it took me a good five minutes to move down the hall to the recreation room, where the only sounds I'd heard from it were jigs and reels played by a retired piano teacher who came to entertain us. Her playing was impeccable and most of my companions seemed to enjoy it, but I found the racket intolerable and excused myself shortly after the beginning of her recital.

I entered, silently shutting the double doors behind me. It was approaching noon and most of my fellow residents were in the dining room, leaving only four in the recreation room. An elderly resident, Mrs. Grant, was speaking to a younger woman I guessed was her daughter. A middle-aged man hovered nearby; perhaps the son-in-law. At the piano was a little girl with long golden hair, wearing a pink, lace-edged dress and black shoes over white stockings. Her feet dangled far above the pedals. The three adults glanced briefly in my direction when I entered. The girl continued to play. I quietly excused myself and made my way across the room to a chair near the piano. I could see the man surreptitiously watching my progress, and I could guess the direction his thoughts were taking because it was evident that, despite my infirmity, I was not much older than him. The chair creaked when I lowered myself on to it and the girl's eyes flashed momentarily toward me, but she did not pause. I observed her face in profile, her childish features made sombre and thoughtful by concentration as she guided her fingers over the keys. Her parents paid her no attention whatsoever. The man wandered about the room and Mrs. Grant continued talking to her daughter. This went on for several minutes as I followed the flight of small fingers from key to key.

Then, without warning, she turned her face to me, full-on, and smiled. I smiled back and felt a link was forged between us. I was her audience. To my knowledge I had never seen her before, I did not even know her name and yet it seemed I did know her, or, at any rate, knew things about her that maybe even her family didn't know. I knew that her confidence was growing and that she was almost ready to play to an audience of strangers. I knew there were times when she needed more encouragement than these people were able to give her. I knew she would be very good someday, not great perhaps, not first rate, but very good, and that she would learn to live within the boundaries of her talent.

Relaxing, I could let myself become entranced by her playing, which now seemed more spirited, if not more accurate, than when

I'd first entered the room. I watched her and tried to understand which part of her sustained the genius that clearly possessed her. I stayed where I was, even after her father abruptly interrupted her. He called her tersely by her name, Ruella, and I was struck by the oddness of it. I noticed then that the women had risen and were standing at the door waiting. Ruella allowed her father to lift her from the stool to the floor. She looked at me again, with large pale blue eyes. As her father took her hand and led her away, her shoes clacking against the linoleum floor with each step, she kept her eyes on me. Then the door closed and I was alone. My first thought was that it had been a dream or that I had been transported back in time. I looked around the room. Other than the raised lid of the keyboard there was no evidence, save for the strains of Mozart echoing through my mind, that anyone had touched this instrument in many weeks.

Idly browsing the shelves one afternoon I made an astounding discovery. It was a commonplace enough collection: tattered volumes of best-selling fiction by forgotten authors, biographies of celebrities long-dead, outdated reference books. But amongst the dross could be found the odd treasure: a modern edition of Plato's *Republic*, works by Tolstoy, Dickens, Forster and others. Imagine my surprise though when I found, wedged tightly between two much larger volumes on an upper shelf that I could reach only by standing on a chair and lifting my limbs as high as they would stretch, a slim volume of poetry, *Rites of Passage: The Collected Verse of Peter Surrey*. I had not thought of this book for many years and, as I stretched one last inch to secure it, I had to scour my memory for its significance to me. Then it came back, the incident in the front hall of Frederick and Pauline's first house, Frederick's befuddlement as I accepted the book from him even though I'd never heard of it, or the author. I could still see myself slipping the book into the pocket of my coat and setting off toward home.

As if it were yesterday I remembered my apprehension and gratitude upon opening it, which I did a few days later. I was worried I would not like it, that the poems—composed in odd moments of reverie by a practising physician—would seem bloodless and clinical. I remember wanting so much to like it because we would then have something in common, something to bring us closer, for at that time I still found his grave manner and sharp intellect daunting. And I remembered my delight when I discovered that this unknown author who produced a single volume of fewer than sixty pages and who killed himself at the age of thirty, was in fact a genius of sorts, an observer of the human condition and a frank chronicler of his own questioning nature, and his pain. Oddly, I never had an opportunity to speak to Frederick about Peter Surrey or his poetry. After misplacing it I then forgot about the book and was mortified to find it two months later under a stack of magazines in my living room. I was so completely embarrassed by this lapse that I walked over to the house that day and left the book with Pauline, as Frederick was out. Neither of us mentioned it again—I felt stupid and he, I suspect, felt he'd forced it on me to begin with. This peculiar episode in our friendship returned to me the moment I ran my hand along the spine and opened the cover.

Frederick's copy had no dust-jacket. Because this one did I hoped to discover more about the author. But there was no photograph and the brief biography on the flyleaf was identical to the one inside the book:

> *Peter Surrey (1930–1960) was born in Hampstead and educated at the Royal College of Physicians. Trained as a surgeon, he lived in Leeds. He published nothing during his lifetime. The poems in the present volume were discovered among his papers after his death by his own hand.*

No editor was named nor was there an address for the publisher, Darkling Press. There was nothing further, except 1961 as the date of publication. I could have asked how Frederick found the book but doubted that information would enhance my enjoyment of the poems. I decided it would not and to this day I have not spoken to him of Peter Surrey.

I've been unable to sleep peacefully since the moment Sophie slipped from my grasp and fell down the stairs. I can't close my own eyes without seeing hers, wide open and staring, and seeing her limbs twisted gracelessly beneath her. I should have done away with myself long ago but, unlike Peter Surrey, I lack the courage for the ultimate step. Death terrifies me. I keep imagining I'll find a way to make amends for what I have done. Sometimes I almost believe that my suffering will redeem me.

Just a thing or two before I set aside my pen for good.

Not long ago I was seated on a park bench between Frederick and Pauline. It was a glorious sunny day in late September. The park was not far from Oak Valley and we had driven there to enjoy the fresh air. I was both relieved and chilled to be in their company, for I love them more than I do anyone and their state of mourning was still palpable. Pauline had lost weight and Frederick had, earlier, confessed to me his worries about her health.

As much as I wanted to I was unable to walk any further and Frederick left us after a few moments to bring the car along the path so I would not have to walk back. I was having trouble breathing but said nothing of this. Pauline sat beside me and we watched some children playing on the wide green area near the water. Their cries and chants filled the air.

"Joseph," she said, and my muscles tensed because I was always, now, afraid of what might be coming. "Joseph, do you ever wonder who your real father is?"

I almost laughed, so great was my relief.

I shook my head.

"No," I said. "What difference does it make now?"

"My mother was wrong for not telling you."

"She must have had her reasons."

"Maybe. But still, she was wrong."

I shrugged. I could feel her looking at me.

"Joseph, I loved you. When we were young I think I even wanted us to get married. But since we were cousins I knew it would never happen."

I didn't respond. I didn't want to know this.

"I suppose I could have said something. It broke my heart to leave you behind. But I didn't know what else to do."

"We were too young, Pauline. We didn't know what we felt. We didn't have any idea what love is."

"It would have changed so much," she said. "We could have had different lives."

I laughed briefly. "Better lives?"

We heard Frederick's car approaching along the gravel drive.

"No," she said as the car drew near. "Not necessarily better. But different."

Our eyes met and we held hands briefly. I was the first to look away.

The pain comes and goes. Sometimes it feels as if all the muscles in my abdomen have just relaxed after being clenched for hours. Sometimes every joint in my body feels like a separate flame. I don't want people to see me like this, sitting on a straight-backed wooden chair, gasping for breath. I suspect by now Frederick has spoken to the doctors and that within a day or two I'll be transferred to the hospital. Yesterday, for the first time, I asked for pain medication. Today it's not as bad. I can move from the bed to the chair and back again. Pauline is here. Her presence grieves me but I can't ask her to leave. There's a light tap on the door and she gets up to see who it is. She leaves the room. Alone momentarily, I allow myself a deeper breath, drawing in the air and trembling as my chest muscles protest the sudden expansion of my ribcage. When I open my eyes, she is standing over me, obviously concerned but I motion to her with my hand that it's nothing. I want to tell her it's no more than I deserve.

"Your friend is here," she says.

"My friend?"

"The one from your office. Lucinda."

She smiles and stands back and I see that Miss Pindar is already in the room, struggling to conceal her shock. Through the months of my decline we spoke on the phone many times and I always managed to discourage her from visiting. I can see on her face that there is some urgency bringing her to my side.

Pauline slips out and Miss Pindar pulls a chair over and sits close to me. I don't know what to think. Her loveliness takes my breath away and makes me regret, for the time it takes me to finally pull some air into my lungs, the impossible distance that my infirmity places between us.

I notice she's crying.

"Don't," I tell her and reach across to take her hand. And I notice something else, about her skin, how it glows, how it's so much smoother and firmer to the touch than mine, which has turned flaccid, like leather worn and stretched loose over my bones. Next to hers, my fingers are attenuated, like spider's legs.

She's wearing a ring. The diamond announces her engagement.

"Joseph," she says. "I'm going away. I came to say goodbye."

I nod. This is as it should be. For a few moments I simply gaze at her. I am not curious about where she is going or who is taking her there. I don't want to know how she intends to fill her days. I don't want her to say anything of a future that does not include me.

"I'll write to you," she says, nodding. "I promise." And for a moment I almost believe her.

I take a breath.

"Did I ever tell you," I say, "about my cousin?"

Her brow creases and she appears confused. But it is her nature to be generous, so she smiles and shakes her head.

And then I tell her.

Acknowledgements

I BEGAN WORKING on this novel while on sabbatical in 1994. I wish to thank the English Dept. at Dalhousie University and especially Chair Ron Huebert for providing a quiet workspace where the initial chapters were written.

It was a privilege and a pleasure to work with Lindsay Brown on the editorial stage of this project. Thank you, Lindsay, for your discerning eye, exacting standards and for pushing me to make every line that much better.

Deepest thanks to the Hawthornden Castle International Retreat for Writers in Lasswade, Scotland, where the first draft was completed in September 1998.

In 2001, I entered *Sophie's Blood*, as it was then titled, in the Writers' Federation of Nova Scotia's annual competition for unpublished manuscripts. It received the HR (Bill) Percy Novel Prize as the top entry. I wish to thank the competition judges and the WFNS for this recognition.

Thanks as well to the judges of the 2022 Guernica Prize competition for their hard work, and to Michael Mirolla and everyone at Guernica Editions.

Over the years the following provided advice and guidance: Steven Heighton, Margaret Hart, Richard Cumyn, Karen Smythe, Brian Bartlett, Stephanie Sinclair.

My wife Collette stayed the course throughout the writing and a decades-long submission process. Without her ceaseless encouragement I might have given up long before this.

About the Author

IAN COLFORD HAS written reviews, essays and fiction for a variety of periodicals and from 1995 to 1998 was editor of the literary journal *Pottersfield Portfolio*. Travels to destinations like Greece, Portugal, Turkey and Italy have influenced his writing. His debut story collection, *Evidence*, published in 2008, won the Margaret & John Savage First Book Award. Other books include two novels and two collections of short fiction. His most recent title is *Witness*. He lives in Halifax with his wife Collette.